THE TRESPASSERS

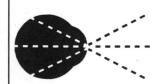

This Large Print Book carries the
Seal of Approval of N.A.V.H.

THE TRESPASSERS

ANDREW J. FENADY

THORNDIKE PRESS

A part of Gale, Cengage Learning

GALE
CENGAGE Learning™

Detroit • New York • San Francisco • New Haven, Conn • Waterville, Maine • London

GALE
CENGAGE Learning™

LIBRARY OF CONGRESS CATALOGING-IN-PUBLICATION DATA

Fenady, Andrew J.
 The trespassers / by Andrew J. Fenady.
  p. cm. — (Thorndike Press large print western)
  ISBN-13: 978-1-4104-1131-0 (hardcover : alk. paper)
  ISBN-10: 1-4104-1131-1 (hardcover : alk. paper)
  1. Treasure troves—Fiction. 2. Large type books. I. Title.
 PS3556.E477T74 2008
 813'.54—dc22   2008035370

Published in 2008 by arrangement with Leisure Books, a division of
Dorchester Publishing Co., Inc.

Printed in the United States of America
1 2 3 4 5 6 7 12 11 10 09 08

*For Don D'Auria
and his bride,
Leah.*

*And for Mary Frances,
bride of the
Toledo Trespasser.*

CHAPTER ONE

Both horses were nearly spent. It had been a long chase under a searing sun. Even the terrain had changed — from dull, flat, monotonous, to mineral-stained, craggy, red stone monuments.

But Jeff Keys, straddling the bay, was narrowing the distance between him and the galloping dun that the big, ugly, grinning bastard, Pete Bass, was spurring.

Keys, who for more than half his nearly two score years had been the pursuer or the pursued, the hunter or the hunted — occasionally both at the same time — reacted as Bass headed his dun toward a narrow opening in the rocky gorge ahead.

It didn't take a seasoned stalker like Jeff Keys to realize that Bass' maneuver was less than smart and skin-close to dumb. The opening led to a dead end where Bass would be trapped, but even though Keys couldn't see it, Bass' grin became even broader as he glanced above at the boulders flanking the slender strand.

But Keys' eyes did catch a glimpse of something reflecting the sun from one of the high lateral boulders.

Bass raced through the loose shale as the dun's shoes kicked up a noisy wake of gravelly dust, and as Keys followed, two riflemen appeared from the flanking boulders with Winchesters aimed at the pursuer.

Man and horse were in perfect harmony, and without breaking stride, Keys had pulled a sawed-off .6 gauge from his saddle boot, fired up to the left, then swung the weapon to the right and blasted off the second barrel in less than two heartbeats.

Both snipers buckled and fell, both hearts no longer beating.

And Bass was no longer grinning. His trap hadn't worked, the odds were no longer with him and he had to face Keys mano a mano.

Bass cursed, wheeled the dun, drew his gun and fired fast, too fast — he missed and before he could shoot again, Keys had dropped his shotgun and in the same motion, his hand had whipped the .44 out of its holster and fired.

Death glinted from Bass' black eyes at the impact, but the impact was not from a bullet alone.

The long, feathered shaft of an arrow stuck out of Bass' back as he pitched from the saddle and landed hard on the harder ground. The dun nickered, lowered his froth-smeared muzzle long enough to absorb the scent of death, nickered again and pumped anodyning air into its aching innards, then moved away from the inanimate creature face down on the dirt.

Keys' gun was still in his hand as he looked up and toward his right.

On a vantage boulder stood a man of color, bow in hand, and even from this distance, his face an insouciant mask. With pantherine grace the man started down, slipping the bow onto the hard lump of his left shoulder near the quiver containing a half-dozen arrows while Keys slipped the .44 into its holster, swung off his mount and moved toward the late Pete Bass.

No word passed between the two men even as the bowman pulled the arrow out of the body.

Keys was a man, big and tall. The other man was bigger and taller, taller by three inches even though Keys wore boots with three-inch heels and the other man was fitted with moccasins.

The two men studied each other for less

than three seconds but that was long enough.

Keys' eyes were deep set and penetrating in a long, lean face set onto a rock-hard body of catgut and gristle with a narrow waist surrounded by a black leather belt that held a black holster hosting an ivory-handled .44. Every other garment he wore from head to heel was beige and blended into the sun-dry hue of the landscape.

The other, bigger man was garbed in buckskin, a gladiator of indeterminate origin, but obviously of blended bloodlines — black and bronze, a tribal compote — African and American Indian. A holstered Navy Colt hovered just below the right side of his waistline.

Keys nodded back toward the two boulders that flanked the gorge.

"They were waiting for me." He glanced at the body of Pete Bass. "And you were waiting for him. That it?"

"That's it." The man's voice was deep and impersonal.

"You could've been of more help with those two." Keys' thumb motioned back toward the snipers.

"Didn't care about those two."

"Or me."

The bowman still held the bloodied arrow

and pointed it toward its former target.

"Just him."

"The manifesto of a true mercenary."

"Five hundred dollars' worth."

"Two hundred and fifty."

"That's fair," the bowman said without hesitating.

"You'd be Elijah." Keys smiled.

Elijah nodded.

"Jeff Keys."

"Yes," Elijah nodded again, "I know."

"You seem to know a lot."

"About some things. Not others."

"About that." Keys pointed to the bow on Elijah's shoulder.

"Mother's side."

"Comanche?"

"Kiowa."

"Father?"

"Slave."

"Not anymore."

"No. He's dead."

"A lot of good men died — on both sides. War's over."

"There's wars — and wars."

"We take 'em one at a time."

"Or they take us."

"Not yet." Keys smiled.

"No, not yet, Mister Keys."

"Jeff."

"Jefferson." Elijah nearly smiled. "Not as in Davis."

"No. As in Thomas."

"I wonder which side he would have been on?"

"I don't."

"You seem to know a lot."

"About some things." Keys was still smiling. "Not others. But about some things I'm sure."

"It's good to be sure."

"And it's good to be alive — and to collect our bounty."

"That we agree on."

Keys motioned toward the boulders.

"Will you help me bury those two?"

"I will."

CHAPTER TWO

Some men know each other, talk to each other, travel miles and miles together for days, months, even years, and never really get to understand each other, at least not enough to feel any kinship between them.

The opposite was true of Jefferson Keys and the man called Elijah.

As the two rode together toward the town of Bootjack, leading the dun carrying the curved body of Pete Bass wrapped in a blanket, they had known each other just a few hours and less than a hundred words had passed between them.

But neither of them had the slightest doubt about the other man's integrity.

Each had heard stories about the other — stories told and re-told and, as usual around campfires and on tiresome trails, stories that evolved with each telling into almost mythical proportions.

Exaggeration was an integral core of the lore of the West.

Keys' eyes glanced to the left at the man riding by his side. No doubt he was much man, but unlike the myths, he was not eight feet tall — and he probably couldn't dance on the moon — nor track a man from this world clear to the next — and chances were that he would ride around a forest fire, not through it. It was unlikely that he could put an arrow into a mosquito flying fifty feet away.

Exaggerations.

The stuff that myths are made of.

Still . . .

Behind every exaggeration, every flowering myth, there is at least a kernel of substance.

The same was true about the tales that Elijah had heard regarding Jefferson Keys

13

— "Big Medicine," the Indians would term him — a man of Homeric deeds during the war for, and against, the Confederacy — scout, spy, Custer's hammer, and later, Juarez's strategist in the liberation of Mexico from Maximilian's stranglehold. A man who could perform miracles with dynamite — destroy an entire village with one stick, and leave only the church standing.

Exaggerations.

The stuff that myths are made of.

Still . . .

In spite of the fact that they had met only a few hours ago, and only a handful of words had passed between them, they knew and respected one another — as the two rode together toward Bootjack.

CHAPTER THREE

Bootjack.

Just about like any other flyspeck town in the West — except that its past had no future and its future had no past.

Bootjack raddled in a cross pattern of buildings, mostly adobe — once a part of Mexico, currently a dirty thumbprint in the middle of the Arizona Territory.

The cross streets were now named Main and Front — formerly *Hidalgo* and *Chupa-*

14

dero — with structures that included a saloon, bank, barbershop, stagecoach and telegraph station, and sundry other enterprises barely subsisting while waiting for a railroad line that would never come close.

The sheriff's office was in an undistinguished structure housing two jail cells and an undistinguished sheriff named John Smith. Smith had been appointed by the town council consisting mostly of his relatives. He looked and dressed the same as most of the other undistinguished citizens except for the star pinned to his coffee- and tobacco-stained vest.

The two identical dodgers that had been in the possession of Keys and Elijah now lay on Sheriff Smith's disarrayed desk.

$500
PETE BASS
WANTED
MURDER and ROBBERY
Douglas, Arizona Territory
Dead or Alive
Tattooed Naked Lady on Left Arm
$500

Upon delivery of the body, Keys and Elijah were informed by Sheriff John Smith that they would have to wait until Doctor James Smith — also undertaker — could confirm in writing that the corpse was actually a corpse and determine the cause of his current condition.

After leaving their horses and some of their weapons — Keys, the .6 gauge, Elijah, his bow and quiver of arrows — at the stable, Keys and Elijah had been sitting for nearly half an hour across the desk from the cigar-smoking Sheriff Smith, waiting for the pipe-smoking Doctor Smith, who was a shorter, older, heavier version of his brother, to return with the official confirmation and cause.

Sheriff Smith was not much of one for conversation or conviviality. He sat and smoked in silence, not bothering to make use of the empty ashtray on his desk.

Keys finally cut through the silence and the smoke.

"Sheriff, couldn't we wait somewhere else?"

"Such as?"

"The saloon. The street. The stable with our horses."

"Best you two wait here. It won't be long now."

"Speaking of horses," Keys looked at Elijah, then back to the sheriff, "what about his horse?"

"Whose horse?"

Keys pointed to the dodgers.

"What about it?"

"Horse, saddle, the rest . . . who do they belong to?"

"Not you two. Just the reward."

The door opened and Doctor James Smith entered and placed a sheet of paper on the desk atop the dodgers.

"It's official," Doctor Smith said as he re-lit his pipe after striking a match on the side of his pants. "Pete Bass is dead at the present time. Cause of demise, a bullet in the heart or an arrow in the spine — or both."

"Imagine that," Keys said. "Now do we collect?"

"Not now," Sheriff Smith said. "You have to wait 'til I telegraph Douglas and get authorization for a bank draft. You know that."

"Sure I do. But I don't know how long it'll take."

"Neither do I. Two or three days, maybe."

"We'll wait."

"Sure you will."

"Now can we leave? Your office, I mean."

"Sure you can."

Both Keys and Elijah rose. Keys smiled as

Doctor Smith went through the same procedure in re-lighting his pipe again, this time with a sucking sound.

"Doctor, thanks for your cooperation."

"It's my job."

"Thanks, anyhow."

"By the way," the sheriff said, "the horse and saddle will just about take care of Bass' burial expenses."

"Sure it will." Keys nodded.

"One more thing, Mister Keys. I know this . . . man here" — he pointed his cigar at Elijah — "has a reputation as a bounty hunter, but since when did you turn tracker?"

"It was something besides money. Something personal."

"But" — Sheriff Smith smiled a cynical smile — "you'll take the money."

"You bet. And when the money comes you can probably find us in the saloon having a drink."

After Keys and Elijah left the office, Sheriff Smith looked at his brother.

"That ought to be interesting," the sheriff said.

CHAPTER FOUR

Years ago when it too was a part of Mexico, the sign had read *HERMANOS CANTINA;* in the years since, after the sign was painted over, its identity proclaimed *PALACE SALOON.* It was a saloon alright, but closer to a pesthole than a palace. Howsomever, it was the only pesthole in Bootjack that served what passed for beer and whiskey.

Keys and Elijah walked through the bat-winged entrance. Along one side, wide wooden planks on six barrels served as the bar, a crude wooden shelf beneath a warped mirror served as back-bar. Sawdust mixed with other matter on a wood floor that hadn't been swept the night before, or months before. Half a dozen tables, all round, with chairs, most of them occupied with dirty denizens. A haze of smoke from cigars, cigarettes, and pipes climbed toward the tin ceiling.

The denizens looked up from their drinks and card games. Two women, both wearing whores' war paint, looked down from a flimsy balcony fronting second-story cribs.

Keys and Elijah both moved to the bar, tended by a square-built man with a square-built face that looked like a block of rancid cheese, wearing a battered green derby.

Cheese-face looked directly at Keys.

"Call it," he rasped.

Keys took a coin from his vest pocket, placed it atop the bar.

"Whiskey. A bottle. Two glasses."

Cheese-face reached over to the back-bar, lifted a bottle labeled "Preferred Stock," removed the cork, set the bottle on the bar, reached back again to a row of glasses, picked up a single glass and set it next to the bottle. He started to pick up the coin.

"Just a minute," Keys said, "maybe you didn't hear me. I said two glasses."

"I heard you. We don't cater to" — Cheese-face pointed to Elijah — "whatever that is."

Elijah smiled and started to walk away. Keys' hand moved slightly toward his companion.

"Hold on."

"Don't push it," Elijah said.

"Good advice."

The voice came from one of two men who had approached the bar. Both nearly the size of Elijah, both with porcine features and protruding hog eyes. One of the two men had a hairlip that made him slightly less homely than the other.

"Take it," Hairlip said. "And take the

bottle if you want and go drink somewhere else."

"You two own this establishment?" Keys inquired.

"No," Hairlip said, "we're customers, and just like all the other customers in this establishment, me and my brother are particular about who we drink with."

"Oh, you're brothers. I never would have guessed, but then, there seem to be a lot of brothers here in Bootjack."

"What're you talkin' about?" Hairlip asked.

"The sheriff and the doctor, you two . . . and I'd like to introduce you to my brother. His name is Elijah."

"Him?!" Hairlip laughed. So did his brother. So did the bartender, the other customers, and the two whores from the balcony.

"We're all brothers under the skin," Keys said. "Aren't we?"

"Not around here," Hairlip said.

"Not unless they got white skin," his brother added. "So if you two is brothers then *you* ain't white either, so you're both . . ."

"Both what?" Keys asked.

"Niggers," Hairlip said.

"Or redskins," Hairlipless added. "What's

worse, I don't know."

"I do," Keys said as his left fist exploded into the brother's nose, squashing it like a tomato.

Elijah's right crashed into Hairlip's hairlip, crumbling a few front teeth.

A dozen other customers swarmed into the melee swinging fists and chairs and bottles. Back to back, Keys and Elijah smashed faces and bodies, propelling them into tables, careening into each other amidst sounds of knuckles against flesh, grunts, groans — crashing the front and back-bars asunder and turning the *PALACE* into a shambles as the sheriff's shotgun went off.

Sheriff John Smith stood at the bat-wings, his finger on the second trigger. Damn few other people were standing besides Keys, Elijah and the two whores on the balcony.

Jefferson Keys and the man called Elijah were in separate, but equal, adjacent jail cells.

The way that Sheriff John Smith heard it, these two vicious predators attacked, without provocation, a couple dozen defenseless — male and female — citizens of Bootjack. In the weight of such testimony the good sheriff had no recourse but to incarcerate said predators in order to keep the good citizens of Bootjack out of harm's way until such time as the extent of damage inflicted on bodies and furniture could be estimated and due punishment determined.

The sheriff was away conducting both assessments as the brace of lawbreakers languished in confinement.

Jefferson Keys stood with both fists clenched around the cell bars while Elijah lay on his bunk, feet extended far over the edge, with both hands behind his head and a relatively quiescent expression on his face.

"Damn sheriff's been away a long time," Keys said.

"You miss him?"

"This is no time for humor."

"Then don't laugh."

"Who's laughing?"

"The gods. What fools we mortals be," Elijah said.

"Now you're a philosopher."

"Not me, nor the conscience of the world."

"What's that mean?"

"It means, I said 'Don't push it.' "

"Just walk away, huh?"

"At least we'd be walking instead of keeping the roaches company in here."

"Don't tell me you always walk away."

"Not always, but I do consider the odds."

23

"We weren't doing so bad." Keys smiled.

"Until the sheriff stepped in."

"Speaking of the sheriff," Keys said, "I think I hear the heavy footsteps of the law approaching."

Sheriff John Smith did approach. He entered the cell area with some papers in his right hand and a brass ring with a large key in his left hand and the butt of a cigar in his mouth.

"Good day, Sheriff," Keys said. "Glad to see you."

No verbal response came from the lawman. He proceeded to unlock both cell doors, then motioned for both liberated occupants to follow him.

They did.

Into his office, where he sat behind his desk as the two men stood and waited for what was to come.

What came was about a minute of further silence before the sheriff spoke.

"Assault and mayhem. Disturbing the peace. Destroying property. Those are just some of the charges . . ."

"When's the trial?" Keys asked.

"Trial's over. You're lookin' at the judge and jury."

"Is that how it's done in Bootjack?"

"That's how it's done in Bootjack, Mister Keys."

"What's the verdict, Your Honor?"

"First off, I stopped by the telegraph office. There's two items that concern this matter." He held up two pieces of paper. "This here's the bank draft for the five hundred reward."

"That's good." Keys looked at Elijah and nodded.

"The verdict is guilty and the five hundred will just about cover the damages unless you two choose to be confined for a long, long time."

"That's not good. But we don't. Do we, brother Elijah?"

Elijah shook his head no.

"Didn't think so — so both of you sign the draft right here over to me. Can you both write your names?"

They both nodded and both signed with a pen provided by the lawman.

Sheriff John Smith folded the draft and tucked it into his shirt pocket.

"Now you two can leave Bootjack in a hurry and forget about ever comin' back — or even comin' close."

"You've seen the last of us, Sheriff." Keys pointed to the other piece of paper. "But do you mind telling us about that second item from the telegraph office?"

"Oh, that."

"Yeah, that."

"Almost forgot. It's a telegraph forwarded to you, Mister Keys, askin' you to be somewhere and get paid one hundred dollars for showin' up. Couldn't help but read it."

"I'm sure you couldn't. Too bad you can't collect that hundred, too."

"Just get your animals and get out of Bootjack in a hurry."

"We're on our way, Sheriff, but just one thing . . ."

"What?"

"Do you mind handing me that telegraph you couldn't help reading?"

Half an hour later both Keys and Elijah were mounted and at the edge of the friendly community of Bootjack.

"Well," Keys said, "it's been pleasurable if not profitable."

"That it has, and at least we're better off than Pete Bass."

"About Pete Bass . . ."

"What about him?"

"You were after him for the reward."

"That's the ticket."

"When the sheriff asked, I told him that with me it was also something personal.

26

Remember?"

"I remember."

"You never asked what."

"You said it was personal."

Keys nodded.

"Well, I want you to know."

"That makes it different."

"The guard he killed in that bank robbery in Douglas was named Tom Green. Tom was in Custer's Wolverine Brigade at Yellow Tavern and Appomattox . . . and so was I."

"Heard you were."

"Tom Green was a good man."

"Pete Bass wasn't."

"No, he wasn't." Keys pointed to the fork in the road. "Which way you heading?"

"North, to Fisbee. Know a marshal there provides me with fresh dodgers."

"That's helpful."

"I provide him with part of the reward."

"That's business."

"Yep." Elijah nodded. "The way of the world. You?"

"South." Keys took the telegraph from his shirt pocket. "Going to meet a couple of fellows . . ."

"And a hundred dollars?"

"That's what it says." He put the telegraph back in the pocket. "Well, maybe again sometime . . ."

27

"Not in Bootjack." Elijah smiled.

"No, not in Bootjack. But maybe somewhere else."

"Sure." Elijah nodded. "It's a creation-big world, but trails cross."

Keys extended his hand.

They shook.

"Adios, Elijah."

"So long, Jefferson."

The man called Elijah rode north. Jefferson Keys rode south.

Chapter Five

Once again Jeff Keys rode alone.

After the war there were thousands like him from North and South. But like snowflakes and cinders, no two were exactly alike — and unlike Keys, thousands had served with the South and lost. But they were the luckier among the losers; at least they had survived. Keys was on the side of those who won — if anyone on either side wins without losing at least a part of himself.

Both sides had buried and left their brethren behind in fields, on hillsides, near streams and forests, north and south of the Mason-Dixon Line. Eternally asleep by one another. Countrymen again forever.

North and South, they had come from the

streets of cities and villages, from factories and farms, rich and poor, the reluctant and the eager — some heeding the call of the Confederacy, but more, many more, responding to the creed of Union Forever.

Many of the officers on opposite sides, including Robert E. Lee and Ulysses Simpson Grant, had once worn the same uniform at West Point and later during the Mexican campaign. Lee had at one time been the commandant at West Point and was even offered command of the Union Forces at the outbreak of the Civil War, declining after a monumental struggle with himself and writing, almost apologetically to his beloved sister who lived in the North, *". . . with all my devotion to the Union and the feeling of loyalty and duty of an American citizen, I have not been able to make up my mind to raise my hand against my relatives, my children, my home."*

Jefferson Keys, although only a lieutenant, also made his decision.

After those first years of the conflict when he did irreparable damage to the enemy serving as scout, spy and dynamiter for the Union, Keys managed to secure a commission as captain, and join the command of the "Boy General" George Armstrong Custer in time for the campaigns and charges at

Yellow Tavern and Appomattox.

It was at Yellow Tavern, the night before the fateful charge, where he sat up with Tom Green and talked. The night before each battle soldiers seldom slept. They wanted to savor life, to breathe, to smoke, to remember. Young Captain Green wore a sunny-faced perpetual smile, even on what could likely be their last night on earth. Green, an orphan, talked about going West — building a ranch, and later a family to call his own. Keys mostly listened, but they promised to keep in touch — if they survived.

They did survive.

But "Jeb" Stuart, the South's charismatic cavalier, didn't. General James Ewell Brown Stuart, the Confederacy's boldest, most beloved cavalry commander, whose Black Horse Raiders hit like bolts of lightning into the Northern blue ranks and won victory after victory for nearly two years, until the "Boy General," with Keys and Green at his side, charged against Stuart's Invincibles at Yellow Tavern and brought down Stuart himself.

It was said that after Jeb Stuart died the South never smiled again.

But Tom Green kept smiling and after the war he did go West and did keep in touch with Jeff Keys. For years Green's letters caught up to Keys before and after Keys had been to Mexico, and in the last letter he said that he had gone bust at ranching, was still hoping to have a family of his own someday, but in the meantime he'd taken a job in Douglas, Arizona Territory, as a bank guard.

Tom Green's last letter caught up to Keys after the sender was already dead — killed by Pete Bass.

That's when Jeff Keys rode to Douglas, Arizona Territory, picked up a dodger and did what he knew he had to do — kill a son of a bitch named Pete Bass.

Once again Jeff Keys rode alone.

CHAPTER SIX

There were no signs of Indians — which meant that there was a damn good possibility that there were Indians around.

This had been their home, their heartland until the invaders came from this and other continents. Mexicans. Spaniards. Bringing horses and gunpowder. And finally those who came to stay. Americans, the most determined. Land-hungry. Unyielding. Undaunted. Wave after uncountable wave. A perpetual procession of seekers. Cattlemen. Entrepreneurs. Farmers. Outlaws and

31

lawmen — all under the invisible escutcheon of something called "Manifest Destiny."

As early as 1845, an article appeared in an Eastern newspaper declaring: "Our Manifest Destiny is to overspread the continent allotted by Providence for the free development of our yearly multiplying millions. We will realize our Manifest Destiny."

Nothing at all was said about the destiny of the Indians. Not that these so-called indigenous tribes had ever lived a pacific existence among themselves. Apache, Comanche, Kiowa, Navajo, Cherokee and all the rest raided, robbed, raped and did their best — or worst — to destroy their red brethren. Even within themselves there was internecine warfare. Mimbreño, Chirachaua, White Mountain, Tonto — all Apache — but not all at peace with each other.

During the war between North and South, the Union Army needed all the manpower that was available, especially if that manpower had already been exposed to the ways of war.

Much of that manpower was in the West. Ergo, almost all of the Western forts were abandoned or reduced in ranks, allowing the hostiles to become even more hostile.

But in the years since, the onslaught of

settlers and entrepreneurs had resumed with even greater momentum, and so had the presence of the U.S. Military.

But the West, including the Arizona Territory, was far from won, particularly the territory adjacent to the Mexican border — the territory into which Jefferson Keys rode.

An improbable sight.

Even for the eyes of Jefferson Keys, whose eyes had seen many improbable sights, during war — wars — and what passed for peace.

The Arizona desert. Known, yet unknown. Unfrequented. Unpopulated. Untamed.

Full many a flower is born to blush unseen
And waste its fragrance on the desert air.

The desert is the birthplace of strange deceptions — sometimes called mirages, sometimes illusions, delusions, chimeras, sometimes madness.

Water where there is no water. Castles where there are no structures. Loreleis where there are no women.

Just as he had topped out on a hillock, Keys reined in his horse, stopped, and studied what appeared in the distance.

He gazed for more than a minute, shook

his head, blinked, and gazed some more.

Still there.

Not a delusion.

Not a mirage.

Not madness.

This had to be the destination specified in the telegraph.

The country had been united by steel tracks and a gold spike at Promontory Summit on May 10, 1869, long after the Union Pacific had pushed west out of Omaha and the Central Pacific had pushed east from Sacramento. In the brief time since then, as time is measured, short-line track had been spoked in all directions throughout the country — still it was an improbable sight, less than a mile away in the midst of a forlorn sea of sand and stone.

The sun shone down on a railroad spur in the hub of nowhere. Keys rode slowly to get a better view of what occupied the gleaming tracks that, no matter how unlikely, definitely did not constitute a mirage.

A locomotive, still belching smoke, but stationary, was coupled to the engine, a utility car, and a brilliant red and black private coach. The engine idled near a water tower. Close by, a large blue tent had been set up. A chef and several assistants were working over and around a spit, preparing all the trappings of a regal banquet.

As Keys rode closer, passing the water tower, he caught sight of something even more improbable — and breathtaking — a beautiful female taking a noontime shower.

She was tall for a woman, but there was no doubt about her womanhood. If she wore anything, it was of gossamer, clinging material that did nothing to conceal the composition of her voluptuous body. Much as he thought it wise to immediately avert his eyes, Keys couldn't help visually consuming, for just a little longer, the shimmering vision, water splashing onto the flowing red hair that fell in burnished waves onto her alabaster shoulders. She turned slowly so that her sun-lit body glistened. Her full-moon breasts swayed uninhibited over a small circle of waist, then blossomed into healthy hips tapering down long lovely legs.

From this distance, Keys could not determine the color of her eyes, but that really didn't matter. He knew those eyes had seen him, and that didn't matter either, not to her. Not as she was revolving and making no attempt to conceal her activity — or her endowments.

Keys had seen females of all colors and shapes, but this one was more than worth the trip even if he didn't collect the hundred dollars.

Howsomever, he intended to collect, and proceeded toward less inviting activity and individuals a hundred or so feet away.

At the banquet area, shaded by the huge open flap of the tent, sat two gentlemen involved in discussion — closer to debate.

Although Keys didn't know it at the time, the two gentlemen were partners named Waxer and Kline.

Willard Oliver Waxer and Simon Ignatius Kline, partners, highly successful partners in sometimes highly dubious enterprises — speculation, development, cattle, mining, and all-around flimflam — partners who rarely started out agreeing on anything and always ended up disagreeing on nothing. Partners who outwardly had nothing in common, particularly their appearance.

Willard Oliver Waxer was a tall, dyspeptic tabernacle of a man, huge of girth — at least three hundred pounds — heavy of brow and jowls, with a full head of blue-grey hair — most of it underneath a black deer stalker cap. His body was shrouded in a black suit made of enough material to fashion a fair-size sail. Every movement was a major effort and his voice was deeper than a grave, coming from some inner darkness.

Simon Ignatius Kline was a ferret of a fellow with narrow face, darting eyes behind steel-rimmed spectacles, and sparse, straight, pale hair that matched his complexion. He was just a tad over sixty inches tall — or short — string-thin and didn't weigh a hundred twenty pounds before his morning bowel movement. He wore a tilted brown homburg and a blue four-button pinstripe suit of barely enough material to make up a vest for Willard Oliver Waxer. Kline seemed to be in ceaseless motion as he spoke with the voice of a constipated canary.

Waxer sipped from an oversized glass of milk while Kline gorged himself on cheeses and fruits and whatever else he could lay his hands on as each took opposite sides on the issue of their current debate.

Another thing that Keys didn't know at the time was that he was an integral part of that debate. Waxer was in favor of Keys while Kline trumpeted the qualifications of someone else.

The debate continued until Keys dismounted and stood in front of the banquet table.

Waxer looked up and smiled approvingly. Kline stood up in squinting appraisal, through his steel-rimmed spectacles.

"You must be Keys." Waxer beamed.

Keys nodded.

"We appreciate your coming all this distance."

"It was just a cat jump." Keys removed the telegraph from his pocket and placed it on the table. "It says one hundred dollars for showing up here at noon today."

There were two stacks, five double eagles in each stack, on the table.

Waxer's fat hand pushed one of the stacks toward Keys.

Keys reached down, took the gold coins and placed them in his pocket.

"Anything else?"

"Yes," said Waxer.

"Maybe," said Kline.

"There seems to be a divergence of opinion."

The beautiful girl, draped in a wet garment that failed to conceal much, walked to the edge of the table and gave Keys the up and down.

Her eyes were green. A cool, but inviting green.

Since he was being surveyed, Keys took the opportunity to do a little more surveying himself. More than her eyes were inviting. She knew what she had and knew how to use it. Even when she was standing still she seemed to be moving.

She couldn't have been more than twenty-one or twenty-two, but she exuded the haughty confidence of a dauphin's favorite courtesan.

The introductions did not include the lady.

"Mister Keys, I am Willard Oliver Waxer and this is my partner Simon Ignatius Kline. You may have heard of us."

"No, I haven't."

"You haven't?!" Kline squealed.

"No, but then I don't get around much."

"You're too modest," Waxer said. "We happen to know that you do 'get around.' "

"Not in the same circles as you two fellows . . . and, by the way, just what circles are those, gentlemen?"

"We're . . . businessmen. Big business."

"Well, I'm just a small businessman, trying to stay in business."

"Maybe we can help you do that." Waxer smiled.

"Maybe." Keys didn't smile. "You looking for another partner?"

"No," Kline quipped.

"No." Waxer still smiled. "We're quite successful as we are. You see, some years ago we started bidding against each other in a certain enterprise — until we realized it was smarter to pool our resources and out-bid the opposition — so we were that much stronger than the opposition — and the strong take it from the weak."

"But," Keys said, "the smart take it from the strong."

"There's been nobody stronger or smarter," Kline chirped.

"There's always a first time." Keys glanced at the beautiful lady.

"Not always," Kline said. "So don't get any smart ideas."

"I'm just here to listen . . . one hundred dollars' worth."

"You may not know much about us, Mister Keys," Waxer said as he picked up a sheaf of papers from the table, "but we made it our business to find out quite a bit about you. We have a rather complete dossier."

"I see." Keys pointed to a second sheaf of papers on the table. "I also see that you have another dossier . . ."

"We'll get to that later if you don't mind."

"It's your call." Keys shrugged.

"As I said it's rather complete, but I'll just review some of the salient points." Waxer squinted, brought the papers nearer to his owlish face then adjusted the distance a little farther away until his eyes found the proper focus. "Skip this part, skip that part," he mumbled, "uh-huh, start here . . . ran away from the farm at age fifteen . . . joined up as teamster on a wagon train bound for California gold country . . . sidetracked in Arizona by irate Comanches . . . became an Army scout . . . then secured appointment to West Point . . . grades near the top of his class first two years . . . roommate there, Cadet George Armstrong Custer, grades near the bottom of his class . . . after outbreak of war went on special assignment . . . acted as scout and spy and dynamiter throughout the Southern states . . . during third year of war sought and secured commission with rank of captain in his old friend Custer's Wolverine Red Scarf Brigade . . . received several commendations and rose to the rank of major after Charge at Yellow Tavern . . . was present at Lee's surrender to Grant at Appomattox . . ." Waxer looked up at Keys. "Fair appraisal?"

"I guess that about sums it up."

"Oh no, not by a long shot, the most interesting part is still to come." Waxer looked back down at the papers.

". . . after the war between the states, another war at another place . . . Mexico . . . joined the forces of Benito Juarez against

Maximilian, pretender to the 'throne' of Mexico . . . during that war married a Mexican girl, one Dominique Ruiz, who along with their unborn baby was killed in the last days of fighting between Juaristas and Maximilian's mercenaries . . ." Waxer glanced up again. "Oh, I am sorry, Mister Keys."

"Alright you're sorry and we're getting pretty close to the end of that hundred dollars."

"Yes, well, just a trifle more, sir."

Back to the dossier.

". . . left Mexico two years ago, and since then has hired out as . . ."

"As what?" Keys looked from Waxer to Kline, then back at Waxer.

"The term that comes into play," Waxer smiled, "is . . . mercenary."

"Gentlemen, I believe time's run out on that hundred dollars. Now do you two businessmen want to tell me about what, if any, business you have in mind?"

"We're considering you for a job, Mister Keys," Waxer said, "a big money job."

"We're also considering somebody else." Kline nodded. "Somebody else who's also familiar with Mexico. He fought for Maximilian."

"You did hear" — Keys smiled — "that

42

they lost."

"Ah, yes" — Kline nodded — "but he came out much better off, financially that is, than you."

"Sounds like you've already made your choice, Mister Kline, so . . ."

"Please," Waxer took a ponderous step forward, "don't be rash, sir, I assure you that no choice has been made as yet."

"Not afraid of a little competition, are you, Mister Keys?" Kline darted up a couple of feet. "Competition is good. Take away competition and you stifle incentive."

"Depends" — Keys glanced at the beautiful girl — "on how you define incentive."

"I thought we were talking about money," Kline said.

"*You* were talking about money, I . . ."

"In any case," Kline interrupted, "we can stop talking for the time being." He pointed toward a rider approaching, not fast, not slow.

They did stop talking.

They stood silent and watched as the rider, saddled on an ash-white stallion, moved closer and dismounted.

He was tall and erect, with a hard, lean face, perfectly symmetrical, steel-gray eyes, a long, thin nose, a knife-blade mouth, and clean-shaven except for close-cropped sideburns that extended well past pointed earlobes. There was a prominent scar high across his left cheek that might have been caused by a sabre or gunshot. He was dressed all in gray except for the black gun-belt with two low-slung holsters out of which curved two gray-handled .44s.

"And you, I imagine," Kline said cheerfully, "are Mister Valance, Amory Valance?"

The man nodded, removed a telegraph from his vest pocket and placed it on the table.

"Good. Very good," Kline said as he took up the remaining stack of double eagles and let them drop into Valance's out stretched palm.

Valance pocketed the coins.

"I am Simon Ignatius Kline and this is my partner Willard Oliver Waxer." He pointed to Keys. "And this . . ."

"Long time." Valance smiled at Keys.

"Not long enough."

"Obviously you two gentlemen know each other," Waxer observed.

"Mexico," Valance said.

"Ah, yes, Mexico," Kline clucked. "And that is the subject at hand, at least for one of you. We —"

"Good-bye, gentlemen." Keys started to move.

Kline picked up a piece of cheese.

"You haven't heard our proposition." He took a bite.

"Not interested."

"Sir," Waxer said, "this opportunity involves a great deal of money."

"It doesn't involve me." Keys started to move again.

"Keys doesn't want to go back to Mexico," Valance said. "He lost something down there . . ."

Keys stepped close to Valance.

". . . his guts." Valance smirked.

Keys' left exploded into Valance's scarred face, and a right smashed into his gut and another left crashed into his jaw, propelling him into the dinner table, but Valance came roaring back into a primal whirlwind of a contest.

Damn little in the immediate vicinity was spared. The table, the spit, the chairs, the tent, even Waxer and Kline were leveled. The chef and his assistants fled. All but the beautiful girl, who stood still in the eye of the desert hurricane.

Valance absorbed more punishment than seemed possible, but when it was over, he lay battered and unconscious amid the ruins.

Both Waxer and Kline staggered to their

feet as Keys wiped the blood from his mouth.

"Well, boys," Keys pointed to the inanimate heap on the ground, then looked up at Waxer and Kline, "there's your man, except he has the habit of losing wars — first with the Confederacy, then with Maximilian."

Keys moved toward his mount and passed the beautiful girl.

"Nice visiting with you, ma'am."

CHAPTER SEVEN

As he rode back across the desert, Keys couldn't help reflecting on what Waxer had read about him from the sheaf of papers.

One phrase burned in his brain . . . *during that war married a Mexican girl, one Dominique Ruiz, who along with their unborn baby was killed in the last days of fighting between Juaristas and Maximilian's mercenaries . . . one Dominique Ruiz . . . one Dominique Ruiz . . .*

As if those words could sum up the existence of the woman Keys had loved more than anything in this world and of their child who never came into it.

For years Keys had been trying to erase that pain from the tables of his memory, a

pain that he knew could never be erased —
from his brain or his heart.

Killed in a raid by a force that included
Amory Valance in its ranks.

Keys didn't want to think of that, now, or
ever. But he couldn't help smiling now, or
when Waxer had mentioned the name of
George Armstrong Custer. Custer was
known by a lot of other names, the first of
which was Autie — because when he was
just learning to talk he couldn't say Armstrong; it came out Autie, and it stuck —
later came Curly, Suicide Custer, Cinna-
mon, Goldie Locks, and up north the Sioux
called him Yellow Hair.

Custer, who always rode to the sound of
the guns. Toward glory. Who saw glory in
every campaign. But that was later. Keys
thought of the times at West Point with
Custer, the best cavalry man there since Ulysses Simpson Grant, but unlike Grant, a
dashing, spirited, carefree cavalier, a prank-
ster who time after time courted trouble
not only for himself but also for his roommate, cadet Jefferson Keys. One of those
pranks involved a superior officer who took
great pride in a flock of prize hens and a
buff cock he had dubbed "Mister Chanti-
cleer," which kept Custer and the other
cadets awake with his boastful crowing until

cadet Custer took it upon himself to kidnap the cock, dispatch and pluck it, prepare the unfeathered remains in a stew pan and, with Keys' assistance, devour the result, and subsequently enjoy the uninterrupted sleep of satisfaction, if not innocence. The superior officer had his suspicions as to the identity of the culprit, but lacked sufficient evidence of proof.

But there were two things that Custer was serious about. His beautiful wife, Libbie, and war. He gloried in both.

In one battle after another, starting as barely more than a teenage lieutenant at Chickahoming, he led charge after charge as he became the "Boy General" through bloody encounters including Gettysburg, where Custer's Michigan Red Scarf Wolverines charged again and again and prevented Stuart's Invincibles from hooking up with Pickett in that valiant charge that would have sealed the doom of the North if it had succeeded. It did not succeed because of Custer.

Through those earlier years of the war Keys had acted alone without uniform as scout, spy and single-handed devastator of bridges, railroads, ammunition depots and other strategic elements of the South. But all that time he yearned to don a uniform and confront the enemy face to face and sword to sword.

It finally happened, after he had been captured, identified, and managed to escape before he could be shot as a spy. He was given a commission and uniform and granted his request to join Custer's Red Scarf Brigade in time to ride at the side of his former West Point roommate at Yellow Tavern and Appomattox.

At Appomattox, Custer stood by Grant and Sheridan when General Robert E. Lee signed the Terms of Confederate Surrender on a small writing table inside McLean's house.

Afterward Sheridan paid McLean twenty dollars for that same table and presented it to Libbie along with a note that said, in part, *". . . permit me to say, madam, there is scarcely an individual in our service who had contributed more to bring about this desirable result than your gallant husband."*

No one could ever speak of Jefferson Keys' contribution at Appomattox, but those who knew, particularly Ulysses Simpson Grant, could never forget.

After that war Libbie went West with her husband when he took over the Seventh Cavalry at Forts Hays, Harker, Wallace, Dodge and Riley. Custer was still leading charges as he quickly mastered the art of Indian fighting in successful campaigns against the Cheyennes, Arapahos, Kiowas and Comanches — until last year, when in defiance of an order, Custer faced a court marshal and suffered the loss of a year's pay because he had made a mad dash to join Libbie at Fort Riley and escort her safely through Indian Territory to Fort Wallace.

It was only due to Sheridan's intervention that Custer's Army career was suspended, not ended.

Meanwhile Custer was languishing in Michigan waiting until the Indian hostilities heated up enough for the Army to realize Custer's worth to the West far exceeded his transgression for the love of his Libbie.

In letters they had exchanged, Autie had asked his old roommate and comrade to join him if and when the Army saw fit to give him back his command of the Seventh. Jefferson Keys replied that he would give the matter serious consideration . . . if and when.

In his saddlebag Keys still carried a folded Red Scarf that had once been a part of his uniform when he rode alongside Autie.

But now, after his encounter with Messrs. Waxer and Kline, the beautiful wet lady, and Valance, Jefferson Keys rode toward the not-so-far-off hamlet of Claypool, which consisted of much clay and no pool.

Howsomever, Keys did have five double eagles in his pocket, more than enough — much more than enough — for a good hotel room and a hot tub bath.

Chapter Eight

Jefferson Keys, bootless, his bruised and aching body stripped to the waist, poured another bucket of hot water into the tarnished brass bathtub that had been set in the center of the hotel room — the best room in the hotel, but not a very good room.

He had only been in Claypool a couple of hours, but between the Waxer and Kline episode and his introduction to this community, he had already had enough excitement to round out a full day — and the day wasn't quite over yet.

Most towns in the West — and other places — are where they are for some good reason: a river, a stream, a spring, a trail — something.

There was no discernable reason for Claypool's location — or existence. It just happened to be there — as if a group of nomads got tired and decided to stop and rest, and then decided if they moved on they'd just get tired someplace else, so they might as well stay here.

Claypool grew, but not very much. It's been said that nature builds things crooked and men build things straight.

Claypool and whoever designed it gave lie to whoever said that. It looked like it had been built without benefit of yardstick or miter. But like every other town that could be called a town, the wood and adobe structures included a saloon, a stable, a general store, a two-story hotel, and a sheriff's office with a sheriff who leaned back on a shaded chair on the boardwalk in front of that office. Any strangers such as Jefferson Keys who rode into Claypool could tell he was the sheriff by the badge pinned onto his canvas vest. He also wore a .44.

He tipped the chair forward on all four legs as he spoke, but did not rise, not at first.

"You!" The sheriff spit out the word, then a splash of tobacco juice. "Hold up, there!"

Keys reined in his mount.

Then the sheriff did rise.

"Step off that animal."

Keys stepped off.

"Stranger, aren't you?"

"Around here, not in other places."

"Don't get smart with me, sonny."

"I'll try my best."

"What's your name?"

"Keys. What's yours, Sheriff?"

"Rawlins. Say, didn't I see you ride through here about first light this mornin'?"

"Camped just outside of town." Keys nodded.

Over the last part of the conversation, a burly, red-headed fellow approached and stood just to the side and behind Sheriff Rawlins.

"You were headed west," the sheriff noted.

"That's right."

"Where you headed now?"

"No place."

"Gonna camp outside of town?"

"Nope."

"We got a law against vagrants here in Claypool."

"Vagrants arc indigent, aren't they, Sheriff?"

"In-dig-ent. What's that mean?"

"Means broke."

"That's right."

"Well, that's not me, Sheriff." Keys withdrew the five double eagles from his pocket and let them drop into his other hand, then back, then replaced them into the pocket.

"Uh-huh." The sheriff spat out another

splash of tobacco juice. "How long you gonna be in town?"

"Long enough to stable my horse, get a drink or two, spend the night in your hotel up the street, then move on."

"Sounds right."

"Say, Sheriff, is that fellow your deputy?" Keys pointed to the red-headed burly fellow.

"Nope. That's my cousin. Keep your nose clean while you're in town."

"You bet."

After that, Keys did just as he said he would do.

The stable. The saloon where he bought two quarts of whiskey; then he headed toward the hotel carrying the saddlebags, the whiskey in a sack and the sawed-off .6 gauge.

The sun was starting to settle in, throwing long shadows, and as Keys started to walk across one of the shadows near an alley, he heard movement, whirled just in time to see a burly figure bringing a gun barrel down toward his head. Keys ducked, took the blow on his shoulder, dropped everything but the shotgun and swung it hard into the burly man's red beard.

The burly, red-bearded man went down like a shot buffalo.

Just then the sheriff appeared.

"What the hell's goin' on here?"

"Ask him." Keys pointed to the sheriff's cousin, who was trying to stagger to his feet.

He finally did, with the sheriff's help.

"It's all a mistake . . ." Red-Beard mumbled. "I thought he was somebody else . . . I thought . . . let's just forget it . . ."

"That alright with you . . . Mister Keys?"

"Sure, Sheriff, no harm done, except one of my whiskey bottles got broke."

Keys picked up everything but the broken whiskey bottle and headed toward the hotel.

Now as he reached down to bring up another bucket of now-tepid water, he stopped midway and instead reached into his pocket, pulled out the four remaining double eagles and the considerable change from the one he had cashed in at the saloon and used to pay for the hotel.

The proprietor of the saloon, Claude Crenshaw, had stood bug-eyed at the sight of the gold coin, and after biting into it, had to go to the safe in the back room in order to procure the proper change after deducting three dollars for the two quarts of rye. The dozen or so other occupants of the saloon were no less mesmerized at the sight of such coin of the realm.

The hotel room for the night including

the hot tub bath came to one dollar fifty cents, so the remainder from the double eagle — including the twenty-five cents Keys had tipped the boy who lugged up the buckets of hot water — amounted to just over fifteen dollars.

Keys tossed the four double eagles and change onto the bed and reached again for the bucket when he stopped abruptly. He noticed the knob of the door handle turning silent and slow.

The boy who brought up the buckets had left the door unlocked and so had Keys, who now picked up the .6 gauge, moved off to the left and leveled the weapon toward the door that was being pushed open.

In the ensuing split second, at least two possibilities raced through Keys' mind.

The first possibility: burly Red-Beard, who might have decided not to forget the shotgun smash in the face and now sought reprisal. The other, more deadly possibility: Amory Valance, who had recovered sufficiently to track Keys, seek him out — and do him in.

Jefferson Keys was completely unprepared for an alternative possibility that now appeared in the doorway.

It couldn't be said that he wasn't surprised . . . and pleased.

She stood there with basket in hand. This time dry but still alluring.

The beautiful girl closed and bolted the door behind her.

"Thought you might be hungry."

"What've you got? Leftovers?"

"I'm not just talking about what's in the basket."

"Neither am I."

Not only could she talk, she spoke with a soft, lilting cadence almost as inviting as the look of those green eyes and the rest of her. She wore a clinging light blue blouse and a darker blue skirt that did nothing to conceal the curves underneath.

"You've got a good build for a man your age . . . or any age."

"Vice-versa. But then, of course, you know that."

"I know a lot of things."

"Such as?"

"This." She set down the basket, took a step closer and started to undress, first herself, then him.

CHAPTER NINE

The double eagles and the rest of the money once on the bed had ended up on the floor.

Keys had known many women. But none

like this one. A cat. A tiger. A tiger, tiger burning bright. A hungry tiger. A sweet savage. Gleaming and groaning. Giving and getting. With a seething tenderness and a raging tranquility. She was pleasure and pain. Softness and strain. Fire and ice. With body and soul. More woman than Keys had ever met. She was all woman and Jefferson Keys' cup ranneth over.

Still later, Keys lay on the bed leaning against the headboard, eating a chicken leg.

The beautiful girl was in the brass tub taking a bath.

"You are the washingest woman I ever met."

"You know what they say about cleanliness . . ."

"Right. Well, let's get to it."

"To what? I thought we already . . ."

"You didn't come here to take a bath or meet the right man."

"There are no right men, bucko, there's just men. Now roll us a cigarette and I'll tell you a story."

Keys built a cigarette, lit it, walked close to the tub, handed it to her, then sat on a chair nearby.

"Why don't you start by telling me your name."

"I'm called a lot of things."

"What do they call you mostly when you're at home?"

"Home, that's just a word, but first let me get to the story."

"I'm listening."

"It's a long story."

"I got all night."

"It starts during the Civil War. By February of 1865 even the leaders of the Confederacy realized that their cause was doomed. But some of those leaders had a plan.

"They would move all the Confederacy's gold that they could get their hands on out of the country into Mexico and make a deal with the sympathetic Maximilian to establish a new country within the Mexican border.

"So in March of '65, Colonel Leigh Shelby led an expedition through Louisiana, across Texas and into Mexico carrying five million dollars, more or less, in gold bullion.

"When his wagons broke down, Shelby ordered the gold be buried near the spot and the expedition was to proceed south toward Mexico City and Maximilian.

"But before the expedition could proceed, a band of killer Yaqui raiders led by Mangus attacked the expedition. The Yaquis murdered all but one.

"Elizabeth Shelby, Colonel Shelby's

59

daughter, was the lone survivor. She was barely fifteen when she became the wife of Mangus. For nearly six years Elizabeth Shelby survived in the mountains and desert — the only white woman in the bloody camp of Mangus.

"During that time, Maximilian's government fell. Maximilian was executed and Juarez became president of Mexico.

"One night in January of '70, the Juaristas attacked Mangus' camp. Mangus was wounded and taken prisoner, but Elizabeth Shelby escaped and made her way to the Texas border.

"Six months later she was working in Madam Pleasant's high-class whorehouse in San Francisco.

"That's where she met Simon Ignatius Kline of the firm Waxer and Kline. And that's when and how Elizabeth Shelby figured a way to get out of the world's oldest profession and into something a lot more comfortable.

"Waxer and Kline agreed to underwrite a secret expedition to go back into Mexico, through the heart of bandit and Indian country, and bring out the gold.

"That's the story — so far."

"Every story," Keys said, "has to have an ending."

"The ending might depend on you. I suppose by now you know my name is Elizabeh Shelby . . ."

"And you were married to Mangus."

"That's what they called it. I never said 'I do.' "

"But you did."

"I didn't have any choice and you didn't have to say that."

"I'm . . . sorry."

"Skip it, Mister Sorry." She let what was left of the cigarette drop into the tub of water. "We still need someone to take charge of the expedition into Mexico . . ."

"*We?* You planning on going?"

"I'm the only one who knows the whereabouts of the gold."

"You could draw a map."

"I could if I trusted whoever had the map. But you see I don't trust anybody."

"Not even me, Liz?" Keys smiled.

"Don't call me Liz . . . sounds like a slattern. Elizabeth."

"Yes, Elizabeth."

"My partners still want to talk to you. Will you come back and listen to their proposition?"

"What about Valance?"

"Back there you eliminated him, so they'd like you to go back and talk some more."

61

"Last time they sent a telegraph offering a hundred dollars. This time they sent you."

"Nobody sends me. It was my own idea and I didn't bring any hundred dollars. I brought something else." She stood up naked in the brass tub. "Isn't this better?"

"Haven't made up my mind . . . yet."

"I'll help you." Her body glistened as droplets of water dripped back into the tub. "Hand me a towel."

There were two towels lying over the back of a nearby chair. One towel was very large, the other very, very small.

He tossed her the small one.

She caught it and stepped out of the tub, stood there a few seconds, then extended the towel.

"Dry me off."

Keys stood up from the chair, took the towel and lightly dabbed it on one of her shoulders, then on the other.

"Something else I can't make up my mind about," he said.

"What?"

"Whether you truly enjoy doing it, or . . ."

"Or what?"

"Whether you are truly a great actress."

"Some of both — more of one than the other."

"Which one?"

"Does it really matter?"

"Not right now." Keys tossed the towel on the bed.

"One more thing you ought to know . . ." she added.

"What?"

"This is all you get — once we leave this room — 'til we get the gold."

"I haven't said I'd go."

"You haven't said you wouldn't."

CHAPTER TEN

" 'Gold! Gold! Gold! Bright and yellow, hard and cold,' " Simon Ignatius Kline quoted. " 'Sought by young, hugged by old.' And it's particularly sought by President Ulysses Simpson Grant's administration. Too much gold has been flowing out of the United States and many of the strikes since '49 are playing out. With that bullion buried in Mexico we could carry great influence and make a great deal more money in the doing."

"I understand that, Mister Kline," Keys said, "but doesn't President Grant figure that that bullion belongs to the U.S. Government since the so-called Confederate States now are also a part of the U.S.?"

"Gold, Mister Keys" — Kline bit into a

piece of cake — "is where you find it — or where you grab it. You let us worry about that once we are in possession of the bullion."

"Now, sir." Willard Oliver Waxer sipped from a glass of milk, then rumbled, "Would you be good enough to listen to our proposition?"

Keys looked across at Elizabeth Shelby.

"That's why I'm here."

Here, this time, was the inside of Waxer and Kline's private railroad car. All black and red and all lavishly appointed.

Waxer, Kline, Elizabeth Shelby and Keys were the only ones present.

"Very good, sir, very good." Waxer subdued the effects of gastric acidity then went on, "Besides yourself and Elizabeth, how many others would you need for the expedition?"

"I'd say the two of us," he looked at Elizabeth Shelby again and back to Wexler, "and three more — each an expert in his field."

"Very good, sir, I . . ." Waxer's stomach growled again.

Kline waved off his partner and picked up the conversation.

"We'll advance one thousand dollars apiece for you and the other three . . ."

"A thousand apiece for the other three,"

Keys said, "and fifteen hundred for me. That's before we go any further. Agreed?"

"Agreed." Kline nodded.

"What about expenses going in?"

"Such as?"

"Such as supplies — guns, ammunition, wagons, livestock, dynamite . . ."

"Dynamite?! What do you need dynamite for?"

"Always need dynamite — blow things and people up."

"Two thousand cover it?"

"Close enough."

"Done . . . that's sixty-five hundred out-of-pocket . . . our pocket." Kline pointed to Waxer, then himself.

"What about percentages?"

"Oh, yes, percentages . . . Elizabeth's share is 10 percent . . ."

"That," Keys said, "sounds a mite skimpy."

"Without us she gets nothing. Ten percent of five million is half a million out of which she pays each of you ten thousand . . ."

"You've agreed to this, Elizabeth?" Keys asked.

Elizabeth nodded.

"Of course" — Kline smiled — "we cannot put any of this in writing, you understand, a verbal contract will have to suffice, but you have our word . . ."

"And the advance, sir," Waxer said.

"And," Keys said, "possession of the gold, until we get paid off."

"That's true, sir." Waxer smiled as he and his partner both nodded.

"We'll advance forty-five hundred now for you and the recruits." Kline moved around the coach biting into an apple. "The balance will be on deposit at Fort Canby. We own the sutler store there and the bank . . ."

"Is there anything you boys don't own?" Keys said.

"If there is" — Kline took another bite — "we're working on it."

"Is the deal done, sir?" Waxer intoned.

Keys glanced at Elizabeth Shelby. She smiled in approval.

"Done." Keys rose, put on his hat and turned back. "Come to think of it, I may need four instead of three going in . . ."

"You thought of it too late." Kline cackled. "Deal's done. You should've thought of it in advance. Anything else comes out of your share. Now would you care to join us in something to eat?"

"No thanks. I didn't think of it in advance so that's not part of the deal. But I'll take that forty-five hundred — in advance."

"Of course." Kline darted toward a safe at

66

one corner of the coach.

After Kline counted out the currency, Keys put it in his pocket.

"You'll hear from me."

"Wire us at Fort Canby," Kline said.

"I'll do that."

"Oh, Mister Keys."

"Yes, Miss Shelby."

"I'll walk you to your horse."

"What do you think, Jeff?"

"Oh, it's Jeff, now, huh, Lizzie?"

"Don't call me Lizzie, it's worse than Liz."

"Alright, Elizabeth, what do I think about what?"

"The deal."

"You say you met Kline at Madam Pleasant's."

"That's right."

"I hope you charged him plenty."

"He got his money's worth."

"Well, I hope you do too — out of this deal, I mean."

"I know how to take care of myself."

"So did Marie Antoinette," Keys interrupted.

"You heard what Kline said. Without them I don't get any part of that gold. But with half a million . . ."

"Minus our shares."

"Even minus your shares, I'll be —"

"Like that other Elizabeth. A queen. The Virgin Queen."

"It's a little late to worry about that . . . Jeff, Jefferson, Mister Keys . . . there was a poem I read from a book in Madam Pleasant's high-class whorehouse, of all places. It went like this . . .

I traveled through a Land of Men,
A Land of Men and Women too,
And heard and saw such dreadful things
As cold Earth wanderers never knew.

"With that money I won't have to travel that land ever again."

"Miss Elizabeth . . ."

"What?"

"You are plumb full of" — Keys mounted — "surprises. I'll see you at Canby."

"Where you heading?"

"Make a deposit." He patted the money in his pocket. "Then Fisbee."

"Why Fisbee?"

"That's where I start doing some recruiting . . . I hope."

Chapter Eleven

Three days later Jefferson Keys was in Marshal Creek's office in Fisbee. Marshal

68

Charlie Creek looked more like a bank clerk than a lawman.

"That's right, Mister Keys," Elijah went through some dodgers and picked out one like this." Creek handed the dodger across his desk.

$200 reward
THE DARCY BROTHERS
TOM and TIM
Wanted for
Stage Hold-Up and Murder
Dead or Alive
Hadley Stage Line

"Not much of a reward," Keys said after he read the poster.

"Not much of a stage line." Creek took off his eyeglasses and put them on the desk. "But I'm empowered to pay on delivery. Them Darcys is mean polecats. Somebody thought he spotted 'em up at a line shack out Rincon way."

"How far?"

"Not far."

"Why didn't you go after them, Marshal?"

"Rincon is just out of my territory. Been a star packer for a long time. Intend to stay a star packer for a long time to come, and not by goin' out of my territory lookin' for trouble. But I've done business with Elijah before."

"So he said. You have any objection if I follow after him?"

"What for?"

"He did me a favor once. Maybe I can be of some help."

"That's up to you, them Darcys is . . ."

" 'Mean polecats' . . . any objection?"

"Hell, no. I'll even draw you a map."

Since riding out of Fisbee, Keys had reined up his horse three times, looked at the map Marshal Creek had drawn, and did his best to follow directions.

Creek might be a tolerable lawman, Keys thought to himself, but he was an almighty poor mapmaker. Actually, Keys didn't think much of Charlie Creek as a lawman either. The more lawmen like Creek, the longer the West would stay lawless.

Then Keys heard gunshots. Two. Three. Then echoes.

He topped out over the rim of a rise and looked across the down slope.

A line shack — almost backed against a fifteen or so foot rake of rocks ramping up above it. And from where he was, Keys could make out the figure of a man behind another configuration of rocks facing the line shack but hidden from it.

Even from the distance the figure looked familiar.

Two more shots from the shack — and echoes.

No return fire from Elijah.

Out of sight of the shack, Keys dismounted and led his horse toward the outcrop of rocks Elijah used as cover.

When he got near enough, Keys gave out with a bobwhite whistle, knowing that Elijah would know it was no bobwhite that whistled.

From his crouched position Elijah turned, spotted Keys and smiled. Keys tied his horse to a branch of a scrub oak, stooped and made his way closer, then settled near the bounty hunter.

Elijah's bow and quiver of arrows lay on the ground beside him. He held the Navy Colt in his right hand, but it was out of effective range of the shack.

Two more shots came from the shack that slammed into the rocks now sheltering the two men.

"They got rifles, huh?"

"Yep," Elijah answered. "You come out here to cash in on that big bounty for the Darcys?"

"Nope."

"Then what?"

"To offer you a job."

"Already got a job. The Darcys."

"I mean when we finish with them."

"We?"

"Any objection?"

"What've you got in mind?"

"One of the three Ss."

"What's the three Ss?"

"Well, there's speed, strength and strategy. This situation calls for strategy."

"I'll say it again. What've you got in mind?"

"Have you et?"

"Have I what?"

"Et. Eaten?"

"Not lately."

"Don't go away. I'll be right back."

"Sure."

Without being seen, Keys made his way to his horse, removed his shotgun from its boot and some other items from his saddlebag and made his way back.

"Now what?" Elijah said.

"First off, we eat."

Keys held up a can of beans, an opener and a spoon.

They shared the cold beans, alternately using the same spoon.

"Now what?" Elijah asked again.

"Now, the strategy." Keys pointed to the shack. "I see the Darcys got a little fire going." There were wisps of smoke coming out a short pipe stack sticking out of the roof. "Probably enjoying a pot of hot coffee."

"Probably."

"And so far they don't know there's two of us out here."

"Right."

"Give me a few minutes."

"You got 'em."

Keys went to work — using the empty bean can, taking apart the shotgun shells and adding powder from some of the .44 cartridges from his belt. He poked a hole into the lid and crammed it back onto the top of the container, then fashioned a wick out of a strip of cloth.

And then Keys explained the strategy to Elijah, who right away began to implement the plan.

He allowed himself to be seen moving away from the cover of the rocks, making his way among other rocks far to the right, then up the slope behind the shack until he was above it.

The Darcys had obviously spotted him but couldn't get a clear shot.

From the stone ledge above, Elijah lit the wick to the can, dropped onto the roof and plunged the container down the protruding stack.

The ensuing explosion was formidable but not deadly, formidable enough so the Darcys didn't know what the hell hit them or what was coming next. They skeltered out the front door, rifles in hand and turned back to aim at the roof.

But Keys was now behind a tree in front of the shack pointing his .6 gauge.

"Hold it up, boys!" he hollered.

But the boys had no such notion. One fired at Elijah on the roof, the other wheeled toward Keys.

Both Tom and Tim collapsed, one from Keys' shotgun, the other from Elijah's Navy Colt.

Neither of them moved, ever again.

CHAPTER TWELVE

There were four horses in the small stable near the line shack — four horses and two corpses. Two of the horses belonged to Keys and Elijah — the other two horses and corpses belonged to the Darcy brothers.

Keys and Elijah had decided to bunk in what was left of the line shack and get a fresh start the next day. But that night they had some things to chew about on the cud of deliberation.

"Marshal Creek gets his commission, 20 percent off the top, that leaves a hundred and sixty," Elijah said. "So your share comes to eighty dollars. Right?"

"Wrong."

"You want more?"

"Nope. This one was pro bono."

"What's that mean?"

"Means free. But I'm here to offer you a job that's worth more. A hell of a lot more — if you'd care to listen."

"I'd care." Elijah smiled.

Keys then proceeded to tell Elijah about the entire venture — from Colonel Leigh Shelby and the five million in Confederate gold, Maximilian, Mangus' attack, Elizabeth Shelby, Madam Pleasant's high-class whorehouse, Waxer and Kline, even Amory Valance and then the deal he had struck for the expedition back into Mexico. He didn't bother with the details about Elizabeth Shelby's visit to his hotel room.

"One thousand apiece going in!" Elijah whistled when Keys was through.

"Fifteen hundred for me."

"Yeah, so you said . . . one thousand dollars! You know, Jefferson, never in my entire life did I ever have, or hope to have, one thousand dollars all at once."

"You got it now if you say yes."

"I say yes."

"Good."

"What about the other two recruits we need?"

"I'll go after one, you go after the other. We'll meet at Fort Canby. My man's named Doc Zeeger. He's in Tucson. Yours is in Silver City, so I'm told. Ever hear of a young fellow called Bickford, Billy Joe Bickford?"

Elijah whistled again.

"Yeah, I've heard of Billy Joe Bickford. He's made some reputation with a gun in a short time — a very short time."

"So he has."

"Supposed to be nobody faster — or straighter."

"There's always somebody faster and straighter."

"He's left a long dead line of them who thought so."

"That he has."

"Hear he's awful independent."

"Yep."

"You do know he's from the South?"

"I know."

"And you still want me to go talk to him?"

"Yep."

"What makes you think he'll come?"

"Mention my name."

"You friends?"

Keys just smiled.

CHAPTER THIRTEEN

Keys had offered Elijah the thousand in advance but Elijah said he'd make do with the hundred-sixty net for turning in the dead Darcys.

So, Keys had ridden to Fort Canby and deposited thirty-five hundred at W-K SAVINGS AND TRUST. His share, Elijah's, Billy Joe Bickford's — who was the most problematic of the potential recruits — but, knowing his customer, Keys carried Doc Zeeger's thousand with him on his way to Tucson.

It had been nearly a year since Keys had seen Doc and Doc hadn't looked so good, but then he hadn't in some time.

Keys smiled as he rode toward Tucson and thought about the tall, stooped, pale, raw-boned, enigmatic man he had met in Mexico a handful of years ago.

Doc Zeeger was not averse to talking — he was just averse to talking about himself. Rumor had it that he had been a veterinarian in Kansas. Some said he rode with Quantrill — others had it that Doc's family was wiped out at Lawrence by Quantrill's guerrillas.

Nobody knew or asked. Doc Zeeger's shadowy past was buried in bleeding Kansas.

The two of them had met when Doc brought down a remuda of surplus U.S. Army horses to sell to the Juaristas.

It was Keys who negotiated the deal on behalf of the beleaguered forces of Benito Juarez and found Doc to be a fair and honest trader, a man of his word. But Doc was also a gambler. He lost all the profits from the horse venture and decided to stay in Mexico until his luck changed. Howsomever, Lady Luck proved to be an elusive would-be companion and Doc decided to join up with Keys and the Juaristas, even though Maximilian's bunch would have ponied up considerably more for his services.

Nobody could count all the bullets Doc cut out of the flesh and bones of wounded Juaristas — and a surprising number of those wounded survived — including Jefferson Keys.

Slowly, bloody battle after bloody battle, the tide began to turn against the pretender to the phantom crown of Mexico, Ferdinand Maximilian Joseph, and in favor of Benito Pablo Juarez, a native Mexican, who had been duly elected then deposed by Maximilian's army backed by Napoleon III.

But Doc had come down with consumption and left for the dry and potentially salubrious climate of Arizona. He managed to survive, if not thrive, these past years.

When Keys last saw him, Doc had a card game and a woman in Tucson. For the expedition Keys needed a man like Doc, but there was no other man quite like him — and maybe Doc was good for one more war . . . if it was a short one.

That last time, Doc was living at the hotel above the Appaloosa Saloon, which made it handy for him to attend the all-day — and some times all-night — card games that persisted at the Appaloosa.

As Keys came through the bat wings Doc Zeeger chanced to be playing poker at one of the tables, with his woman sitting nearby watching.

The game was seven-card stud. Two cards in the hole, four up and the last card down.

All the players except one other and Doc had dropped out. There was a messy but considerable pile of money atop the table. The remaining player, Bart Vogan, had two jacks showing. Doc had a pair of aces up. All seven cards had been dealt.

Doc bet fifty. Vogan paused, then raised a

hundred. Table stakes. That's all the money Doc had left. He started to shove it into the pot and spotted Keys.

"Just a minute, Bart," Doc said. "I'll be right back."

Doc walked over to the bar where Keys stood, smiled, and extended his still sleek hand.

"Jeff Keys, you old cabin robber, what're you doing in Tucson?"

"Recruiting."

They shook.

"Going to war again?"

Keys nodded.

"Where's this one?"

"Mexico."

"It would be."

"Pay's good, Doc. Thought you might be interested, might come along."

"You know I haven't got much time left."

"One way or another, this won't take long."

"What's the rate?"

"A thousand going in — ten thousand more when we get back."

"What are the odds?"

"Long, but . . ."

"But what?"

"A lot better if you deal yourself in."

An impatient voice carried across from

the card table.

"Are we playing poker?"

"Yeah, Bart." Doc's plentiful eyebrows arched. "Be right there." He smiled at Keys. "If I win this hand I'll be flush."

"If you lose?"

"We go to war."

"Good luck."

"Don't need it," Doc whispered. "I've got the third ace."

Doc Zeeger walked back to the table, sat down, shoved the money into the pot.

"Call," he said and turned over the third ace.

But Bart Vogan's two jacks had company. He turned over two more jacks.

Without pause or alteration of expression, Doc rose and walked back to Keys.

"That thousand. You got it with you?"

Keys nodded.

"Melinda."

With the grace of a dancer she came off the chair and made her way to Doc's side.

"Give it to her," he said to Keys. Then to the woman: "Pack my war bag."

"Doc," she murmured.

"Do it."

"Sure."

They were saddled and ready to ride.

She stood nearby and looked at Doc.

He hadn't kissed her good-bye, touched her, or said anything else.

Keys couldn't remember seeing any more melancholy eyes, or a more plaintive expression. She was part Indian or Mexican or both. Maybe forty, maybe less, not tall, not robust, but with an inner strength that shone through, a strength that subdued any betrayal of outward emotion.

It was more than likely she would never see him again.

Where or how they had met Keys didn't know. That's another thing that Doc had never spoken of. But only once before in the eyes of his own wife had he seen that look. Keys was hard-pressed not to say anything, but he knew that's the way Doc wanted it.

Apaches never say good-bye. Neither did Doc. He spurred his horse and started to ride.

Keys followed, then the two rode together toward Fort Canby.

Chapter Fourteen

All day they had ridden without a word passing between them. When the sun reached its highest arc Keys looked across at Doc.

"Want to stop for a noon meal?"

"Let's keep going."

Keys knew that it was hard for Doc to leave what he had in Tucson and that he wanted to put as many miles behind him as he could as fast as he could — so they kept on going and kept silent until that night when they sat at the campfire and finished the evening meal.

Keys rolled a cigarette. Doc lit his pipe.

"You think it's a good idea?"

"What's a good idea?" Doc said.

"To smoke?"

"Don't think it'll make a hell of a lot of difference in the long run . . ." Doc smiled for the first time, ". . . or the short run."

That cut through the heavy atmosphere.

"Doc," Keys said. "You haven't asked where we're heading now."

"Where" — Doc puffed on his pipe — "we heading now?"

"Fort Canby."

"Uh-huh."

"You haven't asked what the job is."

Doc took another puff and stretched out his legs.

"What's the job?"

Keys spent the next few minutes telling

him about the job and about the people involved — so far.

When Keys finished, Doc just nodded.

"We had some good times in Mexico — some not as good."

Keys nodded.

"Never thought I'd go back," Doc said.

"Neither did I."

"Jeff . . ."

"What is it, Doc?"

"If we do the job — and you think I've done my share — and I don't make it back — will you see she gets whatever is coming to me?"

"I will, Doc."

"I know you will . . . amigo."

CHAPTER FIFTEEN

The Waxer-Kline engine, utility car and luxury coach had moved and was now located just outside Fort Canby in proximity to Nogales and the Mexican border.

In addition to the military quarters, Fort Canby consisted of civilian buildings and business enterprises. It had been and still was the site of considerable activity, legal and illegal. It was also the sometime headquarters of Colonel George Crook, whose mission was to maintain a reasonable amount of law and order and safety for the citizens — white, red, brown and assorted hues — who dwelled or passed through hundreds of thousands of acres in the Territory.

Two of those current dwellers were Willard Oliver Waxer and Simon Ignatius Kline. Their entourage included the locomotive engineer, fireman, brakeman, a chef, Jean Pierre, and butler-factotum, Raymond — and also at the present time, Elizabeth Shelby, whose acquaintance Mister Kline had made at Madam Pleasant's high-class whorehouse several months past.

Elizabeth Shelby was provided with a small compartment in the utility car, along with accommodations for the rest of the crew and staff.

Waxer and Kline each had an ornate bedroom in the private coach.

Part of the arrangement since San Francisco had been periodic visits by Elizabeth Shelby to Mister Kline's quarters, sometimes for an hour or so, and sometimes overnight, depending on Mister Kline's inclination and appetite.

Once again Kline had instructed Raymond to inform Elizabeth of his desire for a nocturnal rendezvous.

But on this occasion the outcome was

unexpected — at least on the part of Mister Kline.

He lay naked beneath a silk sheet as she responded to the summons, closing the door behind her — not moving toward the bed.

After what he perceived to be too long a wait:

"Well . . ."

"Well, what?"

"You damn well know what."

"Simon." She addressed him by his first name for the first time. "The time has come to talk of certain things, not cabbages and kings."

"Get undressed."

"That's one of the things. In view of recent events, our previous arrangement is no longer in effect."

"Says who?"

"Says Elizabeth Shelby, who is about to risk life and limb in a business venture south of the border — and who no longer intends to provide you with certain services."

"Pretty independent attitude for a whore."

"Former whore. Current partner."

"Partner?"

"Well . . . associate, shall we say?"

"You don't have to say any more."

"Good."

"I know what you're thinking."

"Do you?"

"I do. I know how much money you've accumulated in the past months — most of it mine — because most of it is in one of my banks — just over five thousand dollars, so . . ."

"So what?"

"You're thinking that's just about enough, along with the help of Jefferson Keys, to finance your own expedition and retrieve the five million in gold."

"Is that what I'm thinking?"

"Yes!" He threw back the silk sheet and stood naked in his bony frame. "But I'll also tell you what you haven't thought about."

"Go ahead."

"The whole thing's preposterous, because even if you and Keys did succeed, you'd be completely helpless."

"Would we?"

"You would. Because the two of you would have no idea what to do with it — or how to do it. You can't hide five million in gold under a bushel basket — or dispose of it in an orderly manner. You don't have the knowledge or wherewithal. But we do — banks, companies, contacts — the United States government still has a claim on that gold, a valid claim — and *we* know how to invalidate that claim without landing in prison. So, Miss Independent Former Whore, you'd better think again. You can take that suddenly sacred body of yours out of here and do with it what you will — I can get along without it — but don't get any grandiose schemes about getting too independent or you'll find yourself in jail or back in Madam Pleasant's whorehouse. Now think that over."

"Why, Simon" — she smiled — "I don't have to think anything over. I had no such notion — about the gold, I mean — just about our little . . . social arrangement. That's all."

"That better be all. In the meantime you can find other accommodations at Fort Canby until Keys gets back."

"I'll do that." She opened the door. "Good night, Simon. Pleasant dreams."

The door closed behind her.

CHAPTER SIXTEEN

At Silver City rifle shots rent the air as a crowd was gathering at the town square near the two men who were the center of attention.

One of the two was a corpulent gentleman in a top hat, the other a tall angular man dressed in frontier garb, armed with a Winchester rifle.

"Come one, come all," the corpulent man proclaimed, "you are about to witness a demonstration you'll remember the remainder of all your born days! Courtesy of the Winchester Arms Company. Allow me to introduce myself. Amos Aikins. And this gentleman is Mister Kit Cummins, who holds in his possession a Winchester rifle.

"As you can see we've set up a target fifty or more feet down the street with a bull's-eye square in the middle.

"Mister Cummins is reloading the rifle of which I speak. But this is no ordinary rifle, ladies and gentlemen. This is the Blue Boy, Winchester's latest model. The fastest, most accurate gun in the world. Seventy-five dollars a lick. And at that a bargain to top all bargains east or west of the hundredth meridian.

"Prepare to be amazed, to be astounded."

The crowd seemed to be prepared.

"Now, Mister Cummins, there's the target. Show the good citizens of Silver City what can be done with Winchester's Blue Boy."

Kit Cummins raised the rifle and began firing, rapidly cocking the lever action, and firing again and again.

The bullets all smashed into, or near, the target's bull's-eye, as the spectators all reacted with applause and whistles.

"Ah, but that's not all!" Amos Aikins added. "There is a standing offer from the Winchester Arms Company of one hundred dollars, payable here and now to anyone who can shoot faster and straighter with any other gun. One hundred dollars, coin of the realm. Anyone in the crowd care to try?" He held the currency with his hand high into the air for all to see.

"I'd care to try." A voice came from the crowd.

A handsome young man, no more than his early twenties, with a strangely twisted smile stepped forward. Sunny-faced and lean, with slightly sloping shoulders.

Amos Aikins looked at Kit Cummins, smirked and motioned to the young man.

"Alright, young fella, move right on up here."

The young fella did, as Aikins looked him up and down.

"Well," Aikens said.

"Well, what?"

"Go get your rifle."

"I'll use these."

The young man's palms gently touched the butts of the two guns strapped to his sides. The belt that sustained the guns was black and the brass buckle that sustained the belt was oval with the raised letters CSA — the buckle worn by officers of the Confederate States of America.

Kit Cummins smiled. Amos Aikins laughed and so did most of the crowd.

"Handguns" — Aikins pointed — "against a Winchester?"

"I got twelve shots in here."

"And you're going to go against Kit Cummins with his Blue Boy?"

"For one hundred dollars." The young man nodded.

"Sure thing, sonny." Aikins motioned. "There's the target. Speed and accuracy. Both of you unload at the count of three.

Aikins winked at the rifleman and started to count.

"One, two, three!"

Kit Cummins began to blaze away. But by the time he got off three shots, the young man had drawn with his right hand and fanned six times, then repeated the action with the left hand and holstered while Cummins was still shooting.

And all the young man's shots were plumb center on the target.

The crowd cheered, clapped and whistled.

"Pay him! Pay the hundred!" they thundered.

The young man reached out and Amos Aikins placed the money in his palm.

"Sonny," he said, "you ain't human."

The young man pocketed the money, reloaded and started to walk away from the still buzzing crowd.

"Mister Bickford."

Billy Joe Bickford stopped and looked at Elijah.

"Mister Bickford," Elijah repeated, "can I speak with you?"

Before Billy Joe Bickford answered, another man with a bigger man beside him interrupted.

"Say, young fella, my name's Seth Crandall. This is my general manager, Joe Munger. I just saw that exhibition you put on. You're Billy Joe Bickford, ain't you?"

Billy Joe Bickford nodded.

"Well, I own the Silver Queen mine and I got a job for you."

Bickford looked at Elijah, then back to Crandall.

"What kind of job?"

"Guarding our diggings. Four trips a month from the Silver Queen into town. Two hundred dollars a trip."

"Two hundred?"

"Right. That's a lot of money. Payable in silver. We been having some trouble lately. Two hundred a trip. How does that sound?"

"Sounds generous."

"Too damn generous," the general foreman murmured.

"Never mind, Munger," Crandall said. "What about it, Billy Joe, we got a deal?" He extended his hand.

"Mister Bickford," Elijah said, "do I tell Mister Keys that you're not coming?"

Billy Joe's face turned dark.

"Who?"

"Mister Keys. Jefferson Keys. He's waiting for you."

Seth Crandall's hand was still extended as Billy Joe looked back at him.

"Mister Crandall, you'll have to excuse me."

"But we got a deal . . . you agreed . . ."

"I'm sorry. Something's come up."

"More money?" Crandall's voice rose. "Is that it?"

"Sure that's it!" Joe Munger moved closer. "I didn't . . ."

"You told Mister Crandall that . . ."

"Step back," Bickford said.

"Like hell I'll step back." He grabbed Bickford's right arm. "Dirty little welcher, I'll . . ."

Suddenly a gun was in Bickford's left hand and he crashed the barrel across Munger's forehead.

Munger folded and hit the ground hard.

Billy Joe Bickford looked at Elijah and holstered the gun.

"Let's not keep Mister Keys waiting."

CHAPTER SEVENTEEN

Two more opposites never sat across a campfire.

The American Southwest became the American Southwest with the Mexican War of 1846 and the Gadsden Purchase of 1854. Those two events increased the United States by more than the size of most European countries.

But much of that territory was just that — territory — not states — and this included the Territory of Arizona.

Prior to the Civil War there had been reluctance to admit new states and upset the balance of free and slave states. Since the cessation of hostilities in 1865, two new states had been admitted: Nebraska, the thirty-seventh, and Colorado, the thirty-eighth.

Neither of them a part of the American Southwest.

There were elements who craved statehood and the advantages that went with it.
But there were those who were vigorously
opposed. Statehood meant more government supervision, taxes, and regulation and
less independence for pioneers and fron-
tiersmen who forged the westward movement. Hundreds, thousands, of those on
both sides of that issue and other issues now
peopled the vast Arizona Territory — some
came to stay, others came to plunder and
move on.

Ranchers and rampagers, cattlemen and
cattle rustlers, miners and marauders, some
lawmen and many more lawless men, some
who came to help build an empire — and
some who came to help themselves. Those
who welcomed the presence of the U.S.
military, and those who looked upon the
Army uniform as a symbol of infringement
— those who looked upon the Indian tribes
as brothers, and those who considered them
a plague to be wiped out — those who had
sided with the cause of the Confederacy,
and those who fought for the Union.

But two more opposites never sat across a
campfire.

The man known as Elijah and the young
man who called himself Billy Joe Bickford.

Tomorrow they would be in Fort Canby,

but tonight they sat in silence broken only by the plaintive call of an unseen coyote wailing through the desert night.

Billy Joe was cleaning one of his guns. Elijah sat cross-legged and watched. Billy Joe had unloaded the gun he was working on and had set the cartridges on the ground but within reach. He glanced up at the man across from him.

"Back there in Silver City you spoke good enough — haven't said much since."

"I was asked to deliver a message. I delivered it."

"You always do what you're asked?"

"Not always."

"You got nothing else to talk about?"

"I just didn't think you'd favor talking to me."

"Got nobody else to talk to — except that coyote. What's your name?"

"Elijah."

"Got any other part to that name?"

"None that I use."

"Slave?"

"Was."

"I wasn't," Billy Joe said.

"I suppose your people didn't have any slaves."

"We did. Too many. Damn near broke us."

"Pity."

"We treated our slaves well."

"Too bad I wasn't one of them."

"Yeah."

"You get along better now — without slaves?"

"I get along."

"So I've heard."

"Have you?

"Just about everybody has."

"What've you heard?"

"In the Army a soldier sometimes asks his superior officer for permission to speak freely . . ."

"We're not in the Army and you don't need permission."

"No, I don't."

"Go ahead, when I was a young boy I used to talk to our . . ."

"Slaves?"

"That's right."

"They ever talk back?"

Billy Joe just smiled.

"Didn't think so, Mister Bickford. Not where you came from."

"I came from Virginia."

"So did I."

"Then you know the Shenandoah Valley."

"I've been there."

"Well, it's not like it was before . . ."

". . . the war?"

"Before Sheridan and Custer laid waste to it. When he was done, Sheridan wrote that even a crow flying over it would have to bring his own commissary."

"Yes, I heard that."

"Well, I saw it . . . and all because of . . ."

"Slavery?"

"What else?"

"The Union."

"Oh, that. Well, Elijah, there's no more slaves in Virginia — but there'll always be slaves somewhere — always have been."

"That so?"

"Sure thing. They built the pyramids, the Hanging Gardens, they built the Grecian Navy, they . . ."

"Picked cotton."

"That, too. Back then, Elijah, I wasn't called Billy Joe. No, back then I was William Joseph Bickford."

"Why the change?"

"Thought it was more in keeping with . . ." Bickford held up one of the guns, then started loading it.

"The reputation you set out to make?"

Billy Joe Bickford smiled, holstered the gun and began to unload the cartridges from the other weapon. He paused and studied the features of the man across the campfire.

"You know, Elijah, you don't exactly look like an African."

"My mother was an Indian."

"That's a strange combination. Some might say you were disadvantaged from both sides."

"Some have said it."

"And I don't imagine you took it kindly."

"You can imagine what you like." Elijah pointed to the gun Bickford was working on. "You take good care of those weapons."

"Works both ways."

"I see you break 'em down one at a time."

"You never can tell. I noticed that you carry a bow and quiver among your possibles."

"I do."

"That the Indian part?"

"It is."

"You good?"

"Helped bring me this far."

"Uh-huh. And tomorrow we'll be in Canby. That's where Mister Keys is waiting?"

"That's where he said he'd be."

"Have you known him long?"

"Not so long. Have you?"

"Longer than you," Bickford said. "He a friend of yours?"

"Haven't many friends. But he's one of

'em. What about you, Mister Bickford?"
"What about me?"
"Have you got many friends?"
Billy Joe Bickford held up both guns.
"One for each hand."

CHAPTER EIGHTEEN

The dawn had broken warm and gentle across the compound at Fort Canby. Canby was peopled by civilians, Indians, and miners as well as soldiers. In addition to the barracks, there was a way station, a cantina, a sutler's store, a freight office, livery, corrals, barns, and about a dozen other buildings.

The gates were open and Jeff Keys and Doc Zeeger rode through.

"Can't get much closer to Mexico than this," Zeeger said.

"Not much."

"Who's in command here?"

"Colonel Crook, last I heard."

"Know him, don't you?"

"I know him."

"What's he like?"

"Take a look for yourself." Keys pointed at the Army headquarters. "He's just getting off that mule."

Doc Zeeger took a look as Colonel Crook

dismounted from the mule and a young captain next to him swung off his cavalry mount.

"Imposin'-lookin' man," Zeeger said, "but I asked what's he like?"

"You'll find out."

Keys knew well and good. Crook was the best wilderness officer who ever lived. He wore civilian clothes except for a well-wrinkled, old Army jacket. He stood more than six feet high, erect, spare, sinewy and muscular.

With the exception of the Civil War, he had spent his entire career on the frontier.

During the four-year bloodbath of the Rebellion, Crook distinguished himself at South Mountain, Antietam, Chickamagua, and Appomattox. Then it was back to the Indian campaigns. Against the Paiutes he took to the field with a command of forty men. He didn't see a house again for two years. The Paiutes were made peaceable. Then came successful campaigns in the Southwest against Apaches, Kiowas, and Comanches. Still, no American officer was more respected, admired, and even loved by the red man. Crook made damn few promises but kept the ones he made.

Colonel Crook looked up as Keys and Zeeger reined in their horses and Keys

101

started to dismount.

"Hello, Jeff. Been awhile." His voice was raspy and he was severe in speech but not unkind.

"Colonel."

Crook extended his hand and they shook.

"This is my aide, Captain Bourke."

Both Keys and the young captain nodded.

"Colonel, this is Doc Zeeger, a friend of mine."

"Hello, friend." Crook smiled.

Zeeger touched the brim of his hat.

"How's the Indian situation around these parts, George?" Keys asked.

"Not bad for the time being, but other situations are not as good."

"Such as?"

"Such as comancheros, mostly a skunk calls himself Battu — hits from across the border then back to Mexico. Could use a scout if you care to sign on."

"No, thanks. Got private business."

"Well, from what I've heard lately — keep it on the up and up."

"You know me . . . George."

"I used to . . . Jeff."

"Beg pardon, Colonel." Doc Zeeger pointed at Crook's mount. "That's a fine-looking mule."

"Name's Apache." Crook nodded. "Prefer

a mule to a horse. And you're a good judge of animals." He looked toward Keys. "People, too, I hope."

Crook walked off toward headquarters followed by Captain Bourke.

"Like I said" — Doc smiled as Keys mounted — "he's imposin'."

"Yeah," Keys agreed. "And right now I wish he was someplace else . . . it'd make our job a lot easier."

At the headquarters entrance, Crook looked after Keys and Doc as they rode across the compound.

"Sir," Captain Bourke inquired, "were you and Keys together during the war?"

"Some wars we were — some wars we weren't."

Keys and Zeeger approached the desk clerk at Fort Canby's civilian hotel.

"Howdy," Keys said.

"Yes, sir. What can I do for you?"

"We'd like to register for two rooms."

"Beg pardon, sir. Would you be Jefferson Keys?"

"I would."

"You're already registered."

"That so? Who registered us?"

"I did," Elizabeth Shelby said as she walked down the stairs.

103

"Yes, sir." The clerk handed them two keys. "Rooms eight and nine, second floor."

"Your room is next to mine," Elizabeth Shelby said to Keys as she approached. "If that's alright with you."

"That's . . . fine, but I thought you were staying with . . ."

"Not anymore, but nothing else has changed as far as our deal is concerned."

"That's good. This is Doc Zeeger. Doc, Elizabeth Shelby."

"Miss Shelby, Jeff's told me about you."

"*All* about me?"

"Just enough to get him here," Keys said.

"That's good," she said. "You two can clean up and we'll get down to business."

An hour later Keys, Zeeger, and Elizabeth Shelby were at the livery stable and corral.

Doc was with the owner, John Marley, talking about and looking over saddle horses, wagon teams, and pack mules while Keys and Elizabeth stood some distance away near the gate.

"You didn't ask about what happened between Kline and me."

"None of my business as long as the deal is on."

"He thought you and I might try to double-cross him with the gold."

"I wouldn't. Would you?"

"Not without you." She smiled.

"Then *we* wouldn't."

"Said if we did, we couldn't get rid of the gold anyhow."

"He's probably right about that. Not my line. Yours either. Besides, a deal's a deal."

"Also told him he could find another . . . companion."

"That's between you and . . . you."

Doc Zeeger approached wiping the sweat from inside his hatband.

"What do you think, Doc?" Keys asked.

"I think Mister Marley's got some good stock and some not as good, but we can make do. Prices are a mite high."

"So are the stakes," Keys said. "Let's get something to eat."

Billy Joe Bickford and Elijah had ridden through the fort gates, directed their horses to a large circular watering trough, dismounted and stood nearby as the animals dipped their muzzles into the trough.

A large, crow-faced man took particular notice of the two strangers and most particular notice of Bickford. Crow-face wore his gun slung low on his right side and his right shoulder canted more than his left. He nudged the big man next to him, then moved heavy-legged toward the trough. The big man followed.

"I want to talk to you," Crow-face said to Bickford.

"Talk."

"Couldn't help noticin' that buckle."

"Couldn't you?"

"I've seen some like it before."

"Have you?"

"On some stinkin' Rebs. Most of 'em dead."

"I think you've talked enough."

"I don't. We chased you Rebs clear from Gettysburg through Georgia. CSA. Stood for Confederate States of America. Well, there ain't no such place. And you" — he looked at Elijah — "ain't you heard? Lincoln freed the slaves."

"Just a minute, mister." Elijah took a step forward.

"Shut up, nigger!" Crow-face barked. "I'll stand up for you if you won't stand up for yourself."

"I don't need you to . . ."

"Hold on, Elijah, please," Billy Joe said.

By now a considerable audience, uniformed and civilian, had gathered 'round.

"This man was addressing me," Billy Joe said to Elijah.

"This man," Crow-face smirked, "lost a

brother at Fredericksburg."

"Then the wrong brother died."

"Take it off, Reb." Crow-face pointed. "That Reb buckle. Take it off!"

"That buckle comes with the guns."

Crow-face took a step back, and another two steps.

"Then take 'em off or get ready to use 'em!"

"I'm ready," Billy Joe Bickford said, but even before he was through saying it, his left hand had drawn the gun, thumbed and fired into the gun handle at Crow-face's holster, shattering it to bits and leaving Crow-face stunned and trembling.

Among the crowd that had stood watching were Keys, Doc and Elizabeth Shelby — and through the crowd came Colonel Crook followed by Captain Bourke.

"What the hell's going on here?" Crook wanted to know.

Crow-face stood, still trembling, and Billy Joe Bickford stood silent as Keys came forward.

"Colonel, I witnessed the entire incident . . ."

"You did, did you, Mister Keys?"

"Yes, sir. This bully threatened, insulted and disparaged this young acquaintance of mine who did his best to avoid the confrontation that just took place."

"Rogers here" — Crook nodded toward Crow-face — "is a bully alright. No doubt about that. You got anything to say, Rogers?"

"No, sir."

Crow-face turned purple as a grape.

"Any complaint?"

"No . . . sir."

"And I'll vouch for this young man, Colonel," Keys said, pointing to Billy Joe.

"That so? Who'll vouch for you, Mister Keys? Alright, everybody, break it up."

The two officers walked away as the crowd, most of them still dumbfounded at the display, dispersed.

As Crook and Bourke headed toward Crook's office, Bourke looked back at Billy Joe Bickford and Elijah.

"Colonel, you think that young fellow and the colored man have anything to do with Mister Keys' 'private business?' "

"Don't know, Captain. But I got a feeling there's an awful lot of foxes gathering at this here hen house."

CHAPTER NINETEEN

After Colonel Crook and Captain Bourke had left and the crowd had more or less dispersed — although a number of the spectators still looked at Billy Joe Bickford from a distance and buzzed about the show he had put on — Keys made a suggestion.

"Why don't the five of us go someplace where we can talk?"

They did.

They walked to the bank of a stream that ran through the fort.

"Elijah," Keys said, "you're on schedule."

"You were right, Jefferson." Elijah nodded. "He did respond to the mention of your name."

"Mister Bickford." Keys motioned to each of the others as he made the introductions. "This is Elizabeth Shelby and Doc Zeeger."

Without acknowledgement, Billy Joe took a step toward Keys.

"I've been looking for you, Mister Keys."

"I know."

"You remember some years ago, when I was thirteen, I made you a promise."

Billy Joe hit Keys hard on the jaw. Keys' mouth leaked blood, but he barely blinked.

"I remember," Keys said.

"Jeff." Doc looked from Keys to Billy Joe. "What the hell's this about?"

"Tell them to stay out of it," Billy Joe said.

"They're out." Keys wiped the blood from his chin.

"Alright, we're out." Doc's brow furrowed. "Now will you tell us what we're out of?"

"Sure, Doc," Keys said without hesitation. "Billy Joe's come here to kill me."

Elizabeth Shelby, Elijah and Doc Zeeger looked at each other, then at Billy Joe, who stood calm and confident.

"Just as sure," Bickford said, "as the setting of the sun."

There was a funereal silence as the three of them digested the unexpected turn. Then Doc lifted both palms upward.

"I left a poker game and a warm woman for this?"

"Sorry to put you out, Doc." Billy Joe almost smiled.

"Yeah." Doc shrugged.

"Ma'am." Billy Joe pointed to Elizabeth. "It'd be better if you walked away from this."

"Like hell."

"Your choice, ma'am."

"Now, Mister Keys," Bickford went on, "the outcome is a certainty, but I'm going to give you a choice."

"That's gallant."

"No. I'm just savoring the prospect."

"Do I also choose the time and place?"

"If it isn't too long or too far. So what'll it

110

be? Guns? Sabres? Fists? As they say, choose your weapon."

"Alright. First off I choose logic."

"How's that?"

"Kill me now and what do you get? Revenge."

"And justice."

"Suppose you could get revenge and justice . . . with a bonus to boot?"

"What kind of a bonus?"

"A thousand dollars today and twenty thousand more a short time later. Would you savor the prospect a little longer?"

"For you it's going to end the same."

"But not for them." Keys' finger pointed to each of the others. "Not for Miss Shelby, Doc, Elijah — and not for you. Twenty-one thousand. Think that much over now and I'll tell you about the rest of it later this afternoon."

"How much later?"

"There's a fine old Spanish tradition called siesta. Suppose we meet in the cantina at three o'clock."

The silence hung thick as paste for almost half a minute.

"Then it'll only take ten minutes," Keys said, "for you to decide . . . after just the two of us talk in private."

"I've waited nearly seven years," Bickford

said. "I can wait that much longer." He turned and started to walk away. "Three o'clock in the cantina . . . private."

"Whew!!" Doc Zeeger expelled all the pent-up breath he had suppressed in his impaired lungs. "I never seen anything like this awake or asleep. He does mean to kill you."

"He does."

"Ought I to kill him?" Elijah asked quietly.

"We need him."

"We need *you* more," Elizabeth Shelby said. "So what are we going to do now?"

"Don't know about all of you." Keys smiled. "But I'm going to observe that fine old Spanish tradition . . . siesta. See you at the cantina, after three."

"Are you serious!?" Elizabeth Shelby grabbed his arm.

"I am." He started to move.

"So's he," Elijah said.

"Jeff." Doc scratched the wrinkles on the side of his face. "You think you can talk him out of it?"

"No."

"No?"

"No."

"Why's that?" Zeeger was still scratching.

"Because . . . he's got his reasons."

■ ■ ■ ■

Fully clothed, including his boots, Jefferson Keys lay on the bed in his room, his eyes closed, thinking about those events . . . some of which he knew about at the time and some that he found out later.

CHAPTER TWENTY

Palm Sunday, April 9, 1865. A nation divided and bleeding. A nation less than a hundred years old. A nation whose sixteenth president, a man who wanted peace, but led his nation into bloodstained battle after battle, burying thousands upon thousands of sons and fathers and brothers.

The battles on land and sea, in fields and streams, in cities and swamps — conquests and defeats — on horseback and foot, all the dynamite and destruction, fire and devastation — all led to the inevitable end:

Appomattox.

General Robert E. Lee's men, hungry and worn out, had stayed with the colors only because of their unshakable confidence and love for Lee himself. But Lee had realized that confidence and love were no match for the overwhelming numbers, strength, and power of Grant's army. And so Lee had sent out of his thin lines a Confederate horseman with white flag fluttering — and a letter asking for a meeting to discuss terms of surrender.

General Robert E. Lee was now in the parlor of the McLean house. Lee had been the most distinguished officer in the United States Army — graduated from West Point at the head of his class — served with honor and glory in the Mexican War — became superintendent at West Point. It was Lee who suppressed the uprising led by John Brown at Harper's Ferry. And it was Lee who first was offered command of the U.S. Army at the outbreak of the Civil War. He declined out of loyalty to his native Virginia.

And now, Lee, along with members of his staff, including General William Babcock and Colonel Charles Marshall, waited for Grant's arrival.

Outside, looking toward the north, with a weary rigidness, stood some of the remnants of General Lee's Army of Northern Virginia.

But there were two others in a nearby barn: Major Joseph Bickford and his aide, Lieutenant Daniel Haynes.

Major Bickford sat on a bale of hay, head bandaged and bowed, with Haynes standing to his right.

Slowly Major Bickford raised his head and

spoke in measured cadence.

"Lieutenant, we can't let it happen."

"Let what happen, sir?"

"The surrender. It must be stopped."

"Beggin' your pardon, sir, but there's nothing left to stop it with and you know it as well as anybody."

"Do I?"

"Yes, sir. Jeb Stuart, Hill, Pender, and Rhodes, they're all dead . . ."

"I'm not."

"No, sir, but you're wounded and . . . fevered. All that's left of Pickett's whole army is sixty bone-beaten men . . . and so are the rest of us. General Lee knows that . . . he's done more than could be expected, and, sir, so have we all."

"Maybe not."

Outside, the soldiers of the South reflexively had stiffened, stood at attention and clenched their fists.

Grant and his staff had arrived. Grant, General Philip H. Sheridan, Colonel Ord, Colonel Parker and Colonel Williams were to go inside and attend to the details of the surrender, while General George Armstrong Custer and Major Jefferson Keys, among others with the escort, waited along with the Confederate contingent on the grounds of the McLean house — waited for the rebirth of a nation.

The opposite of Lee in many ways, Grant had graduated near the bottom of his class, but did serve with distinction and valor in the Mexican War — later he was sent to a remote outpost in California, and being for the first time without his bride, Julia, began drinking and was drummed out of the Army. He was unsuccessful in business after business, and at forty-one considered a flat-out failure — until the war when he enlisted as a Colonel. There was never a more tenacious, aggressive, defiant, and determined officer. Lincoln found his new general in chief and Grant found his calling and destiny.

His soldiers went to battle singing:

. . . there's no such word as can't,
we'll ride our mounts to hell and back
for Ulysses Simpson Grant.

And now on the porch of the McLean house, just before they entered, Grant had spoken to Sheridan slightly above a whisper. "You know, Phil, I met General Lee during the Mexican Campaign when we were both in the same army. I was just a captain then; I wonder if he'll remember me?"

"After today," Sheridan responded, "he'll

remember you."

A few moments later the tall, elegant Lee and the shorter, mud-splattered Grant had acknowledged each other respectfully, then sat across the small table while their respective officers stood by.

Lee spoke with a voice trying to disguise the immeasurable anguish.

"I . . . I suppose, General Grant, that the object of this meeting is fully understood."

Grant nodded.

"To ascertain on what terms you would receive the surrender of my army."

"The terms I propose, General Lee, are those stated in my letter of yesterday. That is, the officers and men surrendered, to be pardoned and properly exchanged . . . and all arms and ammunition and supplies to be delivered up as captured property."

Lee nodded, not displeased.

"Those are about the conditions I hoped would be proposed."

"And I hope," Grant added, "this will lead to a general suspension of hostilities, sir. And be the means of preventing any further loss of life."

But in the nearby barn Major Joseph Bickford was contemplating the further loss of life.

One life in particular.

Slow and somewhat unsteady, he rose to his feet.

"The Bickfords of Virginia," he murmured. Then louder: "There have been Bickfords of Virginia before there was a United States . . . I know how to stop it."

"Stop what, sir?"

"And if I don't, I'd be untrue to those comrades who charged with me at Cedar Creek and Cold Harbor. We vowed . . ."

"What are you talking about, sir?"

"Not what. Who. If a Southerner kills Grant there'll be no peace. We'll have to keep fighting . . . and we'll win. And I know how to do it . . ."

"Do what, sir?"

"Kill Grant, of course." There was a fanatic gaze in Bickford's eyes as he moved, but his voice was composed and confident. "I've been in McLean's house this morning where Lee and Grant are sitting in the parlor. I'm going to climb around back to a room right over that parlor, a room in the attic with a vent . . . and with this gun," Bickford drew the sidearm from his holster, "Grant will die and so will the surrender."

"Major!" Haynes moved close and pleaded, "Please, sir . . . give me that gun . . . you can't . . ."

"Can't I?" Bickford smashed the barrel

across the lieutenant's forehead. Haynes fell against the bale then onto the floor of the barn.

"May I suggest, General," Lee said, "that you commit to writing the terms you have proposed so they may be formally acted upon."

"Very well," Grant replied as easily as he could, "I will write them out." He pointed to his manifold order book and addressed Colonel Ord. "Can I have that book and something to write on, please?"

Major Bickford had bound and gagged Lieutenant Haynes, then dragged him out of sight into one of the empty stalls.

Outside, near the McLean house, two officers who had ridden together, but with one of them always leading the charge, stood somewhat away from the Northern officers and even farther away from the Southern soldiers. One of the two Northern officers wore the usual blue uniform with the insignia of his rank on its epaulettes: Jefferson Keys.

The other officer wore a blue sailor's shirt, broad-collared, rolled into a black velveteen jacket adorned by rows of brass buttons and gleaming braid. His legs were covered by

119

britches of the same material, seamed by twin gold stripes and tucked into top boots cupped by silver spurs — and of course, the scarlet scarf flowed from the throat of General George Armstrong Custer.

"Well, Autie," Keys said, "the war'll soon be over."

"One war just leapfrogs onto another, Jeff, but in the meanwhile I won't be General Custer, just Colonel, unless I can get out West."

"You'll get there, Autie."

"Will you come with me, Jeff? You've been mighty lucky for me."

"You make your own luck, Autie." Keys nodded toward the house. "I wonder how it's going in there."

"Only one way it can go, Jeff, but how severe depends on Grant."

"Yeah, Ol' Unconditional Surrender Grant. Wonder if those are his terms this time."

"We'll soon find out."

"I'm going to take a little walk around . . . with your permission, General."

"Permission granted, Major, but don't stray too far."

"Truth is, Autie" — Keys smiled — "I gotta take a leak."

Grant rose with the pencil still in hand and slowly took the few steps to Lee and handed him the paper.

"I have written," he said, "that what is to be turned over will not include the side-arms of officers nor their private horses or baggage."

There were reactions from the Union officers: Sheridan, Ord, Parker, and Williams. And from the Confederates: Marshall and Babcock, and General Lee.

"This will have a very happy effect on my army." Lee looked at the paper then at Grant.

Major Bickford made his way to the rear of the McLean house. There was no one posted there. He went to a trellis, took a final look around and began to climb.

Lee had finished reading. He hesitated as if embarrassed to speak, but did.

"There is one thing, General. The cavalry men and artillerists own their own horses in our army; I know this differs from the United States Army."

Grant nodded.

"I would like to understand," Lee went on, "whether these men will be permitted to retain their horses?"

There was a stilted moment.

"The terms do not allow this, General. Only officers are allowed their private property."

"No." Lee looked back at the paper. "I see the terms do not allow it. That is clear . . ."

Grant's terms were already generous.

"Well," Grant spoke as gently and respectfully as possible. "The subject is quite new to me. I take it that most of your men are small farmers. They'll need their horses to put in a crop to carry their families through next winter. I'll instruct my officers to allow all men who own a horse or mule to take the animals home to work their little farms."

Lee's face was filled with manifest relief and gratitude.

"This will have the best possible effect on the men. It will do much toward conciliating our people."

Major Joseph Bickford moved quickly and quietly from the second-story window of the McLean house to the stairway leading to the attic.

Behind the barn, Major Keys had finished his business and was buttoning the front of his pants when he heard sounds from inside the stable. A soft, then louder, banging against the wall.

The sound stopped, started again, stopped and started even louder. Not the sounds of horse's hoofs. He thought of walking away but then thought better of it. Keys made his way around to the front and opened the barn door, stepped in.

Once inside he heard it louder, then spotted the source of the noise.

Within a stable, a man in uniform, bound and gagged, desperately kicking his boots against the wooden wall.

Keys rushed to the officer whose forehead bled and eyes implored for help. Keys leaned down, tore away the bandana that had been tightened across the lieutenant's mouth, started to untie the knots of the rope that bound his body, but the lieutenant shook his head and pulled away.

"You've got to stop him!" Haynes cried out. "He's going to kill Grant . . ."

"Who is?"

"Major Bickford . . . McLean house . . . up in the attic . . . there's a vent . . . he's crazy! Going to kill Grant. Hurry!! Now!!!"

Colonel Marshall had finished and blotted the inked letter from Lee to Grant, accepting the terms. General Lee put on his eyeglasses and was about to read it aloud.

Jeff Keys hurried as fast as possible without drawing attention — through the ranks of Northern and Southern soldiers — up the nine steps of the McLean house where a Yankee captain stood at the doorway.

"Step aside, Captain," Keys said, "I'm going in there."

"But sir, I . . ."

"Step aside, Captain! That is a direct order!"

"Yes, sir." The captain stepped aside. Keys walked by briskly and went in.

General Lee read aloud in his soft Southern voice. He neither rushed, nor lingered over the words.

Lieutenant General U. S. Grant
Commanding Armies of the United States
General, I have received your letter of this date containing the terms of surrender of the Army of Northern Virginia. They are accepted by me and I will proceed to carry the stipulation into effect.

Yours respectfully,
Your obedient servant
Robert E. Lee

Joseph Bickford had made his way to the narrower stairway that led to the attic room. General Custer, from some distance, had seen Keys take the steps to the porch two at a time, speak briefly to the captain and enter. Custer had paused for just a jot, then proceeded up the stairs to the captain.

"What is it, Captain? What did the major say to you?"

"Said he was going in, sir. Told me to step aside. Said it was a direct order."

"You ever hear of an *in*direct order, Captain?"

"Sir?"

"Step aside."

"Yes, sir." The captain saluted, stepped aside and Custer went through.

General Lee signed the letter of surrender, slowly removed his eyeglasses and started to rise.

Major Joseph Bickford opened the door of the attic room, entered, leaving the door ajar. He moved to the vent, knelt, drew his sidearm and pointed it through the vent as his eyes adjusted to the semi-darkness and started to take aim.

Keys had hurried up both flights of the McLean house and was proceeding along the narrow stairway.

Lee stepped closer to Grant, readying himself for the final gesture of defeat. He spoke as he moved slightly in anticipation of giving up his sword.

"Thirty-nine years of devotion to military duty has come to this . . . and this, too, is my duty . . ."

But Grant gently placed a restraining hand toward Lee's gesture.

Major Joseph Bickford took dead aim at Grant's head.

Grant extended his hand.

"General," said Grant, "the war is over. You are all our countrymen again."

"Like hell!" Bickford said aloud, cocked the hammer and squeezed.

Both shots went off simultaneously.

Bickford's shot missed its mark because Keys' shot hit its target: Bickford's temple.

Everyone in the parlor reacted instinctively, jerked around and looked for the first time toward the vent.

"Good God!" Custer said as he now stood beside Jefferson Keys.

It was decided by all concerned, including Generals Lee and Grant, that no mention of what had happened and what had almost happened, would ever come to light by anyone concerned — in the best interests of both sides and for the best interest of the nation.

Before he left, General U. S. Grant shook Major Keys' hand.

"Major, if I can ever be of service, please

call on me."

Later, General Custer shook his head and smiled at Keys.

"Well, Jeff, now it *is* over."

"Not quite, Autie. There's one more thing I've got to do."

After talking to Lieutenant Haynes, Keys had taken the coffin containing the body of Major Joseph Bickford in a buckboard, with his own horse tied behind, to the Shenandoah — and home.

He stood before a young boy at what was left of a once stately plantation.

"I thought your father would want to be buried on the ground he fought for."

The young boy looked at Keys' uniform.

"You fought against him."

"We both fought for what we believed in. The war is over."

The boy's eyes went to the coffin, then back to Keys.

"For him . . . and you . . . but not for me."

"Son, your father died from the last shot fired in that war."

"How do you know?"

"I fired it."

The boy's eyes closed. He trembled visibly, breathed a solitary breath, then stared into the face of the man before him.

"What's your name?"

"Keys. Jeff Keys . . . I'm sorry, son." He turned toward his horse.

"Just a minute, Mister Keys, I want you to know this . . . and remember it . . . no matter where you go . . . no matter how long it takes . . . one day you'll turn around . . . and I'll be there . . . because just as sure as the setting of the sun . . . I'm going to kill you."

Keys said nothing.

He mounted his horse and rode away from the Shenandoah Valley with the boy's words echoing in his brain . . . *just as sure as the setting of the sun . . . I'm going to kill you.*

CHAPTER TWENTY-ONE

That was nearly seven years ago. Billy Joe Bickford was no longer a boy.

And as he lay on the bed in the hotel room at Fort Canby, Jeff Keys could still hear the words that Billy Joe Bickford had repeated just hours earlier.

. . . one day you'll turn around . . . and I'll be there . . . because just as sure as the setting of the sun . . . I'm going to kill you.

Keys rose from the bed and made ready for what was to come with Billy Joe. He knew what he was going to say to Major Joseph Bickford's son — and no matter what else — he knew what he was not going to say.

Keys was not going to tell him that his father died not as a valiant soldier but as a failed assassin — not bravely in battle — but, from behind cover, a would-be murderer. All those who knew what happened at Appomattox had taken a vow — and Keys would not break that vow even if his life depended on it.

Chapter Twenty-Two

Elizabeth Shelby, Doc Zeeger and Elijah were standing just outside the hotel as Keys stepped out of the door.

"You still goin' to meet him?" Doc asked.

"Nothing else I can do."

"'There's something else," Elijah said, "I can do."

Keys just shook his head.

"Jeff." Elizabeth came closer. "You said he had his reasons . . ."

Keys nodded.

"Tell us."

"I killed his father."

"When?"

"During the war?" Doc asked.

Keys nodded again.

"Hell." Doc rubbed his chin. "I killed a lot of people during the war . . ."

"But not his father . . . Look, it's almost time . . ."

"Jefferson," Elijah said, "you sure you don't want company?"

"Yeah, I do . . ."

The three looked at each other.

"Come visit us after I'm with him for ten minutes."

Keys walked toward the cantina.

Billy Joe stood waiting at the bar. There were about a dozen other patrons, most of whom had seen the young man use his gun earlier in the day and most of them wondered what he was going to do next.

Keys came in, walked to the bar beside Billy Joe and spoke to the bartender.

"Give us a bottle of your best rye and two glasses."

The bartender placed a bottle and two glasses in front of Keys.

"And we'd like the use of your back room for a few minutes." He put a double eagle on the bar. "Will that cover it?"

"Brother" — the bartender picked up the gold coin — "you can stay in there all week."

Keys picked up the bottle with one hand and the two glasses with the other. He moved toward the door leading to the back room. Billy Joe followed. When they got to the door Keys stopped, raised both hands slightly and nodded toward the knob. Billy Joe reached down, twisted the knob, pushed the door open and waved Keys forward.

The room was small, dominated by a round, felt-covered table, surrounded by six chairs.

Keys set the bottle and glasses on the table, uncorked the rye, poured it into each glass, pulled out one of the chairs, and pointed to another.

"Sit down, Billy Joe. Let's talk something over."

"I didn't come here to talk."

"Then just listen. You agreed to that."

Keys swallowed the rye, then poured himself another.

"I did," said Billy Joe. He swallowed his glass of rye and poured another one for himself. "Ten minutes."

"By February of 1865," Keys began, "even the leaders of the Confederacy realized their cause was doomed . . ."

Keys proceeded to tell Billy Joe about the gold, Colonel and Elizabeth Shelby, the wagons breaking down, burying the gold, the attack by Mangus and the Yaquis, Elizabeth Shelby surviving, being taken by Mangus as his wife at the age of fourteen, escaping, meeting Waxer and Kline and the deal Keys had made to retrieve the gold.

Doc began to walk toward the cantina, Elijah followed, then Elizabeth Shelby.

"You stay here." Doc looked back at her.

"Like hell."

The three of them kept on walking.

". . . that's the setup," Keys continued. "There's no better tracker than Elijah. He's an expert with the bow, rope and bullwhip, and he used to be a blacksmith."

"I know." Billy Joe nodded. "On a plantation in Virginia."

"There's no better teamster than Doc Zeeger. He knows animals and can doctor people. We soldiered together in Mexico for Juarez. Took a bullet out of my gut once."

"He looks sick."

"He's got one war left."

"And you?"

Keys pulled two cigars out of his shirt pocket and a match. He offered Bickford one of the stogies. Billy Joe shook his head. Keys replaced the rejected cigar, bit off and spat out the end of the other one, stuck it in his mouth, struck the match on his pants and lit up. He took a long smooth drag and let the smoke drift back up through his nostrils and mouth.

"Me? My specialty's strategy . . . and

132

dynamite."

"And murder."

"Let's table that for now. We still need you . . ." Keys pointed with his cigar, ". . . and those guns. Waxer and Kline said I could pick my men. I picked you."

"She's not a man," Billy Joe said, "and I don't like the girl going in."

"She goes. Won't trust anybody with a map. Don't blame her."

"On second thought, I'll take that cigar."

Keys took it out of his pocket again, handed it to Bickford and even went through the routine of lighting it for him after Billy Joe bit off the end.

Bickford inhaled, then shook his head slightly.

"Not made of good Virginia leaf."

"They will be again . . . someday."

"What's she to you? The girl?"

"Nothing."

"Yeah?"

"Yeah. Just a Southern belle in distress," Keys said.

"To me she's a squaw."

"And a ticket to twenty thousand dollars."

Both men smoked and looked at each other.

"Billy Joe, here's your chance to get back your father's plantation and then some . . .

and to use Confederate gold, now claimed by the U.S. Government, in the getting."

Doc, Elijah and Elizabeth Shelby walked into the cantina, looked around, then Doc walked to the bar with Elijah and Elizabeth following.

"Where are they?" Doc asked the bartender.

"The five of 'em" — the bartender pointed — "are in the back room."

"Five?"

"Two men, a bottle of rye and two glasses."

"One of 'em," Doc said, "don't look old enough to drink."

"Brother." The bartender blinked. "He's old enough to carry them guns — he's old enough to drink."

"A philosopher," Doc said to Elijah, pointing at the bartender.

"Sorry, ma'am." The bartender offered a weak smile to Elizabeth Shelby. "No ladies allowed . . . unless they . . . work here."

"Go to hell," she snapped.

"Yes, ma'am."

Doc, Elijah and Elizabeth looked toward the door to the back room.

"Time," Doc said.

They moved.

"You and me" — Billy Joe flicked the ash

from the cigar onto the floor — "we pick up where we left off when we get back."

"Right." Keys smiled. "The winner gets the twenty thousand and the loser gets buried."

The back room door opened. A gun flashed into Billy Joe's left hand and pointed at Elizabeth, Doc, and Elijah in the doorway.

"Easy, Billy Joe." Keys grinned. "You've already met the rest of the troops. Come in, troops, that's what doors are for."

The three moved in and Elijah closed the door behind them.

Billy Joe holstered the gun and motioned to Elizabeth Shelby.

"You oughta learn to knock."

"Where we're going," she said, "there won't be any doors."

Doc looked at Billy Joe then at Keys.

"Did you shake hands?"

"No." Keys smiled. "We shook fists."

"*Are* we going?" Doc asked.

"Was there ever any doubt?" Keys puffed on the cigar.

"Uh . . . no," Doc said. "Hell no."

"Then we better get at it." Keys picked up the bottle of rye and stuck the cork back in. "We got a lot of preparations to make."

"Yeah." Doc nodded. "This is gonna be some party."

CHAPTER TWENTY-THREE

Politics makes strange bedfellows — the old saying has been proven true time and again.

But there's something else that sometimes makes for even stranger bedfellows.

Greed.

And it is written in the Bible that the love of money is the root of all evil.

Money, and maybe even greed, had prompted Keys, Elizabeth Shelby, Doc, Elijah and Billy Joe to band together. But they could not be defined as evil.

The same could not be said of Willard Oliver Waxer and Simon Ignatius Kline. Evil has been defined as morality bad or wrong, wicked. And that was not an improper definition of Messrs. Waxer and Kline. They had never allowed conscience to impede their pursuit of profit. Seldom did two men with such opposite physical characteristics share such identical amoral propensities. There was no right or wrong, there was only acquisition, appropriation or aggrandizement. They had been called plunderers, pillagers, swindlers, spoilers, robber barons, brigands, and buccaneers. And they didn't give a damn, so long as they came out on top. And they always did.

One of the reasons Waxer and Kline

always came out on top was that they never had a nefarious scheme without the back-up of an even more nefarious scheme.

This scheme would be no exception.

From their private railroad car they over-saw their vast financial empire via telegraph and special couriers and at the same time kept tab on their latest scheme to add five million in gold — more or less — to that empire via a group of fools that Waxer and Kline had dubbed "The Trespassers."

Trespassers — it never occurred to Waxer and Kline that that word better described the two of them.

Trespassers or not — Keys, Elizabeth Shelby, Doc Zeeger, Elijah, and even Billy Joe Bickford put aside their own differences and designs, at least for the time being, and became a team, a team with one purpose — go into Mexico, retrieve the gold, and receive their due — a team under the leadership of Jefferson Keys.

Keys' hotel room had been set up as headquarters where the five met and went over many of the details involved. Keys, Doc, Elijah and Billy Joe spent the days outfitting for the expedition. Supplies, a wagon that Elijah reinforced with heavy springs, axels and wheels, spare parts — animals for the journey — medicines — ammunition and dynamite.

Elizabeth Shelby spent a good deal of time in the bathtub she had ordered into her room.

One night while Keys was going over some notes alone in his room there was a knock on the adjoining door.

Keys got up and opened the door.

Elizabeth Shelby stood at the threshold semi-wrapped in a towel, still dripping wet, the towel and her body.

"Can I come in?"

"Sure, but I thought you said no more 'til we get the gold."

"Don't get your hopes up. That's not why I want to come in."

"Oh, excuse me." He looked her up and down. "It's just that you seemed dressed — or undressed — for the occasion. Do come in for what ever the occasion is."

"Something came to me. Things come to me in the tub."

"I'll bet they do."

"No, I mean about Mexico."

"What about Mexico?"

"Dynamite."

"What about dynamite?"

"Are you sure you're going to bring enough?"

"Lady, one thing I've never been short

on . . ." He paused and studied the shape of her body outlined through the clinging towel. ". . . is dynamite."

"I know you're good at some things . . ."

"Such praise takes its toll on my humility."

"That's not what I meant."

"No? What did you mean?"

"I meant I saw you in action with Valance."

"Oh, that. He was easy."

"And with Billy Joe . . . he's not so easy and I still don't know how you handled him."

"You'll find out one of these days . . . after we get the gold."

"Do you really think" — she took two steps closer and the towel fell to the floor — "we'll get it?"

She made no move to retrieve it.

"Lady." He picked up the towel and handed it to her. "How much more of this do you think a healthy man should have to bear?"

"Oh, excuse me. I didn't mean for that to happen."

"I was sort of hoping you did."

She wrapped the towel around her and turned around.

"Here," she said, "tuck it in in the back."

He did.

She turned and faced him again.

"Where were we?"

"Things come to you in the tub."

"Oh, yeah, I wanted to ask you, are you really good with dynamite?"

"There's a few used-to-be bridges and railroads that can attest to that."

"Tell me more about it."

"About what?"

"About you and dynamite."

"Now?"

"Now."

"It's not exactly a bedtime story."

"That's alright, we're not going to bed."

"Oh, yeah, that's right. . . . Well, she was my first love."

"She?"

"Sure, dynamite is a woman . . . a woman a lot like you."

"Me?"

"Like you." Keys nodded. "Sometimes silent and docile, sometimes unpredictable and volatile. 'Specially nitro . . . hard to handle, but if you know how, a hell of a companion . . . a helpmate in getting things done . . . or undone. Much like you only a lot older. Origins go back to China over a thousand years, but reborn just a few years ago when a fellow named Nobel invented the blasting cap and discovered that mixing nitro with silica would turn the liquid into a malleable paste called dynamite with the advantage that it could be . . ." He looked her up and down again and smiled. ". . . cylinder-shaped for insertion into . . . a lot of things . . . the drilling holes for mining and . . ."

"OK, OK, I guess you know dynamite."

"Yes, Elizabeth . . . my first love, and a hell of a lot like you."

"Just bring plenty . . . and another thing . . ."

"What?"

"You might know everything about dynamite, but don't get the idea that you know everything about me. Take a good look." She took off the towel and stood with it in one hand, her blazing red hair splashing onto her shoulders and green eyes assured. "Take a good look . . ." she repeated. "And think about that."

She turned, walked slowly into her room, closed the door and locked it from the other side.

Keys did think about it . . . and about other things . . . things he had to talk over with Doc Zeeger.

CHAPTER TWENTY-FOUR

"Doc," he said the next day as he sat in his room across the table from Zeeger with the nearly empty bottle of rye between them, "I been thinking about the . . . expedition."

"So've I." Doc nodded. "Well, go ahead. You haven't changed your mind about it . . . not the Jeff Keys I know."

"No, but I been thinking . . . there's two things we need more of."

"Only two?"

"Mainly two . . . what with comancheros, Yaquis, and who knows what else we might run into. One, we need more firepower, and I know where to get it."

"Good. What's the other?"

"Manpower, along with another wagon and somebody who knows how to handle that firepower and the wagon."

"That's funny . . . and coincidental, 'cause yesterday when I stopped by the cantina, I saw somebody who's just come to Canby. Somebody you used to talk about. But he's in pretty bad shape."

Half an hour later Keys walked into the cantina and looked around. He saw what he wanted to see . . . sort of. And in pretty bad shape.

Keys moved toward one of the tables near a corner where a man sat with his head bent into his folded arms on the table and an empty glass in front of him.

Keys sat on one of the chairs at the table and prodded the man's elbow.

"Sandusky."

No response.

Keys prodded harder.

"Sandusky!" he said louder.

The man stirred, then looked up.

Whoever designed his face never heard of handsome, a face crisscrossed with creases and a crop of spiky hair under what went for a hat. He was dressed in faded buckskin that appeared almost as old as he did. The whites of his eyes weren't white, more orange. The eyes blinked and tried to focus.

"Sandusky." Keys smiled. "It's Keys — Jeff Keys — remember?"

"Sure." Sandusky wiped at his nose. "I remember."

So did Keys — remember what he knew about the man, the man he met years ago, known only as Sandusky; born and raised on a farm near Sandusky, Ohio. Horses and wagons, wagons and horses — and guns, all kinds of guns. Yankee sniper during the war, then buffalo hunter. Killed hundreds of men and thousands of buffalo — buffalo for the men who built the railroad — and buffalo for foreign hunting parties, including royalty — buffalo for robes — and buffalo tongues smoked and sent back East, considered culinary delicacies — while heaps of meat lay rotting, more than buzzards and other scavengers could possibly consume.

"Sure, I remember," Sandusky said again. "I remember you kindly . . . can't say that about many I met."

"Well, I thank you and remember you kindly too, Sandusky. I'm glad our trails crossed again, particularly at this time."

"Any particular reason?" Sandusky straightened up some. "I mean at this particular time?"

"Got a job you might be interested in."

Sandusky shook his head.

"If it's got anything to do with buffalo, I'm not your man."

"Nothing to do with buffalo. Got to do with guns, wagons, danger . . . and money."

Sandusky held out his hand, fingers trembling.

"Maybe I'm still not your man . . . take a look."

"One way to stop that . . ."

"Stop drinking?"

Keys nodded.

"Easier said than done." Sandusky stared

at the empty glass on the table.

"Who said it was easy?" Keys smiled.

"Not them ghosts," Sandusky mumbled.

"What ghosts?"

"In the dreams . . . ghosts of men and beasts I've killed. The men, that wasn't so bad, that was war . . . but who declared war on the buffalo? Them poor creatures . . . strong, but short on brains . . . time was when I thought there weren't enough rifles and cartridges to cut 'em all down . . . but now I'm not so sure . . . but I'm sure of one thing."

"What's that?"

"If there's another world . . . I've got a heap of explainin' to do . . . think about it all the time when I'm drunk and dream."

"Do you think and dream about those ghosts when you're sober?"

Sandusky shook his head. His hat almost fell off.

"Then why do you drink?"

"Ask them ghosts. Maybe it's their way of retribution . . . of keepin' me from gettin' that farm."

"What farm?"

"The one I been wantin' to buy back near Sandusky . . . been wantin' to buy it for years . . . and always I ain't got no money."

"How much do you need to buy it?"

"Five hundred dollars."

"That's not so much."

"It is if you haven't got it."

"You've got it."

"Keys, what the hell are you talkin' about?"

"About that job I mentioned. Five hundred in advance, deposited in the bank in your name . . . on a couple of conditions."

"Who do I have to kill?"

Now Keys looked at the empty glass.

"The whiskey man. You just have to stay sober and alive. And you just might have to do a little incidental killing in order to stay alive."

"I don't exactly call this livin'."

"Then you haven't got much to lose."

"Just the smell of ol' guts and dead buffalo."

"Tomorrow you'll be wearing new buckskins, have a brand-new Henry rifle and checking out a wagon and rig. And when we get back — if we get back — there'll be a big fat bonus . . . but first we gotta talk about guns . . ."

"Brother, there ain't a gun that's been invented that I don't know about."

Jefferson Keys leaned in a little closer.

"One gun in particular . . ."

CHAPTER TWENTY-FIVE

During the next couple of days considerable changes took place.

Sandusky had cleaned up. He went through a thorough process at the civilian barber and bath parlor. His spiky hair was no longer spiky. It had been barbered by Antonio Puglia and meticulously parted directly in the center. He no longer smelled of old guts. That offense had been replaced by an abundant aroma of toilet lilac. He was outfitted with store-bought duds, but he did refuse to surrender his good-luck hat. He had become the possessor of a new model Henry rifle — .44 caliber, fifteen shot, weight nine and a half pounds with breech made of golden brass — also the possessor of a bank book with a balance of five hundred dollars on deposit at W-K SAVINGS AND TRUST.

Keys had introduced Sandusky, after he was cleaned up, to the rest of the Trespassers, who accepted him on Keys' say-so — especially after Keys assured them privately that their share of the profits would not be affected. Doc Zeeger, in particular, welcomed the additional manpower, and driver of a second wagon that he felt was necessary.

Only one of the Trespassers wanted something made absolutely clear: Billy Joe Bickford.

"About that twenty thousand," he said to Keys, "that'll be left after we settle our business . . ."

"What about it?"

"This Sandusky fellow, he doesn't get any part of it. Right?"

"Well" — Keys shrugged — "that'll be up to you . . . or me. Won't it?"

"Yeah." Billy Joe's right hand instinctively hovered closer to his holster. "It will."

Another change included the rental of a barn at Fort Canby by Doc Zeeger to be used for storage and supplies — medicine, airtights, ammunition and dynamite — along with the two wagons and animals. Elijah and Sandusky, it was decided, would stand guard and even sleep in the barn. Doc also moved in. Billy Joe took over Doc's quarters at the hotel and Elizabeth Shelby maintained her adjacent room and tub.

The sun rose bright and warm over the eastern sawtooth ridge near Fort Canby. As Keys walked across the compound toward the barn, he paused at the sight and sound of hoofs and traces of the mounted detachment led by Colonel Crook with a young lieutenant at his side. There were three

Apache scouts with the troop.

Crook raised his right hand and the unit came to a stop near Keys. Keys took a couple steps even nearer.

"Good morning, George. Nice day for a picnic."

"It would be," Crook said, "if we were going picnicking."

"Where are you going, Colonel? Or is that a military secret?"

"No secret. Got a report that Battu and some of his comanchcros might be paying a visit this side of the border."

"Where's the captain? Isn't he going with you?"

"Captain Bourke's staying. In charge of the fort. This is Lieutenant Crane." Crook nodded toward the shiny young officer mounted next to him. "He's new out here. Learning the business."

"Aren't we all. How long'll you be gone?"

"That's up to Battu. Will you be here when we get back?"

"I guess" — Keys shrugged — "that's up to him, too."

"I'm told" — Crook pointed toward the barn — "that you and your friends've been awful busy."

"Oh, just getting ready for a little . . . picnic, Colonel." Keys smiled.

"We'll talk about it some more if you're still here when we get back."

"Always nice to talk to you, George." Keys glanced at the young lieutenant. "And nice meeting you, Lieutenant Crane."

"Thank you, sir," Lieutenant Crane said seriously.

Crook nudged his mule, Apache, waved the troop forward, and they moved toward the gates.

That afternoon all the Trespassers except Elizabeth Shelby were in the barn. Keys sat behind a makeshift desk going over a map — Doc Zeeger and Sandusky checking the two wagons, Elijah waxing his bow, and Billy Joe once again oiling and cleaning his handguns — until Elizabeth Shelby walked in.

She wore tight, brown britches tucked into black lizard boots, a green velvet blouse that matched her eyes and did nothing to conceal, and everything to emphasize, what was underneath.

The men couldn't help but take momentary notice, then went back to work, all but Keys, who continued to look as she came over to him with an unlit cigarette between her lips.

"Got a match?"

Keys rose and took the cigarette from her mouth.

"No smoking in here. We don't want this place and all that's in it to catch fire and blow up. You understand?"

"Sure I do. But give me back my cigarette. I'll smoke it later."

He gave it back, touched her elbow, and started to lead her away from the others.

"Now come on over here, I want to talk to you about something."

"Something important?"

"Not very, but . . ." He stopped walking, so did she.

"But what?"

"Do you have to wear an outfit like that?"

"Like what?"

"Like you were wearing it while you took a bath . . . and it shrunk."

"You don't think it's . . . flattering?"

"It's too flattering. Draws too much attention. Not only from these fellows, but from everybody else at Canby. We don't need that kind of attention — or any other kind. You understand?"

"Look, Mister Keys, you can tell me not to smoke in here. I understand that. But don't go telling me what to wear. That's none of your business."

"Everything is my business 'til we get

151

back; that is, if you want us to go . . ."

"Alright. Alright. Tell you what I'll do."

"Tell me."

"I'll wear a jacket, a loose-fitting jacket, over this. Will that meet with your approval?"

"It'll help."

Just then they had unexpected visitors.

An ornate buggy attached to a team of identical black horses, and driven by Raymond, pulled up in front of the open barn doors. The carriage carried two passengers, Willard Oliver Waxer and Simon Ignatius Kline.

Raymond, dressed more English than Western, debarked, walked inside and approached Jeff Keys.

"Mister Keys, Mister Waxer and Mister Kline would like to speak with you."

"Tell them to come in and speak."

"They would appreciate it, sir, if you would come out and speak to them alone."

"Glad to."

Keys started to move out and Elizabeth Shelby started to follow.

"They did" — Raymond cleared his throat — "say alone."

"So they did." Keys kept on moving.

So did Elizabeth Shelby.

As Keys and Elizabeth approached, Kline

hopped off the carriage and continued consuming the reddest apple Keys had ever seen.

Waxer did not hop. Keys even wondered how Mister Waxer had managed to climb aboard the carriage without benefit of a crane.

Raymond had made it his business to walk out of earshot of whatever was about to be said by those involved.

"Good day, gentlemen," Keys said.

"Good day, sir," Waxer intoned from the carriage seat, which sagged perceptibly.

Kline looked at Keys, then at Elizabeth Shelby, then back to Keys.

"Didn't you hear Raymond say we wanted to talk to you alone?"

"I heard."

"So did I," Elizabeth said. "But I'm the only one around here with any secret, and if you ever want to know where that certain something is, there better not be any secrets from me."

"Makes sense," Keys said.

"Yes, it does," Waxer rumbled from above.

"But let me ask you something, gentlemen." Keys looked around. "Do you think it wise for us to be seen out here together? Isn't it likely to arouse some suspicion, particularly if our little enterprise is successful later on?"

"Not at all." Kline took another bite from the apple. "We have business here at the fort, silver mine headquarters, the bank, other interests. Nothing unusual at our stopping by to talk to some of our depositors."

"If you say so." Keys shrugged.

"By the way," Kline continued, "we see by your account at the bank that you've been spending our money with a lavish hand on this fool's errand."

"It takes money, and probably some of our blood, to make money. Besides, if this is a fool's errand then we're the fools. Any time you want me to stop — so does this expedition."

"I didn't say that!"

"Then what did you come here to say?"

"Well . . ."

"Well, what?"

"We were just wondering, when does this 'expedition' get started?"

"Just as soon as we get one more piece of equipment."

"What equipment is that, sir?" Waxer inquired.

"The fewer people who know that, the better."

"Including us?" Kline squinted.

"Including you. Now, gentlemen, I suggest you let us get back to work."

"Very good, sir." Waxer nodded.

Keys also nodded, turned and moved toward the barn.

Elizabeth Shelby started to follow.

"Uh, just a minute, Miss Shelby." Kline threw away what was left of the apple and came closer.

Keys kept on toward the barn.

"Uh, Miss Shelby." Kline wiped at his mouth. "How do you find your accommodations at the hotel?"

"I find them very easily, every night."

"That's not what I meant."

"What did you mean?"

"I was wondering . . . as long as you're going to be here a little longer . . . if you might consider . . . resuming our previous arrangement?"

"I might consider it."

"It would be very profitable." Kline beamed. "I'd be very . . . generous."

"I might consider it, Mister Kline . . ." she smiled, ". . . but I wouldn't do it."

Elizabeth Shelby walked toward the barn, a most beguiling walk.

CHAPTER TWENTY-SIX

They had dismounted near a stream. The horses were being watered and canteens were being filled.

Comancheros. Dirty men in a dirty trade.

They were called comancheros because mostly they did business with Comanches and other Indians on both sides of the border, providing guns, ammunition, whiskey, assorted provisions, and prisoners, mostly women — stolen and kidnapped.

The comanchero camp was to the south in Mexico, but they had ridden into the Arizona Territory days ago on one of their raiding forays in search of merchandise to ply their trade — horses, cattle, chattel, including human chattel that would bring them profit.

Most of the time their forays had been profitable. Not this time, and they were tired and angry — scalawags, highbinders, backshooters and no-good bastards — the worst and angriest was their leader.

Battu.

Years ago he had come into their camp from hell knows where, killed their then leader, cut off his head and attached it to a pole, for all to see and remember, until it rotted.

No one challenged him then — or since. He took what he wanted, including the women in the camp and the female prisoners until he was ready to trade them.

Battu drank by the stream from his canteen that was not filled with water, then looked up toward the two riders who were crossing from the other side. Two riders he had sent out to scout the terrain.

Battu took another deep swallow then screwed on the lid of the canteen as the two men dismounted — Diaz and Charly — no better or worse than the rest of the comancheros.

"Anything?"

"A ranch." Diaz.

"Big?"

"Not big," Charly.

"Small," Diaz.

"Cattle?"

"Not many," Charly.

"Horses?"

"A few," Diaz.

"Damn." Battu pointed to all the comancheros. "I bring half an army for that."

"But something else," Charly.

"Something better," Diaz.

"What better?"

"Women," Charly.

"Two women," Diaz.

"And only one man." Charly smiled.

"Never mind about the man."

"Very nice family. They let us drink from their well. Water our horses." Diaz.

"What about the women?"

"Oh, Jefe . . ." Charly.

"Mother and daughter," Diaz.

"But both very nice," Charly.

"How nice?"

"Both yellow hair," Diaz.

"Both . . . ripe," Charly.

"Don't know which one you'd pick, Jefe," Diaz.

"I'll pick 'em both. Yellow hair, huh."

"Oh, yes, Battu," Charly.

"Very yellow. Very nice," Diaz.

"Bring a good price." Battu smiled for the first time. "After I'm through."

Both men also smiled and nodded.

"How far?"

"Hours," Diaz.

"Six–seven," Charly.

"We go."

The Olang ranch. That's where the comancheros were going. The only current occupants consisted of Karl Olang, a tall, orange-haired man, forty-five years of age, his handsome, flaxen-haired wife, Ingrid, who was four years younger, and their blossoming, blond daughter, Karla, who had observed her sixteenth birthday just one month ago.

Karl Olang and his hired cowboys had rounded up the cattle on his spread, sold them off and the hired hands had left until the next round-up.

But instead of cattle being rounded up at the Olang ranch, there would be another kind of round-up — the kind that comancheros relished.

Below the border, white women with yellow hair were highly prized — as high as one thousand dollars apiece.

Chapter Twenty-Seven

On a field not far outside Fort Canby, but far enough so the shots would not be mistaken for an attack, the Army had set up a target range for rifles and handguns.

The range was silent, windless, and unpopulated at the time except for Elijah and his bullwhip — the bullwhip that he always carried close to his saddle horn instead of a lariat.

But the bullwhip was not now on his mount. It was in his hand.

Along a hitching post, Elijah had set up and lighted six slim candles; he stood just over five feet away, then spoke without turning his back.

"It's dangerous to walk up soft behind somebody."

Billy Joe took a couple of steps closer and stopped just to the left of Elijah.

"Just curious."

"And dangerous."

"What do you intend to do?" Billy Joe pointed toward the flickering candles.

"Don't intend to do anything. Going to do it."

Elijah unlooped the bullwhip and let the business end lay on the ground for an instant; then, as fast as the eye could follow, brought it up and forward, snapping it six times as six flames were snuffed out without touching any of the candles.

Just as fast, Billy Joe drew his right hand and fired six times, biting off the top of each candle — all one inch from the peak.

"Very good," Elijah said as he looped up the bullwhip. "But there's one difference."

"What's that?"

"Your way makes a lot of noise."

"How does it feel, Captain?"

Keys stopped and spoke to Captain Bourke just as the officer was coming out of headquarters.

"How does what feel?"

"For you, a captain, to be in charge of a whole fort?"

"I feel like the son whose father left the store and said 'You're in charge . . . but don't do anything.' "

"You ought to be glad that there's not much of anything to do."

"I am . . . and I'm not."

"What does that mean?"

"It means I pretty much missed out on the war, having just left West Point . . ."

"Too bad."

"It was for me."

"There's another kind of war going on out here."

"Yes, there is, Mister Keys, but being with an officer like Colonel Crook, and I think he's the best there is, doesn't give me a chance to make a single decision."

"Your time will come, Captain, but in the meanwhile, as Colonel Crook said about that young lieutenant, you're learning the business."

"You can only learn so much" — Bourke nodded — "without . . ."

Keys had already turned toward the gates of the fort. So did Captain Bourke, and soldiers and civilians within the compound.

Colonel Crook and the detachment,

weary, smeared with dust — some with
blood — rode in, smaller in numbers, but
smartly.

Keys and Captain Bourke stood at the
entrance of headquarters as the order to
dismount was given and carried out.

Both Keys and Bourke approached the
bone-tired commander. Lieutenant Crane,
who had suffered a slight wound, had traces
of blood at his forehead.

"George." Keys glanced at the soldiers,
then back to Crook. "Did you find them or
did they find you?"

"I'm in no mood, Keys." Crook moved
past Keys toward the door. "Come on
inside, Captain. I want to talk to you."

Bourke followed.

Lieutenant Crane rubbed at his shoulder,
took a deep breath and spoke a little too
loud.

"Battu . . . comancheros . . . sons a
bitches . . ."

"Lieutenant . . ."

". . . snipers, picked us off . . . killed two,
wounded some . . . on a patrol nobody'll
remember . . ."

"You're *bleeding,* Lieutenant."

Soldiers and civilians nearby, including
Doc Zeeger, had heard the remark.

"Better go and see to it." Keys looked

hard at the dazed young officer who understood Keys' meaning and straightened.

"Thank you, Mister Keys."

Keys walked away.

Doc Zeeger fell in step beside him.

"That young fella" — Doc pointed back toward headquarters — "got a lot to learn . . . if he lives."

"Yeah, partly they learn and partly they die."

"You heard what they said about them comancheros . . . Battu."

"I heard."

"Ever meet up with him?"

"Nope. Haven't had the occasion."

"Well, that occasion just might occur on our way to where we're goin', wherever the hell that is. Probably have to pass right through his territory."

"Probably."

"He's got a lot with him."

"That's another reason why we need that piece of equipment. Are you and Sandusky ready to roll?"

"We will be by tomorrow."

"Then that's when we'll get it."

"You figure out how?'

"Yep, but I was hoping Crook would stay away a little longer. He won't make it any easier."

"I reckon not."

"They don't call him 'Grey Wolf' for nothing."

"You sure your friend Sandusky can handle it?"

"I saw him in action up at the Platte. With that thing he's a one-man army."

"Even if he goes to drinkin' again?"

"Hasn't so far, has he?"

"Nope."

"Then we'll just have to see that he doesn't."

"You know what I think, Mister Keys?"

"No. What?"

"I think this is some cockeyed caravan you're in command of."

Chapter Twenty-Eight

The next morning when Elizabeth Shelby walked into the barn the men had already been at work for more than two hours.

The Trespassers watched as she sauntered by, but not nearly as long as they had watched before. She was dressed the same as before but this time with the addition of a loose-fitting corduroy jacket that covered her to mid-thigh.

She ambled up to where Keys sat behind his desk, turned completely around and faced him again.

"Does this meet with your approval, my liege?"

Keys nodded.

"Any more orders?" She smiled.

"Uh-oh."

"Uh-oh, what?"

"Speaking of orders . . ." Keys pointed to Captain Bourke, who had entered and stood near the barn door.

"May I come in, Mister Keys?"

"Certainly, Captain." Keys rose and walked toward the officer, precluding the captain from coming in any farther. "What can I do for you?"

"Not for me. For Colonel Crook. He'd like to see you."

"When?"

"Now."

"Well, then, I'll go see him . . . now."

As the two of them walked toward headquarters, Bourke said nothing more.

"You know what this is about, Captain?"

"Colonel Crook doesn't sometimes confide in his subordinate officers."

"That's not a bad policy . . . sometimes."

"That'll be all, Captain," Crook said from behind his desk.

"Yes, sir." The captain saluted.

Crook returned the salute and rose.

Bourke left the room and closed the door.

The Colonel stood staring at the map on the wall. He picked up an arrow from his desk and ran the point across the line that marked the United States–Mexican border.

"It's an imaginary line, Keys, but for Battu and his comancheros it's real enough. It's sanctuary. And for me it might as well be the Great Wall of China."

"That's how far you got yesterday?"

"That's it. Battu hit the Olang ranch, kidnapped his wife and daughter and staked him out on an ant hill . . . not a pretty sight of what was left when we got there. I don't even want to think about what's going to happen to those two women."

"Why didn't you get lost and follow him across that imaginary line?"

"You were in the Army, Keys. You know better than that. I couldn't cross that border to save my own brother . . . that'd be trespassing."

"Then you've got to catch him on this side."

"Don't I know that."

Crook clutched the arrow between both hands from point to feather as if to break it in two. And he could have easily, this tall, well-muscled man, who now paced up and down in front of the map. There was strength and confidence in every stride, but also frustration.

"You know, Keys, against the hostile Apaches I used Apache scouts and it worked because they knew the Apache ways better than white soldiers ever could. But with these bastards it's different. There are no comanchero scouts that we can recruit for our cause. There's too much profit to be made on the other side. And so Battu and his kind oblige us always to be the pursuers, and unless we can surprise them, the odds are with them and against us. And another thing, you can parlay with the Apaches — from time to time talk things over. But there's no parlaying with Battu. He's got nothing to talk over — he's not the sort that believes in negotiating."

"What about the reward? That ought to be some incentive . . . there *is* one, isn't there?"

"Five hundred dollars."

"That's not much."

"There's not much we can prove. There aren't many who lived to tell about it, not around here. He heads back south."

"Trouble is" — Keys shrugged — "you can only catch him this side of the border."

"And" — Crook whacked the arrow on

the top of his desk — "there's hundreds of miles of border. Battu can cross any place — hit a small town or ranch — a mine — grab his plunder and get out before we even hear about it."

"George, it's a damned shame. You good hombres have to play by the rules . . . the bad hombres don't."

"What about you, Keys?"

"What about me?"

"I didn't call you here just to discuss Battu."

"You didn't?"

"You know bloody well I didn't."

"Why then?"

"To find out what you're up to."

"Oh, that."

"Yes, that."

"Well," Keys said pleasantly, "that's none of your business, George."

"Everything in this territory's my business. I'm responsible for the safety and welfare . . ."

"I know . . . I know."

"And I want to know what you and your friends have in mind. Those wagons — animals — supplies — ammunition — dynamite. First of all where are you getting all that money you're spending?"

"Investors."

"Investors, huh?"

"That's right . . . investors."

"I just might have a suspicion as to who a couple of those investors might be."

"Suspicion all you want, George. Nobody's broken any law."

"And nobody better . . . and second of all what are they investing in? What're you going to do with all those supplies, ammunition . . . and dynamite?"

"We're going to do some mining."

"What kind of mining?"

"Say . . . silver."

"Where?"

"Now, George." Keys feigned mock exasperation. "You just don't tell people where. That's supposed to be a secret."

Crook pointed the arrow at the map again.

"Alright then. Give me a hint." He moved the arrow as he spoke. "East? West? North? Or *south?*"

Keys just smiled.

"Because if it's south . . ."

"There's no law against *civilians* crossing the border. That's not trespassing."

Crook let the arrow fall flat on the desk.

"Depends on *why* they're crossing."

"George, you're all mixed up."

"I am, am I?"

"Why sure . . ." Keys pulled a cigar out of

his pocket and stuck it in the side of his mouth. ". . . I'm one of the good hombres."

"Just don't try and play any games with the Army."

"Why should I, George?" Keys thumb-nailed a match and lit the cigar. "The Army's got nothing I want."

But the Army did have something that Keys wanted.

Something the Trespassers needed.

CHAPTER TWENTY-NINE

The revolving muzzle exploded with rapid fire — awesomely rapid, and astoundingly destructive — countless cartridges blasting from a circling cylinder — blazing out multiple sustained bursts from a hand-driven crank — mashing toward its target — a tree about fifty yards away.

The firepower literally ripped the tree apart.

The Gatling gun was operated by one soldier cranking the multi-barreled machine gun that was situated atop a wagon while another soldier stood beside him and also served as driver of the wagon when it needed to be moved.

Lieutenant Crane and three other troopers served as escort to the Gatling gun wagon — often referred to by the troopers as the "War Wagon."

From a vantage point, Keys, Doc, Sandusky, Elijah and Billy Joe looked down at the piece of equipment that Keys had been talking about.

"Well, Sandusky." Keys pointed. "What do you say?"

"I say it's like meetin' up with an old friend . . . except it's got a Broadwell carriage . . . latest model . . . twelve-degree sweep at twelve hundred yards . . . covers a front of sixty-two feet."

"Six hundred rounds a minute," Keys said. "That, gentlemen, is one helluva lot of firepower."

"Talk about a lot of noise." Billy Joe glanced at Elijah.

"Yeah." Elijah nodded. "Makes those revolvers of yours sound downright dim."

"Cut that tree right in half," Doc said. "Damn thing could cut down a whole forest."

"Or a lot of comancheros, or Yaquis, or anything else that tried to stop us." Keys added, "We need it. We're going to get it."

"Why, Mister Keys" — Elijah smiled — "you don't mean steal it?"

"Borrow it."

"I don't think," Billy Joe said, "your friend, the Colonel, will loan it to us."

Keys started to rise.

"Then let's not tell him."

The Gatling gun was invented, then patented, by Doctor Richard Jordan Gatling at the age of forty-three in 1861. At that time the six-barrel weapon was capable of firing the then-undreamed-of two hundred rounds per minute.

The 1862 version had reloadable steel chambers and used percussion caps. Then came the Blue Arrow model in 1865, one-inch caliber on an artillery carriage.

Ironically, it was Gatling's contention that he developed his deadly weapon for humanitarian reasons, reasoning that it would reduce carnage in the long run by shortening the length of war — or even eliminating war altogether in the face of such devastation. He was wrong on both counts, but Gatling continued with his perfections, such as improved breech bolts that could quickly be removed for maintenance. The Broadwell drum was a circular cluster of twenty vertical feed magazines easily removed for reloading with full magazines.

Even after the war Gatling continued to further upgrade his gun and provide the

Army with the most effective and deadly weapon in its arsenal.

The weapon the Trespassers needed to borrow.

Lieutenant Crane and the Gatling gun crew had finished the target session and the tree, and proceeded on their way back to Fort Canby.

Crane rode to the right alongside the team of horses pulling the wagon. A sergeant called Spud held the reins. Connors, the Gatling gun operator, sat on an ammunition box in the bed of the wagon beside the Gatling, and two troopers, Andrews and Becker, rode on either side as the wagon rolled over loose shale at the base of a sloping rock wall.

Connors, a smiling, freckled, lanky Irishman, fancied himself the best tenor in the company and gave voice to his fancy in the barracks, the cantina, on the parade grounds, and more often to the accompaniment of the horses' hoofs while driving the wagon. He mostly favored the old Irish ballads and on this journey gave out with words and melody of one of his preferred refrains.

She loved a wild colonial boy, Jack Dolan

173

was his name,
A poor but honest baby he was born in
Castlemaine,
He was his father's only hope, his mother's
only joy,
And dearly did his fairies love this wild
Colonial . . .

Two shots rang out.

The team of wagon horses was used to the sound of gunfire and reacted not at all.

But the soldiers did. To the sound and the sight of two riders, their faces bandana-covered, twenty yards ahead, who fired twice again, missed again, then spurred their mounts toward an outcrop of boulders in the distance.

Lieutenant Crane waved to the two troopers and galloped forth as they followed after them.

According to plan, the two riders they were chasing were Billy Joe Bickford and Doc Zeeger, who knew of a cave less than a mile and a half away where they could hide and not be discovered while the rest of the plan was being executed.

Spud, the Gatling operator, and Connors stood atop the wagon with sidearms drawn and ready.

But not ready for what followed.

From above, Elijah had outfitted two arrows with blunt ends. In swift succession he drew back the bow and sped each of the arrows at each of the two men in the wagon. The arrows found their targets — the back of Spud and Connors' heads — rendering both instantly unconscious.

That's when Keys and Sandusky approached from cover, leaped onto the wagon, and jettisoned Spud and Connors.

While Lieutenant Crane and the troopers fruitlessly pursued Billy Joe and Doc Zeeger in one direction, Keys and Sandusky in the Gatling gun wagon, and Elijah on horse back, were heading in another direction — toward an appointed spot where they would all rendezvous — and where Elizabeth Shelby waited with the wagons, supplies and animals.

CHAPTER THIRTY

"WHAT!?!?" Crook had exploded.

Lieutenant Crane, Troopers Andrews and Becker, Spud and Connors with heads wrapped in wet bandanas, stood in Crook's office, their faces drained white, while Crane did his best to explain the incident.

Crook looked from Captain Bourke back to the blanched lieutenant, who visibly

175

trembled beneath his blue uniform.

"You realize, Lieutenant, that this is unprecedented in the history of the United States Army!?"

"Yes . . . sir. I . . . know it won't look good on my record . . ."

" 'Look good on your record?' Lieutenant, chances are you won't have a record, because odds are you won't even be in the United States Army if this gets out, and I'll probably be . . . never mind. Did you try to follow?"

"No, sir. Thought it best to report . . . don't know if they were comancheros or how many . . ."

"Comancheros my mule! I know who they are and where they're headed. South. Captain Bourke."

"Yes, sir."

"Have a detail ready and prepared to leave in ten minutes."

"Yes, sir." Bourke hurried out of the room. "Sir?"

"What is it, Lieutenant?"

"May we go along, sir?"

"Not only you may — you must. And while you're at it, you better hope we get to them before they get to the border."

When Keys, Sandusky, and Elijah arrived at

the rendezvous area, they found Elizabeth Shelby sitting on a rock about ten yards from the two wagons, supplies, and animals.

She was smoking a cigarette, one of many she had smoked while waiting. The rock was semi-circled by nearly a dozen used-up cigarette butts and as many spent matches.

Keys and Sandusky descended from the Gatling gun wagon and Elijah dismounted. She rose, inhaled one last time, dropped the cigarette and squashed it under her black lizard boot.

"You'll notice," she said to Keys and pointed at the two wagons, "I did my smoking far enough away from the . . ."

"Yeah" — Keys nodded — "I noticed."

"How did it go?"

"It went." Keys motioned toward the Gatling wagon.

"Where's the rest of the contingent?"

"They ought to be here in a few minutes."

"Sooner than that," Elijah said as he looked toward the two riders.

Billy Joe and Doc Zeeger's faces were no longer covered by bandanas as they dismounted. Billy Joe wasted no time in reloading the revolver he had fired.

"Are they still after you?" Keys asked.

"Nope," Doc said. "Headed back toward the fort. I'd give six bits to see Crook's face

177

when he heard what happened."

"We don't want to be anywhere near Crook when he gets his hackles up and we got a ways to go before we got to the border, so let's get started. Sandusky, break down that Gatling and we'll help load it and the magazines into your wagon. How long will it take you?"

"Wet your finger. By the time it's dry, gun'll be in pieces."

"What're we gonna do with the Army's wagon?" Doc asked.

"Leave it here." Keys smiled. "That's the least we can do for Colonel Crook."

The bugler had sounded assembly. The detail with Crook and Captain Bourke at the head had mounted. So had three Apache scouts. Other Army personnel and civilians watched as the troopers moved toward and through the gates at Fort Canby.

Among those watching was a new arrival.

Amory Valance dismounted and walked into the entrance of the hotel.

"How do you do, sir?" The clerk greeted him.

"Got a room?"

"You're in luck, sir. Three of our guests left this morning. We have three of our best rooms available."

"All I need is one."

"One of the rooms has a tub already in it."

"Don't need a tub. Just a room."

"Yes, sir. Sign right there." The clerk turned the register book toward Valance.

Valance signed.

"Very good, Mister . . ." he looked at the signature, ". . . Valance. And how long will you be with us?"

"That all depends." Valance shrugged.

But Amory Valance thought to himself . . . maybe it depends on those three guests who left this morning.

Willard Oliver Waxer and Simon Ignatius Kline watched from the comfort of their private car as Colonel Crook and the troop passed by the stationary train, crossed the tracks and headed south.

Kline finished peeling an orange, dislodged a section and stuck it into his mouth.

"Well," he said to his dry whale of a partner, "it appears that another phase of our little enterprise has been put into effect."

Waxer nodded and sipped from the tumbler of milk.

"Yes, but we've still got a long way to go."

"Not us. Our friends. All we've got to do

is wait."

"What about Valance?"

Kline stuck the rest of the orange into his mouth and spoke as he chewed.

"He'll be here. Maybe already is."

In spite of what had happened and the blot it might put on his command, Colonel Crook couldn't help harboring a grudging admiration of how it had been done and the man who had planned it.

Jefferson Keys had been a rambunctious, almost reckless officer while in the U.S. Army — not as rambunctious and reckless as Keys' former commanding officer, George Armstrong Custer — but almost as unpredictable, which was what made both Custer and Keys, at times, such formidable foes to the opposition.

If every commander went by the book in every battle, then the opposing commander could anticipate and act accordingly. Audacity often trumped and triumphed. Both Custer and Keys were masters of the unexpected and both of them had prevailed — so far.

But Crook, in spite of his grudging admiration, had no intention of allowing Keys to prevail in the matter of the Gatling gun. It was his duty — and as always, he intended to carry out his duty — to catch up with Keys on U.S. territory, retrieve the Gatling, and see to it that proper punishment was administered, and in so doing, erase the blot on the escutcheon of his command.

Lieutenant Crane had led them to the place of the attack on the Gatling wagon.

The Apache scouts took it from there. It was a relatively easy task. The loaded wagon had left discernible tracks and had moved slower than the scouts and troopers who were following.

The tracks led to where the empty wagon and still harnessed team of horses stood — near a rock semi-surrounded by cigarette butts and burnt matches.

And after that, there were more tracks to follow.

"Two wagons," one of the Apache scouts said.

"Four riders," another scout noted.

"More animals. Some horses. Some pack mules," the third Apache who had dismounted observed. "Three, maybe four hours ago. That way." The Apache pointed south.

Colonel Crook looked in that direction and gave the order.

"Forward at a gallop — ho!"

Keys knew the exact demarcation.

The imaginary line that separated what real estate belonged to the United States and what belonged to Mexico.

Not only did it constitute sanctuary for the comancheros, but it was refuge — at least temporarily — for the Trespassers.

They were nearly there when Elijah, who had been designated as rear guard scout, raced his mount to catch up with Keys, the wagons and Billy Joe and Elizabeth.

"They're getting close!" Elijah hollered.

"So are we." Keys nodded, then motioned to Doc and Sandusky, in their wagons. "Knock on it! Billy Joe! Elizabeth! Get those animals moving! We're just half a mile away! That stream ahead!"

It wasn't much of a stream — not more than ten yards wide and two feet deep this time of year — but it made all the difference to the Trespassers as they crossed to the other side while Crook and the troopers reined in their mounts when they got to it.

The pursuit had ended.

The Trespassers had succeeded.

Barely.

Crook lifted himself in the stirrups and wiped his brow. Captain Bourke and Lieutenant Crane were beside him.

"I'll be waiting for you, Keys!" Crook shouted.

"That's nice of you, General," Keys called back.

"So'll Joliet. You'll do twenty years for this."

"For what, George?"

"You know damn well what. You stole our Gatling."

"Who, me?"

"Yes, you and that bunch with you."

"No, we don't know anything about that. Musta been somebody else."

"Like hell."

"If you don't believe me, come on over and search us."

"I don't know what you're up to over there, but you'll be back, Keys, and I'll be waiting."

"You said it yourself, George, there's hundreds of miles of border."

"I'll find you."

Keys touched the brim of his hat in a non-military salute.

"We'll give Battu your regards if we run into him."

"I hope you do."

"We'll bring him back and collect the reward — five hundred, wasn't it?"

"It won't spend in Joliet, Keys — and I hope he hangs you by your . . . thumbs."

"Good luck to you too, George."

The Trespassers started up again, this time in no hurry.

Crook looked at Captain Bourke, who just shook his head and said nothing, then at Lieutenant Crane.

"Let's get out of here, Lieutenant."

"Alright, George . . . I mean . . . *yes, sir!*"

"And," Crook added, "if anybody in my command lets word of this get out, it'll be the stockade. Understood?"

"Yes, sir, Colonel Crook!" Bourke bellowed.

CHAPTER THIRTY-ONE

The comanchero camp was isolated in a mountain meadow between the shoulders of the Santa Maduras. Years ago it had been a Comanche *rancheria,* a village of nearly a hundred Indian men, women and children.

It was the base from which the tribe made their raids until part of the Mexican Army made a raid of its own, leaving no survivors, only a common grave beneath the bloody earth.

No other Comanche tribe ever moved into that area again, and neither did anybody else until the comancheros from across the U.S. border found it a strategic hub from which to do business.

Then came Battu.

He took over the camp and the comancheros. While there was no second in command — Battu was the only one who commanded — he did delegate some responsibility to Rinaldi — a beady-eyed, heavily mustached subordinate whose assignment it was to take a dozen men and make a wide circular sweep of the terrain. If Rinaldi came across a transient family or small group, he would overpower and bring them into camp along with their possessions. If the travelers appeared too formidable, then Rinaldi would ride back to camp, inform Battu, and with the reinforcements, led by Battu, do what the comancheros were good at doing.

But, more often, from the camp, Battu would strike across the border and bring back booty to be traded to the Indian tribes and to Mexicans who were not particular about the origin of the comancheros' trade goods — be those goods cattle, horses or humans. They particularly favored men — red, yellow or black — who could work as slaves in gold and silver mines, or women who served other purposes.

Of the camp women, some were Indian, some mixed breed, some Mexican and some even former inhabitants of the United

States, including fugitives from the law, ex-prostitutes and some unfortunate enough to have been kidnapped, raped and held captive — working in the fields, cleaning the huts, and preparing meals, until they either found more or less permanent favor with the comancheros or were traded off.

As was the ancient medieval custom, the lord of the manor took his privileges before any of the vassals or peons had their pick.

And here Battu was the undisputed lord.

The latest prize, actually prizes, in Battu's domain were from the Olang ranch. Mother and daughter, Ingrid and Karla.

All three of the Olang family had been in the kitchen — Karla peeling potatoes, Ingrid at the stove and Karl smoking his pipe in his kitchen chair when the door slammed open.

Battu, Charly, Diaz and two other comancheros charged in, guns drawn, rifles pointed.

Karl Olang leaped from his chair toward a rifle above the fireplace. He didn't get close. The barrel of Charly's rifle crashed into Olang's forehead, splattering blood into his eyes and dropping him to the floor.

Karla rose, screaming hysterically, until Battu's fist smashed into the side of her face, sending her sprawling half across the

186

room into the wall, then onto the floor.

As Mrs. Olang moved toward her daughter, Diaz pinned her arms behind her while Battu slapped her hard, back and forth, until her chin dropped onto her chest, then grabbed the front of her dress and ripped it away, exposing most of the creamy flesh and abundance of her upper body.

Battu was obviously pleased with what he saw.

Another of the comancheros came into the doorway.

"Jefe . . . there's a wagon and pretty good team of horses in the barn."

"*Bueno.* Tie these two up and throw 'em in the wagon."

"Jefe." The comanchero grinned. "There's something else out there."

"What?"

"An ant hill."

As they were moving away from the ranch, Ingrid regained consciousness in the wagon and saw her husband buried up to his neck, and his bloody face covered with crawling ants.

She screamed — and hadn't spoken a word since.

The young girl had been taken to a tiny, but secure cell-like structure with bars on the door and a mat on the floor. Two of the camp women let her out when she needed to go to the toilet and saw to it that she ate a couple of times a day.

Battu had looked her up and down and relished what he saw.

"She's built almost as full as her mother," he had said. "But nobody gets her. Not even me. She's pure and she's going to stay that way. That way she brings more money. Much more."

The mother was another matter.

And Battu intended to make the most of her before putting her on the market.

But there was one problem.

In his hut Battu stood stripped to the waist. He took another gulp from the bottle of tequila, as he bent over the inert form of Ingrid Olang.

And as he had done half a dozen times before, Battu squeezed her face in the palm of his hand and shook it.

And once again her blue eyes fluttered for an instant, her shoulders quivered, then she remained inert.

He ran a hand over both breasts, then pressed his palm against one. She breathed a little harder, but did not stir.

Battu thought that sooner or later this blond Viking would come around.

He would wait.

Meanwhile there were other women in the camp.

Not like this one . . . but other women.

Keys had picked the spot that would be their first overnight camp in Mexico. The wagon teams were unhitched, horses unsaddled, pack mules unpacked — all the animals fed and picketed.

Among the Trespassers, already there was a certain sense of accomplishment and teamwork — even trust.

Together, under Keys' command, they had made the necessary preparations, snatched the Gatling from the U.S. Army, and beat ol' Grey Wolf to the border.

All they had to do now, in this land of revolution and counter-revolution, was to deal with deadly comancheros, and hostile Yaquis who had been at war with whatever government had been in power over the last two hundred years, find the five million in gold — the whereabouts of which only Elizabeth Shelby knew — somehow elude or delude Juarez's military forces — who would more than likely lay claim to the gold if they found out about it — then make their way back to the Arizona Territory and face the wrath of Colonel George Crook, who promised them twenty years' confinement

189

in an institution called Joliet.

Then there was the matter between Jefferson Keys and Billy Joe Bickford — where there would be only one survivor.

But, so far, things were going according to plan.

There was another, more immediate matter to be settled.

Keys walked up to Elizabeth Shelby.

"Miss Shelby."

"Yes, Mister Keys."

"You know how to cook?"

"How's that?"

"I said, do you know how to cook? You must've done some cooking in your time. You must've cooked for your . . . husband."

"I've done a lot of things in my time."

"I hope that cooking was one of them because we've all got to do our share during this expedition. An army moves on its stomach."

"So does a snake. I'll be damned if I came back to Mexico to cook."

"You don't cook — you don't eat — neither do we. We don't eat, we don't get the gold." Keys smiled.

Elizabeth Shelby was not smiling, but it didn't take her long to think it over.

"I'll cook."

"I thought so."

"Until we get the gold . . . you bastard."

"Yes, ma'am. Oh, and there's one other thing . . ."

"What?" she seethed. "What else do you want?"

"I want . . . to give you something." Keys motioned toward Sandusky, who nodded and came closer carrying a gunbelt with a holstered ivory-handled revolver.

Keys took the rig and handed it to her.

"Sandusky picked it out for you back at Canby. A nice little gun, befitting a nice little lady."

"It sure is, ma'am," Sandusky said. "Fine five-shot Colt, good balance and accurate."

"You do know how to shoot a gun," Keys said, "don't you, Miss Shelby?"

"I told you, I know how to do a lot of things . . . and I'll tell you something else . . ."

"What?"

"I didn't cook for my . . . husband."

"No?"

"No. He had other things for me to do."

"He did?"

"Yes, he did. But the Yaquis aren't very imaginative when it comes to sex . . . Of course, I didn't find that out until I went to work at Madam Pleasant's high-class whorehouse."

Elizabeth Shelby turned and walked away, strapping on the gunbelt.

"Well, I've got to get to cooking supper," she said.

Doc Zeeger and Billy Joe had seen and heard the last part of the exchange.

Doc lit up a cigar.

"That's some kind of woman," he said.

"Yeah." Keys nodded. "My kind."

"You mean that?" Billy Joe looked incredulously at Keys.

"She's going to lead us to the gold, isn't she?" Keys smiled.

"I thought you picked Keys for the job," Amory Valance said to Willard Oliver Waxer and Simon Ignatius Kline in their private car.

"Only for part of the job," Kline said as he bit into a slice of chocolate cake. "But there's another part."

"And that, sir," Waxer intoned, "is where you come in."

"What's the most money you've ever made on one of your . . . assignments?" Kline asked.

"Well," Valance reflected, "let me think."

"Go ahead and think." Kline finished off the chocolate cake.

"Down in Mexico I came away with . . .

two, no . . . three thousand dollars."

"Is that all?" Waxer burped and lifted the tumbler of milk.

"How long were you there?" Kline inquired.

"Almost two years."

"That long." Waxer gulped from the glass.

"How would you like to make more, much more" — Kline smiled — "in much less time?"

"Is that why I'm here?"

"That's why." Waxer nodded.

"What do I have to do?"

"Wait," Kline said.

"What?"

"Wait until Keys gets back. If he gets back," Kline added.

"Then what?"

"Can you round up some good men?" Kline asked.

"For some good money."

"There'll be plenty." Kline reached for another piece of cake. "In the meanwhile, just wait. We'll pick up your expenses and advance you . . . two, no, three thousand dollars."

As Keys lay beneath the Mexican sky and looked up at the scimitar moon, he thought

193

about his decision to come to Mexico years ago.

The decision was largely due to a man named Juarez.

Benito Juarez.

The Abraham Lincoln of Mexico.

The man who had ignited the flame of democracy in a country ruled by tyrants for centuries. An Indian born in Oaxaca, who at the age of fourteen could neither read, write, nor speak Spanish. He worked as a servant and was sent to a Franciscan seminary and turned to law instead of the priesthood and became a strong defender of Indian rights. He rose to civil judge, then governor of Oaxaca. He fought against the tyrannical Santa Anna and was exiled to New Orleans. He worked there in a cigarette factory, then returned to help defeat and exile the same Santa Anna. He barely escaped a firing squad to become president of his country, only to flee Mexico City after his forces lost a pitched battle at Silao at the hands of his reactionary enemies who curried the favor of foreign governments. These governments' intent was to once again plunder the resources of a country that had been plundered by the conquistadores and many others since. At the time of President Juarez's worst defeat, Lincoln had sent him a message expressing "hope for the liberty of your government and its people."

But Louis Napoleon had other ideas. He sent an army to spill more blood with the purpose of crowning his cousin, Maximilian, the Archduke of Austria, as emperor of Mexico.

That purpose was achieved during the time of the Civil War in the United States. While Abraham Lincoln was sympathetic to the cause of Juarez, Lincoln was fighting for another cause and was unable to enforce the Monroe Doctrine.

But during the ensuing conflict Juarez carried Lincoln's letter in the hope that when the Civil War ended there would be help from the North.

Lincoln died too soon, and his successor, President Andrew Johnson, was too embattled in the throes of reconstruction and the winning of the West to send an official U.S. military force to Mexico in answer to Juarez's plea.

But other Americans heard and responded to that plea.

However, there also were other Americans who responded to the call of Maximilian's Phantom Crown — and for more money.

Jefferson Keys was one of those who

responded in accordance to his own doctrine.

A short time after the Civil War, Custer was sent West. His wife, Libbie, went with him.

So did Jefferson Keys — not as a soldier of the U.S. Army, but as a scout.

Autie took over the Seventh Cavalry, a ragtag unit that he quickly shaped into the Army's most effective Indian fighting machine. Leading charges with Keys at his side, Custer waged successful campaigns against Cheyennes, Arapahos, Kiowas and Comanches.

It was just after one of those bloody encounters and just before Custer faced a court-martial because of his defiance of orders, that Keys had his last talk with Custer — or, as the Indians called him, Yellow Hair.

It took place during a cold Dakota night just before leaving Custer's tent.

". . . Autie, this time it's not good night. It's good-bye."

"What the hell are you talking about, Jeff?"

"My stomach."

"Your what?"

"I don't have the stomach for it anymore."

"You want to chew that a little finer, my friend?"

"The stomach for hunting down and killing Indians on their own real estate."

"Only hostiles who break treaties . . ."

"Yeah, that's right, sometimes they break those treaties — sometimes we do."

"Not me, Jeff."

"I know that, Autie. But you're not the whole Army." Keys smiled. "Although sometimes you act like you are."

"Only when I have to."

"I know that too, Autie, but I just can't be part of it anymore."

"Look here, Jeff. During the war I had to kill men I went to West Point with, and so did you — men I admired, even loved. But it was war and I'm a soldier who follows orders. Those orders now are to secure the West for settlement. And those hostiles stand in the way of that. They massacre and pillage . . ."

"Autie . . . you forget one thing."

"What?"

"I'm not in the Army. I don't have to take those orders."

"No, you don't, but you're used to war. What *are* you going to do?"

"Head south."

"South?" Custer smiled. "We already won that war."

"Farther south."

"How far?"

"Mexico."

"Mexico, huh?" Custer brushed back the long locks of his hair. "Somehow I had a feeling you were going to say that."

"There's a real war going on down there. Both sides need soldiers. 'Specially soldiers with experience — and they'll pay for 'em."

"Whose side are you going to soldier on?"

"Juarez."

"Maximilian'll pay more." Autie grinned.

"But with Juarez, I'll sleep better."

"Somehow, I knew you were going to say that, too — or something like it."

"Besides" — Keys also grinned — "I'll be upholding the Monroe Doctrine."

"You do that, Jeff." Custer extended his hand. "Somebody has to."

They shook.

"Say so long to Libbie for me."

"I'll do that."

"And, Yellow Hair . . . don't always be too anxious to ride to the sound of the guns."

"It's worked so far." Custer winked.

Those were the last words Keys heard from Custer, just before Custer was court-martialed and sent back to Michigan — and Keys headed to Mexico where he met the woman who was to become his wife.

But now Jefferson Keys didn't want to

think about that.

Beneath the Mexican sky and scimitar of moon, he closed his eyes and went to sleep.

Chapter Thirty-Two

God nodded and the sun topped out over the eastern ridge and barely broke through the still sullen sky, but all the Trespassers had been up and at their tasks for almost an hour.

One of the Trespassers was absent. Even before first light Elijah had mounted and begun to scout the terrain, taking with him only beef jerky for breakfast — and his bow and quiver for the unexpected.

The rest of the camp was having a working breakfast composed of bacon, beans and coffee, served up by Elizabeth Shelby as Keys, Doc, Sandusky and Billy Joe went about getting the equipment and animals ready for the day's trek.

Billy Joe had taken some time out, as was his usual morning custom, to practice his draw, right hand and left hand. Hook — draw — aim — holster. Hook — draw — aim — holster.

Elizabeth Shelby wore her gun rig over her loose-fitting corduroy jacket. She refilled the tin coffee cup Billy Joe had set on a wagon next to him.

"You start off every morning doing your exercises?"

"Just as sure as the rising of the sun."

"Keeping your fingers agile?"

"That's part of it." Billy Joe lifted, then pointed the tin cup toward her waist. "I see that you're carrying a little fella yourself."

"So I am."

"Maybe" — Billy Joe smiled at her for the first time — "maybe sometime I'll teach you how to use it."

"Maybe, sometime" — she smiled back — "I'll teach *you* something, too."

Elizabeth Shelby turned, carrying the coffeepot and walked toward Jefferson Keys.

"More?" She extended the pot.

"No, thanks, but you make good coffee, Miss Shelby."

"Enjoy it while you can."

"I —" Keys stopped short.

He had seen Elijah riding in — and there was something about the way he rode that signaled trouble.

Elijah dismounted, took a couple steps closer to Keys and the rest of them, then motioned back in the direction he had come.

"We're gonna have company."

"What kind of company?" Keys asked.

"Doesn't look good."

"How many?"

" 'Bout a dozen — from a distance."

"Comancheros?"

"I'd say. But I didn't ask."

"They see you?"

"No, but they can't miss us."

"Should I set up the Gatling?" Sandusky pointed to his wagon.

"Not for a dozen. Let's not show 'em our whole arsenal."

"We better show 'em somethin'," Doc said.

"We will. Let's try putting on a little exhibition. Elijah . . ."

"Yo."

"Up there." Keys motioned toward a boulder.

"Billy Joe . . . be ready."

Billy Joe just nodded.

"Miss Shelby, you stay back by that wagon."

"I . . ."

"Don't argue. Just stay back. Doc, to the left. Sandusky . . ."

Sandusky grabbed his Henry.

"I know. To the right . . . and here they come."

From the direction that Elijah had ridden, they approached, about a dozen with one in the lead — beady-eyed, heavily mustached.

They came to a stop and settled in their saddles.

Keys took a step forward.

The leader touched the wide brim of his dirty hat.

"*Buenos dias,* senor."

"It is a good day," Keys said in Spanish. "Or was, up to now."

"Oh, you speak our language." The leader grinned.

"When it's necessary."

"Well, it's not necessary now — you see I speak your language — good too, don't you think?"

"That depends on what you have to say."

"Not much. Only . . ."

"Only what?"

"We . . . say, what's your name? I am called Rinaldi and . . ." Rinaldi motioned at the other riders, ". . . we welcome you to our country."

"Oh, you're a welcoming committee, are you?"

"Sort of like that."

"OK, you welcomed us. Now you can be on your way and so can we."

"Not yet." Rinaldi waved a fat finger. "First we have to do some business."

"What kind of business?"

"The fee."

"What fee?"

"The passing through fee."

"To you, Senor Rinaldi?"

"To the Jefe."

"Where's he?"

"Not far."

"What's his name?"

"Battu. Maybe you hear of him."

"Maybe."

"Say . . ." Rinaldi pointed to Elizabeth Shelby standing near a wagon, ". . . that's a good-looking woman you got with you."

"She ought to be, she's my sister. Now let's get back to that fee."

"*Si,* we collect a passing through fee . . . say, your sister's got red hair . . ."

"It happens. About the fee . . ."

"We collect a passing through fee for Battu for passing through his country."

"I thought this country was Mexico."

"That's true, but this is a country — how you say, uh — inside a country." Rinaldi looked around at his men, his face displaying satisfaction with his answer.

Some of the comancheros understood what he had said and smiled, even laughed. The rest, who neither spoke, nor understood English, also smiled, even laughed.

Keys took the opportunity to light a cigar.

"Does President Juarez" — he puffed — "know about this 'country within a country'?"

"Battu don't care about what Juarez knows or does."

"I see." Keys took another drag, looked at the wagons, then back at the comancheros. "Not that we have any intention of paying but how much is this . . . passing through fee?"

"Well . . . say, what is your name, senor?"

"Keys. Jefferson Keys." He looked from left to right. "And company."

"Well, Senor Keys . . . and company, the fee depends on what you're carrying in those wagons. Suppose we come closer and see." Rinaldi took his boot away from the stirrup.

"Suppose you don't."

"Who's going to stop us?" Rinaldi's eyes grew bleak.

"We are."

"But Senor Keys" — Rinaldi motioned back toward his men, then at Keys and his group — "there are more of us than you."

"Yeah, but I'm talking about quality, not quantity."

"I don't understand." Rinaldi shrugged.

"You will if you come any closer."

"Then tell us what's in the wagons."

"Poison."

Rinaldi looked puzzled for just an instant, then shook his head.

"I think we talked enough."

"So do I." Keys nodded as Rinaldi started to go for his gun.

But Billy Joe hooked, drew and fired in one blinding motion.

Rinaldi's hat flew off his head and landed on the ground, but before it did, Billy Joe had fired again and the hat of the comanchero to the left of Rinaldi also sailed off with a bullet hole in the crown and landed between horses. At the same time an arrow struck the hat of the comanchero to Rinaldi's right. His hat fell to the ground with the arrow still stuck through it.

Almost simultaneously, Elizabeth Shelby drew and fired twice, both slugs kicking up dirt just inches away from the front hooves of Rinaldi's horse, sending the animal prancing backwards.

By then all the Trespassers had guns — and Elijah his bow and arrow — pointed directly at the comancheros before any of them had lifted their weapons.

"I wouldn't make any sudden moves, Rinaldi." Keys had his gun pointed at the comanchero's chest. "The next shots'll draw blood, yours first."

"OK, OK, Senor Keys . . . we'll forget about the passing through fee this time."

"That's agreeable."

"But maybe you'll pass through again sometime."

"Maybe."

"And maybe we see you then . . ." he pointed toward Elizabeth Shelby, ". . . and your sister."

"Maybe."

"Say . . . just one more thing."

"What?"

"Can we pick up our hats?"

"Sure," Keys nodded. "But leave the arrow."

Rinaldi reached down, retrieved his sombrero, and gave an order in Spanish.

Two more sombreros were retrieved and an arrow left on the ground. Amid murmured grumbles and curses, the comancheros wheeled their horses, and led by Rinaldi, rode away from the Trespassers' camp.

Elijah made his way down from the boulder, picked up his arrow, and after a cursory examination, placed it back into the quiver.

Guns were holstered, rifles lowered, as the Trespassers gravitated toward Keys.

"You know," Doc said, "we ain't seen the last of 'em."

"Yeah, I know." Keys lifted his cup and

drank. "Coffee got cold."

"Next time," Doc went on, "there'll be a lot more of 'em."

"Then that'll be Gatling time."

"Want me to heat up the coffee?" Elizabeth Shelby lifted the pot.

"No, we got to get going, and didn't I tell you to stay by the wagon?"

"You did . . . and I did. But you didn't say anything about" — she patted the ivory handle of the Colt — "this, brother."

"No, I guess I didn't . . . sister." Keys looked around at the rest of them. "Good work. Let's go."

"Miss Shelby." Billy Joe drifted closer to Elizabeth Shelby.

"Yes, Mister Bickford."

"About that little fella." He pointed to the Colt.

"What about it?"

"Pretty good shooting . . . for a lady."

"That's progress."

"What is?"

"Calling me a lady."

CHAPTER THIRTY-THREE

Once again Battu had tried to revive Ingrid Olang — and once again he had failed.

His rude hands pressed against her face,

and rubbed against her naked breasts —
and once again her eyes fluttered, but saw
nothing and closed.

That night he had been with another
woman from the camp, an Indian woman,
with eyes dark and wide apart, hair black as
a crow's wing. But even then, he thought of
the flaxen-haired, milk-complexioned, full-
bodied creature he coveted.

Battu walked to the table in the middle of
the room, lifted the uncorked bottle of
tequila, drank, paused for just a second,
then carrying the bottle, went back to the
bed and tipped the bottle just above Ingrid's
face, letting the liquid flow onto her lips,
chin and neck.

She coughed and turned her face away,
breathed heavily, but did not come to.

Battu cursed, then reacted as he heard the
sounds of hoofbeats, then riders dismount-
ing and being greeted by the camp comancheros.

Rinaldi and the other comancheros with
him waited as Battu came out of the hut,
strapping on his gun belt and at the same
time carrying the tequila bottle.

"Jefe." Rinaldi smiled and bowed just a
little.

"Never mind the bullshit." Battu looked
around. "You come back with nothing."

"Not nothing." Rinaldi shook his head.

"I don't see anything."

"But *we* did." He nodded toward his men. "We saw something."

"Looks like something saw you, too." Battu ripped Rinaldi's sombrero off his head and poked a finger through the bullet hole, then slammed the sombrero against Rinaldi's stomach. "What happened?"

"They sort of ambushed us."

"How the hell can they sort of ambush you? How many of them?"

"Uh . . ."

"Uh, what? Were there so many you couldn't count them?"

"No, Jefe. Six of them but they had us surrounded."

"Six men surrounded all of you dumb bastards?!"

"One was a woman, a beautiful woman with red hair, red like a fox. They got two wagons and pack animals."

"What's in the wagons?"

"We didn't get to see."

"Why not?"

This time Rinaldi stuck his finger through the bullet hole in his sombrero.

"Did the woman do that?"

"No, Jefe, but you will want her, red hair like a fox. We go after them now?"

"Where was this?"

"Near Blanco Canyon."

"Which way were they going?"

"South. We go after them?"

"No, not now. I got business first. Send Charly and Diaz to keep track of 'em. We can hit 'em anytime. And get word to Don Carlos Mondego. Tell him to meet me at Chupadero Flats in two days and tell him to bring plenty of money. Tell him I got just what he's been looking for — young and juicy."

"Very good, Jefe. How much you think he'll pay . . . a thousand?"

"If I know Don Carlos Mondego, when he sees that young one with that yellow hair . . . two thousand."

Rinaldi whistled.

"And Jefe, wait'll you see the one with red hair. Not that young, but . . ." He whistled again.

"Alright, get moving. Looks like we got a lot of business to take care of. But right now I'm going to take care of something else."

Battu lifted the bottle of tequila to his mouth and turned toward the hut.

But inside the hut things were not the same as when Battu had left.

For some time Ingrid Olang had not been completely unconscious and inert. She had been aware of Battu's hands, even his breath, as he bent over her and poured tequila onto her lips and face.

She was also aware of what he would do to her if he knew that she was conscious and could respond to his cravings. Most of all she remembered the attack on her husband and the sight of him helplessly buried up to his neck with his bleeding face crawling with ants. No matter what happened to her, she would avenge what Battu did to her husband.

Ingrid Olang had managed to stagger to her feet and look around the hut for something, anything, she could use as the instrument of her revenge.

She saw what would serve her purpose, made her way to a sideboard near the stove, picked it up, weaved back to the bed, and did her best to appear to be in the same condition she had been in when Battu had gone outside.

It took her a time to quell the deep breaths and the quivering of her body, but she managed.

She heard the door open, then close. She heard the heavy footsteps on the crude wooden floor, first moving away toward the table, then changing direction, and moving toward the bed and inevitably closer to her.

Once again she felt a hand on her face, on her breast, and was aware of the foul breath close to her lips.

She bolted and her hand holding the knife sprang from her side toward Battu's chest, but he twisted and took the blade on the meaty flesh of his left shoulder. At the same time he dropped the bottle, and before she could strike again, drew his gun and fired twice point-blank into her heart.

Ingrid Olang slumped back and into the darkness of death — still holding the knife.

The gun gripped in his hand, Battu walked to the door and opened it.

Rinaldi and some of the other comancheros who had heard the shots stood at the doorway.

"Jefe." Rinaldi saw the blood on Battu's shirt. "Are you alright?!"

Battu nodded.

"The woman?"

"Get the dirty bitch out of here."

CHAPTER THIRTY-FOUR

As the Trespassers, all but Elijah, made their way south, a hot, nomad wind whispered around smooth boulders and through forlorn trees and jagged rocks.

Keys rode at the head of the caravan, Elizabeth Shelby not far behind, Billy Joe alongside the string of pack animals, while Doc and Sandusky were at the reins of the two wagons.

Elijah was making his circular sweep, hoping to see or meet nothing, or no one, he didn't want to see or meet.

The sun was at the tip of its arc, bright and hot.

Elizabeth Shelby urged her horse ahead and pulled abreast of Keys.

"I never realized," she said, "how much I didn't miss Mexico."

"Would you prefer San Francisco?"

"You *are* a bastard."

"Why this time?"

"You had to bring up Madam Pleasant's."

"I didn't . . . you did. I was talking about the climate." Keys smiled.

"Like hell you were."

"Have it your way, Miss Shelby."

"I'll tell you what I'd like to have . . . what I've been thinking about since we crossed the border."

"A cold beer?"

"Not even close."

"What?"

"A cold bath . . . in a tub or a stream . . . Just lay there and let that clean water splash over . . . everything."

"Are you trying to drive both of us crazy?"

"Why, Mister Keys, I thought . . ."

"Never mind what you thought, there's something I wanted to talk to you about."

"What?"

"So far we've been moving straight south . . ."

"So?"

"So I don't expect you to draw us a map, but can you get a little more specific about distance and direction?"

"Sure I can . . . when the time comes; meanwhile, we're doing OK."

"That helps."

An hour later Elijah caught up to the caravan.

Keys gave the order to stop near a cluster of shadeless trees.

"Not good," Elijah said.

"How bad?" Keys asked.

"Two of 'em. They're dogging us alright, following tracks but staying out of sight."

"Did you get a good look?"

"Good enough."

"Were they part of the bunch with Rinaldi?"

"Nope. Two new faces but cast from the same mold."

"Want me to punch their tickets?" Billy Joe asked evenly.

"No, Elijah could've done that. Two of 'em can't hurt so long as they keep their distance. Elijah, let us know if any more join up. We'll all be extra cautious on night watch. Let's move on."

But there was somebody else on the move.

Battu.

And he was not alone.

Shortly after he had killed Ingrid Olang, Battu, along with the two women who had attended Karla, entered the tiny cell-like structure.

At the sight of him she rose from her chair.

"I'm afraid, young girl, that I've got bad news for you." Battu took off his hat with his right hand. His left shoulder was bandaged under a different shirt. "Your mother is dead."

Karla Olang slumped back into her chair and began to sob.

"But she died in peace in her sleep. You can visit her grave before we leave." Battu waved his hat around the room. "This is no place for a nice young girl like you. We have made arrangements for you to go to a beautiful hacienda where you will live like a queen under the protection of a powerful, respected man. A man of high esteem and wealth."

Battu turned to the women with him.

"These two will prepare you for the journey — make you fresh and even more beautiful with new clothes and everything you'll need until you meet Don Mondego and he takes you to his hacienda, which is like a palace. He is a rich man with much land and a silver mine."

Karla Olang's head was bent and she still sobbed.

Battu touched her shoulder.

"Do you understand what I said?"

She looked up at him, her blue eyes sodden.

"I . . . understand."

Chapter Thirty-Five

The Trespassers' caravan moved at the accustomed pace in the accustomed order, with Keys in his customary position at the head of the procession. That morning they had covered just over three miles when Keys raised his hand signaling the others to stop — all but Elijah who, as usual, had ridden ahead, and around, to see what he could see, and not be seen.

"What is it?" Elizabeth Shelby pulled her animal to a stop alongside Keys. "What's wrong?"

"Nothing's wrong, far as I know. But we have to confabulate, you and me."

"About what?"

"Well, I know that you don't want to disclose any more about our destination than you have to, but this trail . . ."

Billy Joe had ridden up to Keys' other side.

"Why're we stopping?"

"I was just telling Miss Shelby that the trail divides up ahead there. Since she's the only one who knows our destination, it's up to her to tell us . . . to the left, or to the right?"

"Left." She pointed.

"That'd be somewhat to the east. Thank you, Miss Shelby."

"You're welcome, Mister Keys."

"Doc." Keys looked over at the lead wagon. "How you doing?"

"My ass is getting flatter, but other than that, just fine."

"Good. How about you, Sandusky?"

"Haven't been sober this long in over a year, but other than that, just fine."

"Alright then . . ."

"Aren't you going to ask about me, Mister Keys?" Billy Joe smiled.

"Nope. To the left it is."

"What about Elijah?" Billy Joe inquired.

"He'll find us."

Not far from where the trail divided, on a white plateau, there was located a place called Chupadero Flats.

And there, Battu, Rinaldi, one other co-manchero known as Pierre, along with Karla Olang, had dismounted and waited.

Battu had seldom been more affable. He had done business with Don Carlos Mondego at Chupadero Flats many times before, but this time he anticipated his most profitable transaction.

"Little girl," he assured her again, "you will find Don Carlos Mondego to be a gentleman of quality. His bloodline can be traced back to the royal court of Spain . . ."

Since they left the comanchero camp, Karla Olang had remained silent. Only at her mother's grave had she whispered a prayer. Since then, she spoke not a word — not to plead, nor to protest. She seemed resigned to her fate, which could not be any worse than to be in the clasp of the coman-cheros . . . and Battu.

". . . but you must smile," he went on, "and let your beauty shine through, you'll see . . . ah!!"

Battu saw what he had been waiting to see:

Don Carlos Mondego, mounted on a coal-black, silver-saddled stallion, flanked by two of his "soldados," as he called them — his household guards.

Mondego dismounted and greeted Battu, but his gaze locked on the face and form of the girl who stood nearby.

"Battu." He finally turned toward the co-manchero. "This time your messenger did not exaggerate. She is all he described and more."

"I knew you would be pleased." Battu smiled.

"Senorita." Don Carlos' eyes glistened. "You will excuse us for a moment or two, while Senor Battu and I speak privately."

He was tall and courtly, swarthy, with aquiline features, soft-spoken, but his eyes were dark steel coils, and there was an underlying menace in his manner.

Don Carlos Mondego and Battu walked a few steps away.

"She is untouched, Don Carlos," Battu said, "pure and innocent. You will have great pleasure with this one, you will . . ."

Mondego raised his right hand.

"You needn't say more, Battu. What is the price?"

"For such a face and body . . ."

"What is the price?"

"Only two thousand."

"Never have I paid that much."

"Never have you had one like her."

"That's true. But I have only brought with me fifteen hundred."

"Don Carlos, you and I have done business many times before and we will again. Your word is your bond. Fifteen hundred now, take her with you, and the rest I will send to collect. Is that satisfactory?"

Don Carlos Mondego looked back at the girl.

"That is" — he nodded — "satisfactory."

Battu, Rinaldi and Pierre had ridden back in the direction of the comanchero camp, and Don Carlos Mondego, the two soldados and Karla in another direction toward Mondego's estate.

Mondego had assured Battu that along with the additional five hundred, the horse that the girl rode would be returned to him. Battu didn't particularly care about the horse; it wasn't much of an animal, and besides, he had stolen it.

As they rode on, Karla looked straight ahead and said nothing — but Mondego was full of himself and his plans.

"Do not be afraid." He smiled. "Don Carlos is not some savage who takes his pleasure in the wilderness. You will have silk sheets with feathered pillows, and a bed fit for a princess . . ."

She tried not to look at him or listen, and tried not to think of silk sheets with feathered pillows, and a bed fit for a princess . . . with her naked body providing him pleasure.

She tried not to think of it and tried not to listen, but the more she tried the more he talked about how it would be.

When Elijah completed his scouting circle and hooked up with the Trespassers he had much to report.

They dismounted to give the animals a rest and to listen.

"The two comancheros are still tracking us but keeping their distance. And just ahead there's more company coming this way."

"What kind of company?" Keys asked.

"Didn't get too close. Three men, one of them on a regal horse with a regal saddle, and . . . something else."

"What else?"

"A young female."

"How young?"

"Shy of twenty . . . from a distance . . . and blond."

"Blond?"

"Blond as they get and if you want to see for yourself . . ." Elijah pointed to the four riders about to cross the trail.

But instead, the leader on the black stallion approached the Trespassers with the two soldados just behind him and the young blond female between them.

"Howdy, Senor," Keys said.

"I am Don Carlos Mondego. The land on that side of the trail," Mondego motioned to his left, "is mine. All of it."

"My name is Jefferson Keys, and we're not going on that side, Senor Mondego. Just straight ahead."

"That is good," Mondego said.

But Keys and the other Trespassers noticed that the look on the girl's face was not good.

Her lips were silent but her eyes were screaming.

"We will be on our way now," Mondego said.

"Just a minute, please." Keys glanced at Billy Joe and Elijah, then back to Mondego. "Won't you introduce the young lady to us? She . . ."

"I said we will be on our way now." The coiled springs in Mondego's eyes were wound tight.

"My name is Karla Olang," she said.

"You be quiet!" Mondego commanded.

"Did you say Olang?" Keys looked at her. She nodded.

Mondego streaked for his gun. So did the two soldados.

Billy Joe shot Don Carlos directly between the eyebrows, Keys, the soldado to the left in the chest, and Elijah, the soldado to the right in the forehead.

They fell from their saddles in that order.

Keys, Billy Joe and Elijah holstered their guns.

Doc moved not fast, not slow, toward the three men on the ground. He prodded Mondego's body with the tip of his boot.

"Dead as sausage."

Billy Joe went to the side of Karla's horse and reached up.

"Let me help you, ma'am."

He did, and as she stepped off, he felt her still trembling.

"It's alright, ma'am," he said, "I . . . we won't let anything happen to you."

Keys came closer.

"Miss Olang, we heard that the comancheros had taken you and your mother."

"My mother's dead. They . . . sold me to" — she looked toward Mondego's body — "him."

"Did he . . . ?" Billy Joe couldn't finish the sentence.

"No." She shook her head. "He was taking me to . . ."

"Quit asking her so many questions." Elizabeth Shelby took Karla's arm. "You come with me, honey. My name's Elizabeth and you can meet the rest of these buckos later."

"What're we gonna do with these?" Sandusky pointed his Henry at the bodies.

"Bury 'em," Keys said. "On his land."

"What about the horses?" Doc asked.

"Slap 'em on the rump, they'll head for home."

"Too bad," Doc said. "Damn good horses, 'specially that stallion."

"Don't you think," Elijah conjectured, "that his men'll come after us?"

"Maybe, and maybe not. Maybe they'll be too busy fighting over and dividing the spoils. But just in case . . . let's get as far away from here as we can."

And that's exactly what the Trespassers did.

CHAPTER THIRTY-SIX

The campfire that night was different than the ones before. Now there were two women among the Trespassers. Karla had taken it upon herself to help Elizabeth prepare supper. And Billy Joe had taken it upon himself not to be too far away from Karla.

Keys noticed that there was a different look in Billy Joe's eyes, much different than when he had repeated, "I'm going to kill you, Mister Keys. Just as sure as the setting of the sun." A look that neither he, nor any of the other Trespassers, had ever seen before.

Earlier, while they were having supper and Billy Joe sat next to her, Keys came up to Karla and spoke softly.

"Are you OK?"

"Thanks to you." She nodded. "All of you."

"There's something I have to tell you. We're glad to have you with us, but what we're going to have to do, and where we're going, is no place for a lady . . ." He looked up at Elizabeth Shelby, who stood just behind Karla. "Except for Miss Shelby here, who has to be part of this . . . expedition. But please be sure that we'll keep you with us, and see that you're alright until we can find a safe place for you to stay until you can get home."

"Home?"

She said the word in a voice that quavered.

"Back to Arizona."

"I don't have . . ."

"Karla, it's too soon to talk about it now. We just wanted you to know we'll help you as much as we can."

"Mister Keys, I . . ."

"Just finish your supper and get a good night's rest. You'll need it. We all will."

Keys moved away and sat on his saddle blanket. Elizabeth Shelby followed and sat next to him. She rolled a cigarette and he lit a cigar.

"I saw something for the first time," she said.

"What?"

"A look of humanity in Billy Joe's eyes."

"Is that what it is?"

"You think he still wants to kill you?"

"Nothing can stop him, except . . ."

"Except what?"

"Me."

"I'm not so sure you could . . . and neither are you. Are you?"

"It's a long way back to Arizona."

"And it was a long way to San Francisco."

"What's that supposed to mean?"

"It means, that remark you made earlier wasn't about the climate, it was about me and what I did there."

"You don't have to tell me . . ."

"I know I don't, but you're going to listen."

"Go ahead."

"How I got there is another matter. There was a wagon master who wanted company. I heard that it was a city that sparkled by the bay and the streets were paved with gold. They weren't, and I couldn't even get a job as a domestic because no wife wanted somebody who looked like me around her husband. So I stole. I stole food — an apple — an apple from a stand and this man saw me and came up to me afterward and started talking about what he could do for me like he was doing for other girls like me on the street. And a cop came up to us, a big Irish cop.

" 'Get off my beat,' he said to the man, 'get off and stay off.' The man left and the cop, his name was Riley, said to me, 'You know what he was trying to do to you, don't you? He's a lowlife pimp.' Well, I knew that and I was so desperate I was willing to go with him and I told that to the cop. And Riley said, 'If you're going to do that, you can start at the bottom, or you can start at the top. Come with me.'

"He took me to a place and introduced me to someone. Her name was Madam Pleasant and she was an octoroon and she was high class and she taught me a lot of things about her profession and so I started at the top and that's how I traveled through a land of men and met a man named Simon Ignatius Kline and thought about how a street I'd live on someday would be paved with gold."

"It's funny," Keys said.

"I don't see you laughing."

"I don't mean that kind of funny."

"What kind then?"

"I mean if you hadn't met Kline, he wouldn't have sent for me, I wouldn't have got these fellows together, we wouldn't be here."

"Maybe you'd all be better off."

"Karla Olang wouldn't."

"You're right about that."

"I better be right" — Keys took a puff of his cigar — "about a lot of things."

"Me, too." She snuffed out the cigarette and rose. "About one thing in particular."

Keys stood up next to her.

"You do know where that damn gold is buried, don't you?"

"Oh, I know that alright."

"Well, that's the most important thing."

"Is it?"

She crossed over to the other side of the campfire.

"Come on, Karla, I'll show you where we ladies bunk."

Billy Joe helped Karla rise to her feet.

"Thank you, William," Karla said.

"Did you hear that?" Elizabeth Shelby mouthed to Keys. "William?"

CHAPTER THIRTY-SEVEN

The next morning the Trespassers plus Karla Olang got an even earlier start than usual. Elijah had left while the moon was still visible. Elizabeth and Karla had fixed and served a mobile breakfast, the animals were hitched and saddled and the caravan proceeded as usual except that now Karla rode beside Billy Joe Bickford.

"No, ma'am," Billy Joe said, "it wasn't either a ranch or a farm. It was what was called a plantation, in what was then the most beautiful valley on earth, the Shenandoah."

"Yes, I heard of it."

"So did Sheridan. He destroyed it."

"And your plantation?"

Billy Joe nodded.

"But the land is still there."

"Not mine anymore. Lost it."

"Everybody loses something."

"Yes, ma'am, I . . ."

"I wish you'd stop calling me 'ma'am,'
William. My name is Karla."

"Alright, I . . ."

"How are you two doing?" Elizabeth rode
over next to them.

"Fine," Karla said.

Billy Joe just nodded.

"Billy Joe." Elizabeth smiled. "You forgot
something this morning."

"I did?"

"You did."

"What?"

"Your exercises."

Elizabeth Shelby nudged her horse ahead.

"What kind of exercises do you do, William?" Karla asked.

"Uh, oh . . . uh, just . . . exercises."

Charly and Diaz dismounted, and still holding on to the reins of their horses, moved
closer to the three fresh mounds that were
yards away from the trail.

"I guess that's what those shots were
about that we heard," Charly.

"Yeah. Three shots . . . three graves," Diaz.

"I wonder who they are?" Charly.

"You mean, were," Diaz.

"Yeah, were," Charly.

"I don't know, but I'm not gonna dig 'em
up to find out," Diaz.

"You think we oughta ride back and tell Battu?" Charly.

"He said to keep trackin' 'em," Diaz.

"Yeah, but how far?" Charly.

"I don't know. He didn't say, but we better keep goin' 'til they get there," Diaz.

From the distance up above, Elijah could see the two comancheros near the graves, but could not hear what they were saying.

The Trespassers had covered more than twenty miles that day, camped not far from a stream, had supper and sat, some of them smoking and talking quietly.

Doc and Sandusky.

Billy Joe and Karla Olang.

Keys, Elizabeth Shelby, and Elijah.

"Doc," Sandusky asked, "you think we'll make it?"

"Make what?"

"Make it back?"

"I'd say the odds are seventy–thirty."

"Which way?"

"Against."

"Then why did you come?"

"I've faced worse . . . and for no money. At least this time I already got some for somebody . . . and besides, time's runnin' out on me. Why'd you come?"

"I had to do somethin' . . . besides die

drinkin'. Think I'll get a chance to use that Gatling?"

"I'd say the odds are seventy–thirty."

"Which way?"

"What do you think?"

"Yeah."

"William?"

"Yes, ma'a— I mean, Karla."

"Do you know where we're going?"

"Well . . . in a way, but we're not supposed to talk about it."

"Not to me?"

"Not to anybody."

"Have you known these people long?"

"Not too long . . . except for one."

"Which one?"

There was a pause.

"Keys."

"He's a good man. I'm beholden to him . . . and to all of you."

Another pause. And this time Billy Joe did not respond.

Elijah had told Keys about the two trackers at the gravesites.

He rose.

"You sure you don't want me to do something about those two?"

"Not yet."

"I don't think we ought to let them get back to where they came from."

"Neither do I."

"Let me know when."

"I will. Get some sleep."

"I will. Good night."

Elijah walked away.

"Mister Keys."

"Yes, Miss Shelby."

"We're getting close."

"I presume you're referring to the gold."

"I am, but so are they." She nodded toward Karla and Billy Joe. "And I'm not talking about the gold."

"I wouldn't count on it."

"Sometimes women see things before men do."

"Sometimes."

"How did it happen to you?"

"How did what happen?"

"Doc mentioned that you were married when you were down here in Mexico."

"He did?"

"He did. She still here?"

"She's dead. Get some sleep. I'm taking the first watch."

"Good night, Mister Keys."

She rose.

"Good night, Miss Shelby."

As he smoked, Jefferson Keys thought about the first time he came to Mexico . . . and about his wife.

Through the funnel of his mind he thought about how he had left Custer and joined the embattled army of Juarez, of meeting him, and being assigned to a brigade led by a young captain named Duncan Ruiz, and more importantly, of meeting Ruiz's sister, Dominique.

Duncan and Dominique belonged to what was once the aristocracy of Mexico, but chose to fight with Juarez against the imperial monarchy of Maximilian imposed by Louis Napoleon.

Keys thought of the first time he saw her. It was in a field hospital where she was smeared with the blood of wounded and dying Juaristas.

Keys himself had sustained a wound in his left shoulder and Captain Ruiz had brought him there and said, "Mister Keys, this is my sister Dominique; she will take care of you."

Keys looked around and saw and smelled the odor of torn flesh and bones and death.

He shook his head and started to move away. "Take care of them," he said to her, "they're worse off."

"They will not live to fight again," she said, "but you will, if you stop bleeding — and this won't take long."

Keys was dazed, but not altogether from the wound. It was also from the sight of the most beautiful creature he had ever seen on God's earth: dark, lustrous eyes in the perfect oval face of someone he had never imagined meeting in a place like this or any place.

She moved quickly and quietly, and with a certainty beyond her years. Not ten words passed between them, not at that time. But there were other times. Keys made sure of that.

Between attacks on Maximilian's forces and blowing up bridges and arsenals, he made it his business to make sure he saw her again. And each time there were more words until there was nothing left to say except, "Dominique, I love you. Will you marry me?"

"When this is over."

"No. Now."

"Yes . . . now."

Captain Duncan Ruiz gave his sister away in a half-destroyed cathedral and Keys was the happiest man in Mexico, and even happier when she told him they were going to have a child.

But the child was never born. In a last desperate raid led by a Maximilian mercenary named Amory Valance, Dominique lay

235

dead, and with her a part of Jefferson Keys died.

He stayed on, was wounded again, this time more severely, and his life was saved by Doc Zeeger. Keys lived to fight again as the tide turned inexorably against Maximilian. With the Civil War ended, the United States exerted more and more pressure on France to recall its troops. Also war clouds were darkening over Europe and Louis Napoleon needed to reinforce his army on the continent. He withdrew his troops and financial support of Maximilian, and many of Maximilian's mercenaries, including Amory, got out while the getting was still good.

Maximilian and what was left of his imperial brigades fought on until his last stand; defeat and capture took place on the Hill of the Bells near Queretaro.

Keys and Doc Zeeger were there.

Maximilian, on orders from Benito Juarez, who had been elected president, was executed by firing squad on June 19, 1867.

Keys was not there.

Keys had bade Captain Ruiz good-bye and thought he would never return to Mexico . . . and he didn't, until now.

Since his return to the comanchero camp,

with fifteen hundred dollars in coin of the realm from Don Carlos Mondego, Battu had been celebrating in an orgy of women and whiskey. It was more than enough compensation for what he had looked forward to with the late mother of the girl he had sold to Don Carlos.

When told that Diaz and Charly had not come back to report on the caravan that had been spotted earlier, Battu shrugged it off, saying that right now he had other things on his mind, and went on with the women and whiskey.

There would be time enough for the Trespassers.

Charly and Diaz looked down at the Trespassers' camp from a distance — but close enough to distinguish a newcomer to the Trespassers' camp.

"Do you see what I see?" Charly.

"I see," Diaz.

"The girl that Battu brought back," Charly.

"How did she get with them?" Diaz.

"I don't know." Charly.

"Me neither." Diaz.

When the next dawn broke, Elijah woke Keys.

"She's gone," Elijah said.

"Who's gone?" Keys wiped his face.

"Miss Shelby."

"Are you sure?"

"Damn sure."

CHAPTER THIRTY-EIGHT

The Trespassers' camp had been roused.

Elizabeth Shelby's gun and gunbelt were beside the place where she had slept, and so was her corduroy jacket, but she was gone.

Karla Olang was the first one questioned by Keys.

"No. I didn't see or hear anything until you woke me."

"Who was on night watch?" Keys asked.

"I was," Sandusky said. "On the other side of the camp. But I wasn't watchin' for anybody to leave . . . Still, it's my fault . . ."

"Never mind," Keys said. "The important thing is to find her."

"Looks bad." Elijah had just come back from a quick search. "She left alone alright, but she's not alone now."

"What do you mean?"

"You better come along with me."

"Where to?"

"The stream."

"Alright. The rest of you stay here."

"Should we make ready to leave?" Zeeger asked.

"We're not going anyplace 'til we find her."

"This is where it happened," Elijah said after they reached the edge of the stream some distance from the camp.

"How do you read it?"

"She took off her clothes and went in. You can see some of her clothes are still here."

He picked up a blouse and handed it to Keys.

"Her and her damn baths," Keys muttered.

"When she came out they were waiting for her."

"How many?"

"I make it two . . . with moccasins. They must've knocked her out . . ."

"Or killed her."

"I don't know, but one of 'em carried her. There's only two tracks leading off in that direction."

"Can you follow them?"

"I don't know how far . . . depends on the terrain."

"We're going to try. But first we've got to get back to camp."

■ ■ ■ ■

Keys' and Elijah's horses were saddled.

They had told the Trespassers what had happened, or what they thought had happened.

"Elijah and I are going to see if we can find her. The rest of you stay here."

"Where the hell would we go?" Doc said.

"That's right." Keys nodded. "None of us knows where we were going except her. But be ready for anything. Some of those Indians might come back."

"Yaquis?" Doc grunted.

"What else," Keys said. "Get the wagons and animals back behind those rocks."

"Should I set up the Gatlin'?" Sandusky asked.

"This time the answer is yes."

"What if you don't come back?" Billy Joe wanted to know.

"We will."

"But if you don't?"

"Wait three days then head back for the border."

"What about our . . . business? You and me?"

"If we're not back, then the Yaquis have taken care of it. We're wasting time."

Keys and Elijah mounted and headed toward the stream.

Billy Joe Bickford put his arm around her shoulder.

"Karla, you stay close to me."

CHAPTER THIRTY-NINE

Tigers of the Rocks.

That's what the Yaquis were called and that's what they were.

The Apaches of Mexico.

Fierce. Unrelenting. Bloody.

To protect their lands and customs they had fought other tribes. Tarahumaras, Tepehuanes, Hicholes, and Mayos, the conquistadores too, and all the governments that had been set up in Mexico for over two hundred years. During that time countless military expeditions were sent to decimate and destroy the native marauders. Thousands were slaughtered, still hundreds survived.

Among the survivors and relentless insurgents was Mangus, who had attacked the Confederate contingent led by Colonel Leigh Shelby, and who had killed them all after the Confederates had managed to hide the gold that they had brought with them — all except Elizabeth Shelby.

It was Mangus who took the young girl as his bride until she managed to escape while the Yaquis were attacked, and Mangus was captured.

But since then Mangus had also escaped, regrouped many of his followers, and continued his bloody raids on ranches, churches, and villages, from a remote encampment ensconced at the base of a steep, shroud-like escarpment.

Diaz and Charly were closer to the Trespassers than they had ever been.

From their vantage point they had watched Keys and Elijah ride away from the camp.

They had waited and watched as the wagons and animals were moved behind the protection of an outcrop of rocks — and as one of the wagons was uncovered and a strange-looking weapon had been assembled.

They had no idea of what had happened, or what was going to happen. But it didn't appear that those who had stayed behind were going to move soon.

"What do you think?" Diaz.

"I don't know what to think," Charly.

"Me, too. Now maybe we go back and tell Battu where they are." Diaz.

"What if we do, then they go someplace

else and we lose 'em?" Charly.

"Right. So?" Diaz.

"So what do you think?" Charly.

"I think we stay here and wait." Diaz.

"How long?" Charly.

"I don't know. But for now we wait." Diaz.

"OK. We wait." Charly.

Keys was mounted, Elijah on the ground reading tracks.

Elijah looked up.

"This is it. This is where the ponies were. Two of them. They mounted and headed . . ." Elijah pointed.

"So'll we. Well, at least we know one good thing."

"Yeah." Elijah nodded as he mounted. "We didn't find her body, so she's still alive."

"Can you follow their tracks?"

"Not easy, ponies unshod. But one of the tracks is deeper, just a little."

Elizabeth Shelby had come out of the stream naked, her body wet and glistening as she emerged.

While still wet, she began to put on her clothes, the tight-fitting pants, chemise, socks, boots, and as she lifted the blouse the two Yaquis sprang. Two young warriors. Lupo and Banos.

Before she could scream, Lupo's fist smashed into the side of her face; she dropped the blouse and fell. He carried her to where they had left their ponies, bound her hands with a leather thong after wrapping a red bandana around her mouth, set her on his horse, swung up behind her, and the two Yaquis headed back toward the stronghold with their prize.

A prize that Mangus would appreciate when he returned from a raid.

The men and women in the camp clustered around as Banos and Lupo dismounted and Lupo pulled Elizabeth Shelby, still bound and gagged, off his pony.

They spoke in Yaqui language but the captive understood what was being said as the two related how they had captured and brought her here.

One of the older men, Kavese, made his way through the others, looked at Elizabeth Shelby, smiled in disbelief, then addressed the others, some of whom, by now, had also recognized her.

"This is Tanimara." Kavese pointed. "Wife of Mangus. He will be pleased to see her. She was his favorite wife."

But there was someone there who was not pleased to see her.

Sonsera. Mangus' current wife. Young.

Dark. Not more than sixteen. A full-blooded Yaqui, whose face and form did not compare favorably to the woman who now stood before her.

"Take her to Mangus' hut," Kavese said. "Tie her there until he comes back."

Mangus and thirty of his raiders had been away from the stronghold for nearly a week.

They had swept to the south, mounted and armed, in search of whatever they could use, eat or trade.

Mangus, now somewhere in his forties — no one, including him, knew exactly where — had never, even as a child, been anything but angry, mean, sullen, combative, eruptive and unpredictable — all traits, which as he grew older, grew stronger and reinforced his dominance over the Yaquis who had survived enemies of every sort, due in large part to Mangus' cunning, cruelty, and command.

Even when he had been captured, no other leader rose within the tribe. No one dared try. The Yaquis knew that Mangus would come back — and back he did come, with a saber scar on his face and across his back, tracks of the capturers' whip — more cruel and cunning and merciless than before.

The mistake his capturers made was not killing him.

If he were ever caught again, they would not make the same mistake.

And since he had left the encampment nearly a week ago, his mien had worsened.

It had been the least productive sweep in more than a year.

A raid on a small church had yielded only a dented silver chalice, a gold cross and chain that had been around the collar of an old priest who now lay dead, and the meager contents of a shattered poor box.

Two ranches, littered with a half-dozen bodies, had provided only a few horses, a milch cow, and some rib-lined cattle the Yaquis had rounded up and were herding back to the stronghold. Herding cattle was far from what Yaquis did best and the going was slow. For some reason, a reason known only to Mangus, a reason he had to explain to no one, Mangus blamed the poor results of the raid and the sluggish pace of the trek back to the stronghold on one of the thirty raiders, a Yaqui named Eskimin, who limped from a long-ago bullet wound in the leg and who had dared to mention in front of the others that lately things had not gone well, and in fact things had seldom been worse.

Mangus had overheard and approached

Eskimin. Without warning he slapped the older, crippled warrior.

"Are you blaming me?" Mangus barked.

"I only said . . ."

Eskimin said nothing more.

Mangus had pulled out his knife and made a deep slash across Eskimin's throat, nearly decapitating him.

"Leave him there for the buzzards," Mangus said.

Since then very little was said to, or by, Mangus.

That and the fact that Mangus had not had a woman since leaving camp had made him even more ill-tempered than usual. Sonsera, the fourth wife he had taken since he came back, was not very appealing, but she was young and serviceable and seldom spoke unless an answer from her was required, and so far she had fared better than his three previous wives. After he tired of the first two he sold them to other tribes and the third one was foolish enough to lie to Mangus about a minor matter. He cut off her nose and she died of infection.

Often, since his return, he had thought of that milk-skinned, red-haired, green-eyed girl he had taken from those travelers he had killed, the girl whose body had blossomed beyond his wildest expectations and anticipations — who had learned the Yaqui language and their ways, but was different than all the other women of the tribe, and for that matter, any other woman he had ever taken, or even seen.

The wife he called Tanimara . . . and who, unknown to him, now was a prisoner in his stronghold.

It had become too dark for Elijah to try to follow tracks.

Keys and Elijah unsaddled their horses, fed them grain, set up dry camp and suppered on jerky.

As Keys took another bite of his supper, he grunted.

"I think it tastes pretty good," Elijah said, "compared to some suppers I never had."

"So do I." Keys smiled.

"Then why the comment?"

"I was just thinking about what that little bastard Kline was feasting on back in their private coach."

"Who said life was fair?"

"True. But at least there's some justice."

"Tell me about it."

"That fat bastard partner of his has got an ulcer or something and is restricted mostly to milk."

"Yeah . . . milk and money."

"That's true, too. But I wouldn't trade places with him."

"Neither would I . . ." Elijah paused, ". . . but then again, on second thought . . ."

"Second or third thoughts, you wouldn't, and you know it."

Elijah grinned and nodded.

Then there was silence.

Keys reached for a cigar.

"Want a smoke?"

"Don't think so."

Keys lit the cigar.

"Back there," Elijah said, "you told them three days."

"I figure" — Keys nodded — "by tomorrow, we'll know about her . . . one way or another."

"Or they'll know about us . . . the Yaquis, I mean."

"Yeah. Their camp can't be far."

"What'll we do if we find it?"

"Why" — Keys took a puff, then shrugged — "we just go in and get her out."

Elijah smiled.

"I should've known better than to ask a dumb question."

"I'll take the first watch," Sandusky volunteered. "And this time I'll make sure nothin' comes in or goes out."

"OK," Doc said, "but I can't sleep anyhow. Sit here for a minute or two and let's talk about what Keys said."

"You mean about the three days?"

"That's what I mean."

"Well, that's what he said."

"I know that, too."

"Then after that, what do you want to do?"

"We could go after them."

"Yeah, and we could get killed tryin'!"

"We could get killed anyhow."

"That might be alright by the two of us, but . . ."

"But what?"

"But what about the two of them?" Sandusky motioned toward where Billy Joe sat with Karla Olang. "They might see it different . . . 'specially the kid."

"He might at that."

"So . . . what do we do?"

"Damn if I know," Doc said.

"I do." Sandusky rose.

"What?"

"Pray that, one way or another, they get back."

Billy Joe and Karla sat next to each other, both leaning back against a wheel of Doc's wagon.

"William, I want to ask you a question . . .

and please tell me the truth."

"I don't make a habit of lying."

"That's not the way I meant it. I meant don't just tell me what I want to hear. Tell me what you really think."

"Alright. What's the question?"

"Do you think they'll find Elizabeth and bring her back?"

"That's two questions." Billy Joe smiled.

"Well, do you? Honestly?"

"I honestly don't know. But if anyone can do it, it's the two of them, Elijah and . . . Keys."

"William, somehow I get the feeling, whenever you mention his name . . ."

"Whose name?"

"You know very well: Mister Keys. There's something about the way you say his name . . . and there's a look in your eyes that's . . ."

"That's what?"

"Well . . . different."

"Sure." Billy Joe tried to make a joke out of it. "It's different than the way I say your name and different than the way I look at you."

"That's not what I meant and you know it."

"Karla, it's nothing for you to worry about."

"You just don't want to tell me."

"I just don't want you to worry about it . . . or anything you don't have to, OK?"

She didn't answer.

She was looking in another direction.

"What's the matter?" Billy Joe asked. "What're you looking at?"

"That gun." She pointed to Sandusky's wagon. "What do they call it?"

"Gatling. It's a powerful weapon."

"Do you know how to use it?"

"No, I don't."

Her eyes went to the guns still strapped on Billy Joe.

"But you know how to use those."

He looked away.

"After the war I had to learn to do something. This is what I'm best at."

"Oh, I don't believe that, William. I believe you can be best at anything you want to be."

"What I want the most right now, is to get you out of here."

"We'll get out, William, all of us. I'm sure of it."

With the fingers of his right hand, he barely touched her face.

"It's good to be sure," he said.

But he wasn't.

■ ■ ■ ■

Charly and Diaz weren't sure of anything. They had drunk the last of their tequila and were asleep on their blankets.

She didn't know how long she had been in Mangus' hut.

In addition to the thong binding her hands and the bandana around her mouth, they had fastened a rope around her legs, tied the other end to a post in the middle of the room so she could lie on the dirt floor, but not move very far.

She knew it was still dark outside. There was a single window filtering in what little moonlight shone through.

Elizabeth Shelby thought of the times before — how many times she could not count — in other camps, but mostly in this stronghold, this same hut, where, as the wife of Mangus, the pearl-complexioned, crimson-haired, emerald-eyed wife, unlike any other girl that Mangus or anyone in his tribe had ever seen, he had taken her innocence and for years hoped that she would bear him a son. She never did. But it had become evident it was not Tanimara who was infertile. Before, during and since, he had taken other women, and always with the same result — without issue.

No one among the Yaquis dared speak of Mangus' infertility, and his sterility did not diminish his desire to bed his peerless prize.

As she lay there that night waiting for his return from the raid and what would inevitably follow in that fulsome room, she knew she could withstand what would happen physically, but it was something else that made her cringe even now.

The odor.

The sickening, suffocating odor.

Mangus smelled worse than a goat.

Mangus never washed.

She remembered how she had prayed for rain hoping that nature would do what he, himself, never did. Cleanse him of at least some of the noxious stench that permeated his body.

In the time since she had escaped from Mexico and fled to San Francisco and Madam Pleasant, Elizabeth Shelby had been with all sorts of men.

Tall men. Short men. Fat men. Thin men. Young men. Old men. One-armed men. One-legged men. Drunk men. Silent men. Talkative men. Robust men. Sick men.

She had even been told by Madam Pleasant about men who existed only in myths, the "anthropophagi, whose heads do grow beneath their shoulders." Elizabeth Shelby had learned to steel herself as she *traveled through a land of men and heard and saw such dreadful things.* But the one thing she could never wash away was the lingering, malodorous memory of the man who would come back into that same hut, and the knowledge of what it would be like to be with him again.

Elizabeth Shelby reacted and turned toward the door as it opened — slowly and quietly.

Had Mangus returned from his raid in the dark of the night?

She had heard no sounds of hooves or voices.

But framed against the doorway, for just an instant, someone stood with a knife glinting in the moonlight, then closed the door and walked into the room.

CHAPTER FORTY

Who it was, Elizabeth Shelby could not determine.

But she could determine that it was not Mangus.

It was a woman.

A very young woman.

And as the young woman passed by the moonlit window, Elizabeth Shelby recognized her as the girl who had come up and stood next to Kavese when the old Yaqui had identified the captive as Mangus' favored wife.

Sonsera moved closer and kneeled, still holding the knife. Dark and thin, very thin compared to Elizabeth Shelby, she even smelled like Mangus.

With the blade of the knife just inches away from the white woman's throat, Sonsera's other hand went to her own face, her finger touching her lips.

She whispered in the Yaqui language.

"You speak our language?"

Elizabeth Shelby nodded.

"I am going to take the bandana from your face. Do not make any noise or you will die. Do you understand?"

Shelby nodded again.

Sonsera, still holding the knife, untied the bandana.

"I am Sonsera, Mangus' wife. When he comes back and sees you, he will no longer want me. He will take you as his wife again. If I kill you he will cut off my nose."

Elizabeth Shelby was beginning to understand what the young girl was thinking, but said nothing.

"If I help you get away and you are caught, will you promise not to tell them what I have done?"

"Sonsera," Elizabeth answered, "I will never tell."

Sonsera slashed the thong from Elizabeth Shelby's wrists, then cut the rope. She lifted both the thong and rope and rose to her feet.

"They should not see that the rope was cut. Take it and the thong with you."

"Yes."

Wobbly at first, Elizabeth managed to stand until the circulation returned to her body.

"Can you walk?"

"Yes."

"Come with me. I'll show you the way."

With Sonsera in the lead, they made their way to the door. Sonsera opened it, looked out, then motioned for Elizabeth Shelby to follow.

A cloud had hit the moon shrouding the night in darkness except for the far-away dancing starlights.

Sonsera moved and Elizabeth followed, behind the other huts, where Yaquis lay, some drunk, some with bodies entwined, and others just asleep in the cool desert night.

They made it to the bouldered edge of the encampment.

"Your only chance is on foot. Get far away as fast as you can. When Mangus comes back they will come after you. He will seethe with anger that you are gone and come after you."

As the two of them stood, even in the dark, it was evident why Mangus would favor the red-headed woman with full breasts, well-rounded hips and long, tapered legs over the Yaqui tadpole.

"Thank you," Elizabeth Shelby whispered, turned, and ran, swift and silent, into the bleak, dry sea of desert. She turned and looked back in the direction where she had left Sonsera.

The young girl who had been responsible for her deliverance — so far — was gone.

After almost a mile she realized that she was still carrying the thong and the rope that had lashed her hands and legs. She let them drop to the ground.

Elizabeth Shelby continued to run with Sonsera's words echoing in her brain: ". . . get far away as fast as you can . . . far away . . . fast . . ."

The cold night wind thrashed her face and spilled her hair into a flowing red wake until her legs shivered and her lungs gasped for anodyning air — until she stumbled and hit the ground hard and lay on the cold, barren surface.

But not for long.

Elizabeth Shelby made it to her feet, and began to walk, in which direction she was not exactly sure.

She could only hope it was away from the Yaqui stronghold.

But hope and strength ebbed with the strain of each labored step until every bone and fiber seemed detached from the will and message from her brain, and until her brain was clouded, suspended somewhere between the will to live and the indifference of death.

And she knew that she could no longer control her fate — the deep, dark pit of the desert opened up — and Elizabeth Shelby dropped into it.

Chapter Forty-One

The stars no longer danced in the blue-black bowl of sky.

The spotlight of sun drifted just above the jutting outline of the eastern rim.

A shadow fell upon the inert form on the arid ground — then another.

Hands reached and touched.

A voice.

"Elizabeth."

Not Tanimara.

"Elizabeth."

Keys and Elijah.

She stirred from a netherworld.

Gently, they ministered to her.

With words and water.

Faces she thought she would never see again.

Until she could move, sit up, and smile.

Until she could speak.

"Where . . . ? Where . . . ?"

"You were sent for," Keys said, "but you didn't go. Take it easy . . . we'll get you back. Don't talk now . . . take another sip."

He put the canteen to her lips.

"Not too much. Just take a sip."

He poured water from the canteen onto his bandana, softly brushed the hair from her face, and daubed the kerchief onto her forehead and cheeks and throat, then around her wrists where the leather thongs had left deep red bruises.

After a time, they lifted her onto Keys' saddle. Keys mounted behind her.

Elijah swung onto his horse.

"I've got to tell you . . ."

"You tell us nothing. Get your strength back. Chew on this jerky. Whatever it is, it can wait 'til we get back to camp."

Elizabeth Shelby was not so sure it could . . . but she didn't have the strength to do anything but comply.

At the Trespassers' camp there was relief, then celebration when Keys and Elijah returned with Elizabeth Shelby.

At the Yaqui stronghold there was dread, then outrage when Mangus came back and heard of the capture and escape of Tanimara.

How she had escaped no one could explain, nor was Mangus in the mood to listen. He, now with the dead priest's cross around his neck, and the same raiders, along with Lupo and Banos, mounted and started the search.

Sonsera stayed behind with the others at the stronghold and trembled at the thought of what might happen.

Elizabeth Shelby had put on her blouse and corduroy jacket. She sat with the rest of them: Keys, Elijah, Sandusky, Karla, Billy Joe, Doc and Zeeger.

She told them what had happened — of being recognized as Mangus' wife, of being tied until he came back with the raiders, of being freed by Sonsera, and of giving up hope, and falling senseless — until Keys and Elijah . . .

"That's enough," Keys said. "We'll stay here until you can travel. You'll ride in Doc's wagon . . ."

"I'm ready . . ."

"I'll tell you when you're ready. Then we'll move in another direction as far away from those damn Yaquis as . . ."

"We've got to go back," she said.

The Trespassers fell silent and looked at one another as if she had gone crazy.

"Go back where?" Keys asked.

"The Yaqui camp."

"Why the hell would we do that?"

"Because" — she took a deep breath — "that's where the gold is buried."

Chapter Forty-Two

"How the hell could your father and the rest of those Confederates bury five million in gold," Keys wanted to know, "in the middle of a Yaqui settlement without the Yaquis knowing about it?"

It was evident that the rest of the Trespassers also wanted to know.

"Well . . . has anybody got a cigarette?"

"Forget the cigarette," Keys snapped. "Just tell us how."

"Well," she repeated, "it's not exactly in the middle of the settlement . . . but close."

"How close?" Doc asked.

"Well . . ."

"That's three 'wells' you've dug. Get to the water," Keys said. "Tell us just how it happened and where."

"As I remember it, when the wagons broke down my father and the rest of them had no idea that just around the cove was where Mangus and the Yaquis were. They decided to bury the gold, move on and come back for the gold later . . . but right after they buried it, the Yaquis came screaming in and, well . . . you know the rest."

"Except," Doc said, "exactly where the damn gold is buried."

"That's right." Elizabeth Shelby nodded.

"Why" — Doc wiped at his chin — "didn't you mention before we left that it was buried so close to the Yaqui camp?"

"Two reasons."

"Go ahead," Keys said.

"One, I wasn't sure that the Yaquis would still be using that same camp."

"What's the other reason?" Keys asked.

"I wasn't sure that if you knew about it, you'd be willing to come after the gold."

"That's the best reason," Doc said, " 'cause that'd make us even crazier than we already are. But now that we're here and do know, what do we do?"

Doc looked at Keys.

From their far-away vantage point Charly and Diaz had seen Keys and Elijah ride in with Elizabeth Shelby. They had no notion of what had happened or what was going to happen next.

"What do you think?" Charly.

"I think I want a drink," Diaz.

"Beside that?" Charly.

"Beside that, I don't know." Diaz.

"Me too." Charly.

Before Keys could answer, Billy Joe spoke up for the first time.

"I'll tell you what I say we do." He glanced at Karla, then back to Keys. "I say we forget about the whole damn thing and get back to where we came from, while maybe we can still make it. It's not just us anymore. There's her."

He pointed to Karla.

"I was thinking of that too," Keys said.

"That's it, then." Billy Joe smiled.

"Just a minute." Keys went on, "I said I was thinking about it. I didn't say I decided."

"You better decide quick, because I . . ."

"Why don't you just slow down, Mister Bickford," Elijah spoke softly but emphatically. "You're not in command here."

"I'm in command of me."

"I thought you and I had business to settle," Keys said to Billy Joe.

"I'll settle it when you get back . . . if you get back. Right now I'm thinking of her."

"William, please — all of you." Karla's eyes were moistening. "I appreciate all you've done, but please . . . I don't want you to decide anything on account of me, please . . ."

"Jeff." Doc wiped at his mouth. "I'll float my stick with you . . . whatever you say."

"Me too." Elijah nodded.

"And me." Sandusky shrugged.

"I haven't come this far" — Elizabeth Shelby stood up — "just to . . ."

"Jefferson!!!" Elijah pointed.

"I see it."

In the distance was the dust of a band of riders coming straight at the Trespassers' camp.

"Maybe," Keys said, "Mangus has already decided for us."

CHAPTER FORTY-THREE

"Sandusky," Keys commanded, "get that Gatling ready."

"It's ready." Sandusky started to move.

"Hold on!" Elijah hollered and shielded his eyes from the sun. "They're not Yaquis!"

"You sure?" Doc asked.

"Unless Yaquis wear uniforms."

"Doc," Keys said, "where are those field glasses?"

"Right here." Doc picked up the glasses next to him, put them to his face and focused. "It's a Mexican army troop."

"That's not bad news." Keys smiled.

"It gets better . . . maybe."

"What do you mean?"

"Guess who's in the lead?"

"This is no time for guessing games."

"Then see for yourself." Doc handed him the field glasses. "It's your brother-in-law."

Keys focused the glasses to his eyesight.

As Doc had said, into focus came the face and figure of a man Jefferson Keys never expected to see again.

Duncan Ruiz.

Now Colonel Duncan Ruiz.

Proud, chiseled features, confident eyes, a military mustache over resolute mouth, and cleft carved into a prominent chin. The bearing of a true soldier.

Keys lowered the glasses.

"Sandusky, Billy Joe, toss a canvas over the Gatling."

"I thought Doc said he was your brother-in-law!" Billy Joe said.

"He is, but this is his country and he's a soldier. Let's save it for now."

Sandusky and Billy Joe covered the Gatling.

"Let's give 'em a friendly greeting, everybody." Keys waved both arms. The rest of the Trespassers did the same, waving and hollering.

"Hola!"

"Buenos dias!"

"Welcome!"

"Amigos!"

By then Ruiz and his troop had slowed from a gallop to a trot to a walk.

Colonel Ruiz raised his arm. The troop came to a stop.

The smile on the Colonel's face broadened to a grin. He dismounted and hurried to meet Keys, who moved toward him with both arms outstretched into an *abrazo* when they came together.

"Mano!" Ruiz shook his head in pleased disbelief. "You're the last man I ever expected to see here!"

"And vice versa! *Mi capitán!*" Keys performed an exaggerated salute to go with his smile. "Excuse me — *mi coronel!*"

Ruiz shrugged.

"The army made a mistake."

"You're right. You should've been a general by now. How did you find us?"

"We didn't. We were looking for somebody else."

"Well, believe me, we're glad it worked out this way."

"So am I, *mano.*"

"Why don't you tell your men to dismount and we'll talk things over."

"Like old times," Ruiz said.

"Almost like old times."

"Yes, my friend . . . almost."

"*Federales!*" Charly.

"I see," Diaz.

"Now we go back. Tell Battu." Charly.

"Tell Battu, what?" Diaz.

"About the *Federales,*" Charly.

"What about them?" Diaz.

"They're here." Charly.

"Let's wait." Diaz.

"For what?" Charly.

"To see if they stay here." Diaz.

"We wait." Charly.

■ ■ ■ ■

"Colonel Duncan Ruiz, this is Miss Elizabeth Shelby . . . of San Francisco; Miss Karla Olang, Arizona Territory; Doc Zeeger, you remember . . ."

"I remember Doc Zeeger with fond memories and gratitude of the Republic of Mexico."

"And damn glad to see you again, Colonel," Doc said.

"This is Elijah, a new old friend."

Both men nodded.

"Billy Joe Bickford, he's one of us now. And Sandusky, as handy as they come."

"A pleasure to meet all of Jefferson's friends." Colonel Ruiz smiled and turned to Keys. "But you haven't told me what brings you back to Mexico."

"Let's table that for the time being. You said you were looking for somebody else. Mind telling us who?"

"Not at all. You've heard of him. Everybody has, a Yaqui renegade, no, not a renegade, a beast named Mangus . . ."

The Trespassers could barely keep from saying something, but followed Keys' lead and said nothing as Colonel Ruiz continued.

". . . on his latest raid he hit a church and

two ranches, killed a half dozen, including a priest, and as usual, vanished into thin air."

"Not quite thin air," Keys said.

"What do you mean?"

"How would you like to hit his stronghold, wipe it out . . . and him with it?"

"I would like nothing, nothing better, but we've been trying for years to find it."

"Miss Shelby just came back from paying it a visit."

"Is this a joke?"

"No. It's a fact. Miss Shelby was once Mrs. Mangus. But let's table that for a while too. How many in your troop?"

"Twenty."

"And there's seven of us . . . counting two women."

"There has to be many more of them, my friend, in their stronghold . . ."

"Ah! But we have a few advantages."

"We do?"

"We do. Elizabeth, can you draw a map of the layout there?"

"Every inch."

"It doesn't have to be that detailed. The ways in and out."

"Only one passage in or out."

"That's even better."

"Still," Colonel Ruiz said, "they outnumber us, *mano*."

"That, my friend" — Keys smiled — "never stopped us before. Besides we've got strategy . . . and an equalizer . . . more than an equalizer . . . worth a hundred troops."

Mangus seethed with anger.

In his hands he held the rawhide thong and rope that had been cut away from Elizabeth Shelby while she had been held in the hut.

He knew that she could not have cut herself free.

He knew that someone else had done it.

And he knew who that someone else had to be.

Mangus had split his band into four forces that had zig-zagged in different directions looking for tracks, signs, or for Tanimara herself.

As he stood with the slashed thong and rope, Lupo and Banos with their share of the searchers rode back from up ahead.

They had found the tracks where Elizabeth Shelby had fallen and where two riders had picked her up and carried her away.

They made their report to Mangus.

"Do we go after them?" Lupo asked.

"No. Not now." Mangus fumed. "Now we go back."

Still carrying the thong and rope, he

mounted and rode toward the stronghold.

The rest followed.

"Alright, Sandusky," Keys said, "let's show the Colonel and his boys what we've got."

The barrels of the Gatling revolved and spit out a barrage of gunfire — hundreds of rounds in less than a minute — that ripped a distant row of oak trees into kindling.

"That's enough!" Keys waved his arm and hollered. "Don't waste ammunition."

Sandusky stopped cranking and the Gatling stopped spitting.

Keys turned to Ruiz and his troopers, who stared in disbelief.

"What do you think of that?" Keys smiled.

"*Mano,* I think we could have used that at Chapultepec."

"And," Keys said, "pretty soon we can use it someplace else."

He turned to the Trespassers.

"Miss Shelby, you draw that map of the setup . . . then we'll talk some strategy."

Charly and Diaz were dumbfounded.

"That gun is straight from hell," Charly.

"We got to tell Battu," Diaz.

"He won't believe us." Charly.

"I don't blame him." Diaz.

"We go?" Charly.

"Let's see if they go first," Diaz.

"And which way." Charly.

"I hope it's not our way." Diaz.

"Me too." Charly.

Keys had studied the map that Elizabeth Shelby had drawn. He traced his finger along the paper.

"Those huts go right up to the base of the escarpment?"

"Practically up to the wall."

"OK, then those walls have got to come tumbling down. Elijah, how far will those arrows of yours fly?"

"To the moon."

"They won't have to fly quite that far. Alright now, I'll explain the rest of it . . ."

The Trespassers and Colonel Duncan Ruiz listened while Keys went over his plan.

Earlier, Billy Joe, holding on to Karla Olang's arm, had approached Keys.

"Karla says she won't leave the rest of you . . ."

"And you, William."

"But," Billy Joe asked, "do the two ladies have to go along on the raid?"

"Billy Joe, they'll be far enough away to be safe. And with the Colonel and his men, this is the best chance we've got against

Mangus and his Yaquis, and besides that . . .
that's where the damn gold is."

"Excuse me, Mister Keys," Karla said,
"and it really is none of my business, but
after you brought Miss Shelby back, I did
hear her say something about buried gold.
Is that what this is all about?"

"Well, not *all* about, not anymore, but that
is a part of it, a big part."

"And I've hamstrung all of you, haven't
I?"

"No, in some ways" — Keys looked at
Billy Joe and back to her — "Karla, you've
been a help, a big help. And we appreciate
it, but we'd appreciate something else too."

"Anything. Please tell me . . . what?"

"Don't say anything about gold . . . to the
colonel, or to anyone else."

She put a finger to her lips and smiled.

"Mum's the word," Karla whispered.

"That's the word," Keys whispered back.

Keys finished outlining his plan and turned
to Ruiz.

"What do you think?"

"I think" — the Colonel smiled — "you
ought to stay and join the Mexican Army."

"No, thanks. I've already been in too
many armies."

Keys rose.

"Alright, let's get a move on. Everything rolls."

"You see?" Charly.
"I see," Diaz.
"They're not coming in this direction." Charly.
"No. They're not," Diaz.
"Now we got something to tell Battu." Charly.
"And get a drink." Diaz.
"Drinks." Charly.

Keys and Ruiz rode at the head of the expedition.

Elizabeth Shelby, with her gun strapped over her corduroy jacket, just behind them. Then Billy Joe and Karla, the pack animals, and the wagons — Doc's and Sandusky's — all flanked by ten Mexican troopers on either side.

Elijah was nowhere in sight.

That's where a good scout should be.

Nowhere in sight.

Sonsera turned at the sound from the entrance of the hut.

Mangus stood in the doorway with the slashed thong and rope in one hand, a knife in the other, and venom in both eyes.

Chapter Forty-Four

Mangus flung the rawhide thong and rope at her feet.

"I know," Sonsera said, "you will cut off my nose."

"That will come later" — Mangus nodded — "much later. But first" — he held up the knife — "you will suffer many cuts. Lose much blood."

His left hand signaled toward the door. Lupo and Banos came into the hut. Banos carried a rope.

Mangus walked to Sonsera and ripped off all her clothes. He pushed her up against the post, then motioned to Banos.

Both Banos and Lupo looped the rope around the girl's naked body and post, circle after circle, and fastened it tight with a knot.

When they were finished they looked at Mangus, who pointed to the door.

They left.

Mangus was in no hurry.

When he was ready those outside would hear her screams.

They would hear her plead for the mercy of death.

That was part of the torture.

But Mangus was in no hurry.

■ ■ ■ ■

The caravan moved on toward the hidden cove of the Yaquis' stronghold.

Twice during the day Elijah had scouted far ahead and come back to report no sign of Yaqui activity.

Keys let his horse drift back and away from Ruiz, until he came alongside of Doc's wagon.

Zeeger tried unsuccessfully to stifle a cough.

"How you doing, Doc?"

"How the hell you think I'm doin' after swallowin' half the dust of Mexico?"

"Why don't you put that bandana up around your mouth?"

"Maybe because I'm stubborn or maybe because I just like the taste of Mexican dust or maybe . . ."

". . . maybe I'm sorry I asked, you ol' war-horse. I think this sort of thing agrees with you. You look better now than when we started. Maybe we ought to do it again sometime." Keys smiled and let his horse fade farther back next to Sandusky's wagon.

"Sandusky . . ."

"What is it?"

"Nothing, except you know that a large

part of this operation depends on you and that . . . pop gun."

"Then you got nothin' to worry about except the other parts of this operation."

"That's all I wanted to know."

"Then you know it."

Keys maneuvered his mount so he came up between Billy Joe and Karla.

"We're getting close," Keys said.

"I don't want Karla to get too close."

"She won't . . ."

"I wish you two wouldn't worry so much about me. I'm not a child . . ."

"No, Karla, you're not." Keys looked at Billy Joe, then back to her. "Not anymore. You and Miss Shelby stick close together where I showed you on the map."

Karla Olang smiled and nodded.

"Well, Billy Joe, we're on the same side in this one."

"Not for long. In case you forgot, I'm from Virginia."

"No, I didn't forget. And in case you didn't know, I'm from Virginia too."

"You are?" Billy Joe Bickford wasn't sure he believed it.

"Born and reared in Clifton Forge."

Keys prodded his horse ahead and pulled up next to Elizabeth Shelby.

"Miss Shelby."

"Yes, Mister Keys. You have any last-minute instructions?"

"Nope. We couldn't've come this far without you . . ."

"I know that."

"But . . ."

"But?"

"There's nothing more you can do until after this is over . . ."

"Then we get into bed again, is that it?"

"No, that's not it . . . I mean that's not what I mean. I mean you and Karla stay put, out of harm's way 'til it's over."

"Oh, that?"

"Yeah, that."

"Sure I will and I know why you want me to do that. Not because you're madly in love with me, but because I still haven't told you exactly where the damn gold is buried. That's it, isn't it, Mister Keys?"

"If you say so, Miss Shelby."

Keys kneed his horse forward and alongside Colonel Duncan Ruiz.

"All of your people ready, *mano?*"

"Willing and anxious." Keys nodded.

"You still haven't told me, amigo, what you and your people are doing down here."

"Well, we're helping you, *mi coronel.*"

"That means you still don't want to tell me."

279

"Maybe, *mañana.*"

"I wouldn't count on it." Ruiz smiled.

"There's something you can count on."

For the third and last time Elijah had come back with his report.

The caravan came to a stop and Elijah reined up.

"Well, the entrance is just like Miss Shelby said it was. Could hardly spot it even if you were looking for it. And from what I could tell, those huts go right back up against that rock wall."

"Mangus' is the farthest one in," Elizabeth Shelby said. "The back wall is part of the mountain."

"Looks like," Elijah said, "they're getting ready for a barbeque. Slaughtered some beeves."

"Good." Keys nodded. "Let's hope they've got plenty of whiskey to go with it. Well, we'll wait until dark and get into position."

CHAPTER FORTY-FIVE

Hunter's night.

A night to see and not be seen.

The spits where steers were being turned above the flames of the fire pits gave off eerie reflections against the rock walls. There was chanting, drinking, even dancing among the hundred or so Yaquis in the stronghold.

But not in the hut of Mangus.

Mangus was disappointed as he took another drink and made another slice into the frail, bleeding body of Sonsera tied to the post.

Each slice deeper and bloodier than the last.

Disappointed because Sonsera, still barely conscious, and severely suffering, had not cried out, had not screamed, had not supplicated.

For hours she had borne torture in agonized silence.

Her face, shoulders, chest, arms, her midsection and legs, leaking red rivulets of blood.

Her teeth biting into her thin, twisted crimson lips.

And still, she would not give sound to her suffering.

From the time she had turned and seen him in the doorway with the severed thong and rope in his hand and that look in the eyes on his scarred face, she knew that one way or another her life was over.

Anything she could say or do would be useless. Sonsera did not know whether the white woman had escaped or was dead.

But she knew that even if she told Mangus why she did it — because she wanted to stay with him as his wife, regardless of the way he had treated her — the Yaqui way, as chattel — she was still the wife of a tribal chief — she was above the other women — she had known no other man — and she wanted to stay with him as long as she could — it would make no difference to Mangus. In his eyes, she had betrayed him, and he would make her pay in the cruelest way he could think of.

The way he was doing it now.

All she could hope for was that she would soon fall into oblivion and cease suffering.

But, disappointed as he was, Mangus was determined to prolong her suffering as long as possible — until he made that final cut.

The Trespassers had taken their assigned positions, as had Colonel Ruiz and his men.

The most dangerous and important assignment had fallen to Elijah and his skill in stealth and with the bow and arrow — arrows.

Luckily for him, and for Keys' overall plan, it was a night of feast and even celebration for the nearly hundred men, women and children of the tribe — and without the immediate presence of Mangus, they had become even more lax than was their custom.

With pantherine movement, Elijah stealthily made his way up the rim of boulders that nearly circled the encampment, until he was close enough for the flights of his arrows to carry out their missions.

He settled along the shield of one of the boulders and made ready.

The others had been ready and waiting.

Keys. Doc. Sandusky. Billy Joe next to Sandusky, where he would feed the magazines into the Gatling. Ruiz, his troopers nearby, rifles and guns drawn.

Only Elizabeth Shelby and Karla Olang had been positioned away from where the combat would be joined.

Sonsera was sustained only by the rope that bound her body to the post. She was between two worlds — and a part of neither.

With his left hand Mangus lifted her chin — and with the knife in his right hand, he raised it toward her face.

Elijah lighted the wick of the first stick of dynamite attached to the first arrow, strung the arrow into the bow, pulled it back as far as it would go, and let it fly high toward the wall of the escarpment. Then within seconds, the second, third and fourth fiery flights followed — and so did the explosions as the missiles struck, blasting the cliff asunder and sending avalanches of stone hurtling down into the settlement, smashing huts and scattering screaming Yaquis amuck as if the world were coming to an end.

The ceiling of Mangus' hut collapsed. He was thrown to the ground, but survived.

Sonsera didn't.

Still tied to the post, she was buried beneath the debris of roof and rock.

Mangus managed to get to his feet and stagger toward what used to be the doorway.

Outside, panic had spread throughout the camp and their only thought was to escape through the passage that led to the safety of the open desert.

But it was not the women and children who fled first.

The warriors, some with guns, some without, overran the weaker survivors and stampeded toward the narrow corridor while the others wailed and weaved after them.

The encampment had become a cauldron of confusion and chaos. Chunks of razor-sharp rocks and boulders tumbled onto the spits spreading fire across what huts still stood. Mothers took hold of crying children, clasped them to their breasts and tried to avoid being trampled by the men scurrying toward the passageway.

Lupo and Banos were in the forefront, slamming aside the women and older men in their path. Kavese fell hard and could not rise.

When a couple dozen warriors, Lupo and Banos among them, charged into the open, the Gatling roared and the night was shredded by hundreds upon hundreds of deadly thunderbolts. The barrels swung from side to side in a twelve-degree sweep and covered a front of sixty-two feet, nearly the entire width of the passage. Lupo and Banos were among the first to die.

Keys, Doc, Ruiz and his troopers opened fire from all directions.

Some plunged to the ground dead, others lifted their arms in surrender. None chose to fight on against the firepower of the attackers.

From the time of the first explosion, Karla had closed her eyes and buried her face into both palms.

When she lowered her hands and opened her eyes, Elizabeth Shelby was gone.

Still dazed and bleeding, Mangus stumbled through the camp toward the passage.

He heard a voice.

"Mangus!"

He turned and saw her.

"Tanimara!"

"No," she said. "Elizabeth Shelby."

Elizabeth Shelby raised the gun and fired into his face and body until he fell and the gun was empty.

CHAPTER FORTY-SIX

The squadron of buzzards that had been circling above since before dawn were denied.

The dead were buried in a common grave within the settlement. What had been a stronghold was now a cemetery.

The male survivors stood stolid and silent. The women wept and wailed.

Colonel Ruiz and his troopers, none of whom had suffered so much as a scratch, would march those survivors to another settlement. This one set up by the Mexican government and reserved for recalcitrant members of Yaqui tribes.

Doc had been ministering to the injured and wounded — this time women and children first — most of whom, at first, couldn't believe that one of those who was responsible for the devastation would now relieve the pain and suffering of the enemy.

That was not the Yaqui way.

Sandusky had broken down the Gatling and loaded it on his wagon.

Elizabeth Shelby had reloaded her revolver and waited for Keys to upbraid her for leaving her station and risking her life doing what she did. Keys said nothing about it — so far.

At that time Keys was talking to Elijah, who was unstringing his bow.

"Giving it a rest?"

Elijah smiled and nodded.

"It deserves it. You know something, Elijah, I do believe you *could* hit the moon."

"Why not? It's a pretty big target."

"Well, you hit the target last night. Four times. Those walls came tumbling down."

"First time I ever tried it with a stick of dynamite tied to an arrow. Took a little . . . adjusting."

"We all might have to do a little more adjusting before this trip is over."

"That's what makes life interesting, isn't it? If you survive."

"Better yet . . . succeed."

Just after the Mexican troopers had mounted and were about to escort the Yaquis to the south, Colonel Duncan Ruiz stood next to his horse as Jefferson Keys approached and the other Trespassers and Karla stood nearby.

"Well, *mano,* it's *mañana.*" Ruiz smiled.

"So it is." Keys nodded.

"Now do you want to tell me?"

"Tell you what?" Keys asked in mock innocence.

"You know what." Ruiz pointed to the Trespassers. "I don't think you and your friends came to Mexico to help President Benito Juarez." Ruiz motioned toward the stronghold. "Although, I must admit, you have been of great help. Do you want to tell me more?"

"Best I don't."

"Best for whom?"

"All around. But I can tell you this, you and I are going in different directions. You're going south. We're going north."

"You're going back?"

"Soon. Very soon. Let it go at that, *mano.*"

"I will. But don't break any laws."

"Not even bend 'em?"

"I'll be looking the other way." Ruiz smiled.

"One more thing . . ."

Keys touched the arm of Colonel Ruiz.

"I know what you're going to say, *mano.* Rest assured. So long as I am alive and able, there will be fresh flowers on the grave of my sister — your wife."

Ruiz mounted. Gave the order. The column of troopers and Yaqui survivors headed south.

Billy Joe Bickford came forward and stood next to Keys.

"I don't even know kitchen Spanish," he said. "What does *mano* mean?"

"It's short for *hermano.*"

"Hermano?"

"Means brother."

"Come on over here." Keys led Elizabeth Shelby away from the rest of them. "I want to talk to you."

"I wonder what about."

"No, you don't."

"No, I don't."

"You're a damn fool."

"If I weren't, we wouldn't be here."

"I told you to stay up there with the Olang girl."

"So you did."

"And so you didn't."

"No, I didn't."

"You could have been killed . . ."

"That's the chance we both had to take . . . you and me."

"Why?"

"Because I wanted to see him. I wanted

to smell him. Because I wanted to kill that son of a bitch. Me. Myself."

"More than you wanted the gold?"

"More than anything. Now I want to ask you something, if you'll shut up a minute."

"Go ahead."

"You want to stand here and bawl me out or . . ."

"Or what?"

"Or do you want me to show you where the damn gold is buried?"

CHAPTER FORTY-SEVEN

They didn't have to go far.

As the crow — or buzzard — flies, less than a mile.

But on horse back or wagon it was a little over a mile, just around the jutting peninsula of rocks and boulders in the cove next to what was the Yaqui stronghold.

They were all there. The entire caravan. Keys. Doc, Elijah, Billy Joe Bickford, Sandusky, Karla Olang — waiting for Elizabeth Shelby to point down to the ground where the gold was buried.

But Elizabeth Shelby didn't point down.

She pointed straight ahead to the side of the cliff.

They looked at her.

Then they looked at the side of the cliff.

Then they looked back at her.

"Is there a secret cave in there, some-where?" Doc asked.

"Nope." She shook her head.

"Then what?" Billy Joe asked.

"I think," Keys said, "I've got a pretty good idea of what happened."

"Why don't you let us in on it?" Doc suggested.

"I take it," Keys said to Elizabeth, "that your father, Colonel Shelby, besides the gold, was carrying some dynamite when those wagons broke down."

Elizabeth Shelby was genuinely surprised.

"How the hell did you know that?"

"From looking up top of that cliff," Keys said, "my guess is when the wagons went bad, instead of leaving them here and bury-ing the gold, he had the wagons pushed to the side of the cliff with the gold still in one or two of them . . ."

"Just one."

". . . planted some dynamite up high, set it off, and blew half the mountain down. My guess is the gold is still in one of those wagons buried, not under the ground, but under the side of that mountain."

"That's a damn good guess," Elizabeth Shelby said. "Because that's exactly where it is. Actually, the Yaquis heard the explosion and that's what brought them here. But they didn't know anything about the gold being buried."

"How the hell" — Sandusky scratched at his chin and asked Keys — "did you figure it out?"

"Well," Keys pointed up above and said, "any good dynamiter could tell you that's what happened to that cliff."

"Sure," Billy Joe said, "now all we've got to do is dig it out from under all those tons of rock."

"No, my lad." Keys smiled. "Digging is for miners. We don't dig."

"What *do* we do?" Billy Joe asked.

"We dynamite. Dynamite blew it under. Now dynamite is going to blow it away."

"What about the gold?" Billy Joe pointed. "Won't that get blown away?"

"Not the way I do it," Keys said, "in increments. That bullion won't even have a scratch on it. That's a promise."

Charly and Diaz stood in front of Rinaldi, who stood in front of Battu's cabana.

"But we have much to tell him," Charly.

"Very much," Diaz.

"Tell him when he's finished."

"Finished?" Charly.

"Finished what?" Diaz.

"What do you think?"

"Oh," Charly.

"Oh, ho!" Diaz.

"He would not be in a very good mood if you disturbed him now."

"We'll wait," Charly.

"How long?" Diaz.

"*¿Quién sabe?*"

An hour later Battu and Rinaldi sat near the campfire across from Charly and Diaz.

Battu half filled a tin cup from the whiskey bottle and passed the bottle to Rinaldi, who poured whiskey into his cup and passed what was left in the bottle to Charly and Diaz.

"You've been gone a long time," Battu said after he drank. "Where did you go — to China?"

"Where's China?" Charly.

"The trouble with you two is, you're uneducated."

"*Sí,* Jefe," Diaz.

"Tell me what you saw and don't take all night."

"*Sí,* Jefe. We saw much," Charly.

"Very much," Diaz.

"Report."

"The gringos with the wagons traveled far," Charly.

"We heard three shots," Diaz.

"Heard? What did you *see?*"

"Graves," Charly.

"Three graves." Diaz.

"Gringos?" Battu took another swallow.

"No, Jefe," Charly.

"Not gringos." Diaz.

"How do you know if you didn't see?"

"Because all the gringos were still alive later," Charly.

"Very much alive," Diaz.

"Continue the report."

"We continued to follow," Charly.

"But now they had somebody else with them," Diaz.

"Who else?"

"The girl you sold," Charly.

"To Don Carlos." Diaz.

"What?! You're sure?"

"*Sí,* Jefe. We're sure." Charly.

"We seen her." Diaz.

"Then I think I know who is in one of those graves."

"Who, Jefe?" Charly.

"Who?" Diaz.

"Don Carlos. How else would they get the girl?"

"Maybe he sold her to them," Charly.

"Maybe." Diaz.

"Don Carlos would never sell such a girl.

You're both stupid. You hear me?"

"*Sí*, Jefe." Diaz.

"*Sí*, Jefe." Charly.

"And he still owes me five hundred. God damn him. Continue the report."

"The girl with red hair disappeared from the camp," Charly.

"But they brought her back." Diaz.

"Who brought her back?"

"The two gringos," Charly.

"One white, one colored." Diaz.

"Go on."

"Then came the *Federales*," Charly.

"A troop. Maybe thirty, forty." Diaz.

"What next?"

"The gringos fired a gun from hell," Charly.

"Many bullets." Diaz.

"At the *Federales?*"

"No, Jefe." Charly.

"At trees." Diaz.

"Trees?"

"Cut the trees apart." Charly.

"Many bullets. Many." Diaz.

"Then they all rode off." Charly.

"Gringos and *Federales* — together." Diaz.

"Where did they go?"

"We don't know." Charly.

"That's when we came back to report."
Diaz.

"That's when you ran out of whiskey."
Battu took another drink.

"That too, Jefe." Charly.

"And to report." Diaz.

"The gringos' gun is from hell." Charly.

"Many bullets. Many." Diaz.

"I know of such a gun," Battu said. "The army has such a gun."

"So do the gringos." Charly.

"Many bullets." Diaz.

Rinaldi spoke for the first time.

"What do we do, Battu?" he asked.

"I have to think about it. They have the girl and that son of a bitch Don Carlos, dead or alive, owes me five hundred."

Jefferson Keys kept his promise.

It took three precisely set dynamite explosions but the wagons were no longer covered by the mountainside they had been under.

The Trespassers did have to do a little digging but the five million in gold bullion was now in the possession of the Trespassers. Shiny as ever, and soon to be stacked and covered in Doc Zeeger's wagon.

It was an amiable task and each of them did his share of the work. It took almost three days and they did not work in silence, not during the day, nor around the campfire at night.

For the first time since they started the trek, none of them was averse to talking.

"What you thinking about, Doc?" Keys lit a cigar.

"I'm thinking about living a little longer than I expected. But hand me one of those cigars anyhow."

Keys did, and lit it for him.

"I'm thinking" — Doc inhaled — "about playing some poker and not caring whether I win or lose, because for the first time I think we've got a chance of getting back . . . and so for the first time I'm thinking about a Colonel named Crook."

"Oh, him."

"He said something about a prison called Joliet . . ."

"Oh, that . . ."

"Yeah, that."

"Think about that poker game instead."

"And a warm woman." Doc smiled.

"That too."

"I might even be thinking about getting married."

"Beats Joliet."

Keys rose.

"William, after we get to Arizona, will you

be going back to Virginia?"

"There's something I've got to do first. Settle a score."

"Does settling a score seem so important anymore?"

"Karla, can we talk about something else?"

"Anything you want." She smiled.

"Anything?"

Billy Joe saw Keys walk by.

"There is something I want to talk about, but . . ."

"But what?"

"It'll have to wait."

"Alright, William."

"Sandusky."

"Jeff."

"How you doing with those ghosts?"

"What ghosts?"

"Good. About that deal we made before we left . . ."

"What about it?"

"You know how much that gold is worth?"

"So?"

"So, I want to change the deal."

"I don't. A deal's a deal."

"We'll see."

"Nothin' to see. Good night."

"Good night, Sandusky."

■ ■ ■ ■

"Elijah."

"Jefferson."

"Cigar?"

"No, thanks . . . I've never seen anything like it."

"Like what?"

"Like the change in the look of that kid's eyes."

"Oh, that."

"Yeah, that. From the way he looks at her, then when you walk by, the way he looks at you. From magnolias to murder."

"He's pretty set in his ways."

"I know how to 'up-set' him and his ways."

"Now, Elijah." Keys smiled. "You wouldn't do anything . . . rash?"

"I wouldn't do anything . . . unjustified."

"We needed him to get in. We're probably going to need him to get out."

"Then what?"

Keys shrugged.

"Every squabble's got to have an end."

"His? Or yours? Besides, this isn't exactly what I'd call a squabble."

"You sure you don't want a cigar?"

"That I'm sure of."

"Good night, Elijah."

"Good night, Jefferson."

"Got a light?"

She closed her lips around the end of the cigarette she had rolled and took a couple of steps behind Keys.

He turned, blew the ash off the edge of his cigar, and let it touch her cigarette until it was lit.

"Thanks."

"You smoke too much."

"Good advice." She smiled. "I'll quit if you will . . . smoking, I mean."

"You know what I think?"

"No, what do you think?"

"I think you'll walk right up to the devil himself, and ask for a light."

"You think I'll get it?"

"The light?"

"What else?" She smiled. "And, besides, it might be the angel Gabriel."

"It might at that . . . or maybe Simon Ignatius Kline."

"You just can't forget him, can you?"

"Why would I want to forget him? He's the one who brought us together . . . isn't he?"

"Maybe it was . . ."

"What?"

"You know what the poet said . . ."

"A lot of poets said a lot of things."

"This one said, 'There is a destiny that shapes our ends.' "

"No, he didn't."

"He didn't?"

"Divinity. 'There is a divinity that shapes our ends, rough-hew them how we will.' Hamlet."

"I knew that, besides . . . destiny, divinity, what's the difference?"

She turned and walked a couple of steps, then turned back, took a deep drag.

"Good night, sweet prince."

I'll be damned, Jefferson Keys thought to himself.

The next morning, all the gold bullion was in Doc Zeeger's wagon, covered and tied down with a heavy tarp and rope, as was the Gatling in Sandusky's wagon. The pack animals were ready and so were they.

The Trespassers started the journey back north.

CHAPTER FORTY-EIGHT

"Well, sir," Captain Bourke said, "lately things have been quieter than they have been since we got to Fort Canby."

Colonel Crook had invited Captain

Bourke and Lieutenant Crane to have supper with him in his quarters.

"I noticed that." Crook cut another slice from his steak.

"Apaches seem settled in on the reservation . . ."

"For the time being," Crook said.

"Yes, sir, and nothing from the comancheros since they hit the Olang ranch. No sign of them at all . . ."

"You think Battu has retired?"

"No, sir. But maybe he's operating someplace else . . ."

"Maybe."

"Permission to ask a personal question, sir?"

"Go ahead, Captain."

"You once mentioned that when things settled down you'd think about sending for Mrs. Crook to come out from Ohio."

"Yes, I did."

"Well, I wonder, sir, if and when you did . . . if it would be alright if I sent for my wife. You know that Cynthia and I had only been married a short time before I joined up with you."

"Yes, I know. What about you, Lieutenant? Are you married?"

"No, sir. I'm not, I . . . I . . ."

"You what?"

302

"I don't even have a . . ."

"Sweetheart?"

"Yes, sir. I mean, no, sir. I don't."

"Too bad. They could all come out and start a sewing circle . . . or something."

"I take it, sir," Bourke concluded, "that you don't think . . ."

"I don't think the time is right, that's right, Captain. I've been in this kind of situation before. The young bucks on the reservation could get restless at any time. So long as Battu is alive he could come back. I keep wondering why Waxer and Kline are hanging around and the same goes for that snake of a gunfighter, Valance."

"He rode out this afternoon, sir," Lieutenant Crane said. "I saw him."

"Good work, Lieutenant. Another thing, I still haven't reported that missing Gatling . . ."

"I'm sorry about that, sir."

"So am I. And I don't know what Keys and his gang are up to, but it's probably up to no good. So I'll tell you something, Captain."

"Yes, sir."

"This could just be the lull before the storm. You're a good officer and I know you miss your bride. So when I do think the time is right and I send for Mary, then you do have my permission to bring out your Cynthia."

"Thank you, sir."

"And as for you, Lieutenant."

"Yes, sir."

"You'll be a good officer too."

"Thank you, sir."

"Someday."

Waxer and Kline waved farewell to Amory Valance as he rode away. Valance did not wave back.

"You think he can round up those men and pull it off?" Waxer asked.

"Either way, we've got little to lose . . . and a lot to gain."

"You're right, Simon." Waxer took a sip of milk. "There's nothing like hedging our bet."

CHAPTER FORTY-NINE

Elijah once again had made his customary circular sweep and joined up with the Trespassers just as they had come to a stop and were about to make preparations for supper and night camp.

With him he had brought three good-size rabbits . . . all three dead.

He held them out toward Elizabeth

Shelby, but Karla intercepted them.

"I'll take 'em. Pretty plump for prairie rabbits . . . they'll make for a good pot of stew . . . after I skin them."

"You skin?" Billy Joe said. "As well as cook?"

"Can't cook" — Karla smiled — "unless you skin. Otherwise it'll make for a pretty hairy stew."

"Let me skin 'em for you, ma'am." Sandusky took hold of them. "Nothin' to it after skinnin' buffalo."

"Thank you, Mister Sandusky."

"Just plain Sandusky, ma'am. Just like the city . . . only it ain't a city. More like a village, back where it's round on the ends and high in the middle . . . O-hi-o."

Karla went on with her preparations as Sandusky went about his skinning.

"Karla," Billy Joe wondered, "back at the ranch, didn't you have any kitchen help?"

"Sure. *I* was the kitchen help. I helped my mother. Sometimes it was just for the three of us in the family, but there were other times when we had to make ready for seven or eight ranch hands at round-up and branding."

"Sounds like it kept you pretty busy."

"Oh, that's besides the other chores. Milking. Feeding the chickens. Slopping hogs.

Carrying . . ."

"Stop! I'm getting tired just listening."

"Didn't you have to work, William?"

"First we had help to do the work, then after the war there was nothing to work on . . . thanks to the Yankees."

"Well, there's some work to be done around here. If you've a mind to, you can peel those onions."

"OK." He nodded. "I'll be your kitchen help . . . only we don't have a kitchen."

They both laughed.

Sandusky brought back the skinned rabbits.

"Would you believe," he said, "that Elijah fella shot these jacks with a bow and arrow?"

"Quieter that way," Elijah said, as he came forward. "In case there's somebody around."

"Was there?" Keys asked. "Somebody around, I mean? See anything?"

"Nothing with two legs."

"Good," Keys said. "Let's hope it stays that way."

"It won't." Doc grunted.

"What makes you say that?" Keys said.

"Experience."

"Just the other day you said you thought we were going to make it."

"No. I said there was a chance we were going to make it."

"Well." Keys smiled. "We're going to."

"You're damn right we are," Elizabeth Shelby said, holding up a ladle, then pointing it toward Doc's wagon, "even if I have to pull that wagonload of gold all the way to Arizona by myself."

"I believe" — Doc wiped at his whiskers — "she could at that."

"So do I." Keys smiled, then looked at the onion peeler. "Say, Billy Joe, what're you crying about?"

Later, as Keys was spreading out his bedroll, Billy Joe Bickford came up beside him.

"I want to talk to you."

"Sure, Billy Joe. What is it?"

"About something you said earlier."

"You mean about crying?" Keys smiled. "I was just joshing. Don't take it . . ."

"No. Not that. Something you said earlier."

"OK, but I can't imagine what it is."

"Can't you?"

"No, I can't. Shoot . . . now don't get me wrong. I don't mean that literally."

"Never mind the jokes."

"Alright, if this is going to be serious, go ahead and be serious."

"Were you serious when you said you were from Virginia? Born and raised."

"Clifton Forge. You can't get much more Virginia than that."

"That being the case, I've got one more question to ask you."

"Ask away."

"What is it that makes a Southerner, a Virginian, turn into a skunk and go against his own kind . . . against his neighbors, against his native soil? Will you answer that, Mister Skunk?"

"I will, Mister Bickford. I'll answer for some of us other skunks at West Point. First of all, let me tell you that two of my best friends at the Point were George Armstrong Custer and J.E.B. Stuart. At the Point if I had to choose between the two of them, I don't know which one I would have picked. But that wasn't the choice."

"What was?"

"The choice was between my native soil and neighbors, as you put it, and something else . . . actually two something elses. Two pieces of paper."

"What the hell are you talking about?"

"One of those papers said, *'All men are created equal.'* The other said, *'In order to form a more perfect union.'* The Declaration of Independence and The Constitution.

That's the choice I had to make, a lot of us had to make. Your father chose gray. I chose blue."

"Not if it meant the destruction of your home."

"It *did* mean the destruction of my home . . . but not of my country. I respect your father's choice. I think he would have respected mine. Does that answer your question?"

"No."

Billy Joe turned and walked away.

Elijah came out of the shadows.

"He just won't let go," Elijah said.

"I didn't expect him to."

"What do you expect?"

"Right now, I expect . . . to get some sleep."

CHAPTER FIFTY

It hit like a tornado.

That's because it probably was a tornado — or a part of one.

Sometimes called twister — whirlwind — duster — tempest — sirocco — squall — dust devil — sometimes son of a bitch.

But whatever they want to call it, it comes out of nowhere and wants to leave nothing, or little, in its wake but destruction.

Luckily, they saw it coming.

Elijah did.

He rode back like his saddle was on fire.

"Get behind those rocks!" he yelled and pointed to an outcrop. "Everybody, everything, behind those rocks!"

Keys took up the cry and did his best to herd the caravan to the leeside of a formation of brown boulders.

Elizabeth Shelby, Billy Joe, Karla and the pack animals, Doc and Sandusky with the wagons, all headed for what shelter there was, and there wasn't much. Not from the roaring maelstrom.

It sounded like a freight train and hit like a spout out of hell — seething — churning — swirling — pitching — plunging — roiling — penetrating.

Pummeling everybody and everything with dust — dirt — sand — grime — painting and penetrating — blinding — all of them huddled close to the ground, bending with hands across faces, backs to the holocaust.

For how long, they couldn't tell. There isn't that kind of time in clocks. It seemed like hours, but in fact, it was less than ten minutes.

Then as suddenly as it appeared, it disappeared.

The dust, dirt, sand and sound — all gone. Silence.

Then Keys' voice.

"Everybody alright?"

"No. Goddammit!" Doc's voice. "Not alright. At least not the animals and sure as hell not the supplies."

Doc walked all over, inspecting and cursing — spitting dirt out of his mouth between curses.

"Take it easy, Doc," Keys said, "or you'll have a heart attack."

"I've already had two."

"Well, take it easy or you'll give us all one. Now, how bad is it?"

"It's bad enough, but give me a few minutes and I'll tell you exactly. Sandusky, I'll need your help."

"Got it."

"Miss Shelby?"

"Yes, Mister Keys."

"Are you alright?"

"This time I really need a bath."

"Other than that?"

"I'll survive."

"Karla? Billy Joe?"

"I'm fine," Karla said, "thanks to William. He was practically on top of me."

"Nice going, Billy Joe." Keys smiled. "Elijah?"

Elijah nodded.

"Good," Keys said.

"Bad," Doc said. "Everything's ruined. All our supplies except for the air-tights, and we ain't got too many of those. All the food full of dust and dirt and can't be separated out. Not fit to eat. Dirt went right through the burlap and deep into everything. And the animals need attention — some damn nearly went blind or will unless attended to. And the wagons, wheels, axels — all covered with dirt. Got to be cleaned and greased. We're dead in the water — except there ain't any water — and that about covers it."

"It sure as hell does," Sandusky chimed, "except for the Gatling."

"Alright," Keys said, "alright. We're still afloat and we're still going to make it."

"How?" Billy Joe inquired.

"I'll tell you how. We've been avoiding towns and villages all along the line. Well, there's one not more than five miles from here — Villa Nueva — remember, Doc?"

"I remember. We had a little set-to there. Store. Saloon. Stable. Not much else."

"We don't need much else. Doc, can you come with me?"

"Hell, no. Sandusky and me have got to stay here and tend to the animals and wagons."

"And the Gatling," Sandusky added.

"Right. Make out a list of the supplies we need most. Elijah and I'll ride — no — Elijah, you better stay here and guard the camp."

"I'll go with you."

"Alright, Billy Joe, you and I'll ride in with a couple of the pack mules, the ones in best shape, and bring back enough for us to keep going." Keys smiled. "Just as sure as there's an 's' in Mississippi."

"Did you say 'ass'?" Elizabeth said.

"That too," Keys replied.

Chapter Fifty-One

Of the five or so miles from camp to Villa Nueva, Keys and Billy Joe Bickford on horse back and with the pack mules had covered about half the distance with less than a dozen words, not counting those to the mules, who wanted to move at their own pace, if at all.

Finally Billy Joe broke the silence between them with a complete sentence.

"Are you sure we're on the right road to this place . . . what's it called?"

"Called Villa Nueva and I'm sure."

"You said it was five miles."

"I did."

"Seems to me as if we've already come five miles."

"Just over three."

"Seems like five."

"Maybe it's the company," Keys said.

"Maybe it is at that. Heard Doc say you had a little 'set-to' there."

"And other places."

"In Mexico?"

"In Mexico."

"One war wasn't enough for you?"

"Even one war is one too many."

"Then why . . . ?"

"Why fight?"

"Yes, that's right. Why?"

"Somebody has to. As the man said, there is a special place reserved in hell for those who do nothing. The trick is to pick the right side."

"You mean the winning side."

"Not always."

"Seems like you do."

"Not always. Sometimes the lost causes are the ones worth fighting for."

"Like my father did?"

"Like your father did. Villa Nueva is just beyond the next bend."

"What sort of a 'set-to' was it?"

"At Villa Nueva?"

"At Villa Nueva."

"Nothing that'll ever be remembered in any history books."

The rest of the way they rode in silence — except when they spoke to the pack mules.

Keys and Billy Joe pulled up in front of the combination General Store–Stable, dismounted and tied the animals to the hitching post.

Billy Joe looked up and down the main street.

"Seems like everybody in town is taking a siesta."

"Too early for siesta."

"Then why's the street deserted?"

"Don't know. But the store's open."

Keys went in. Billy Joe followed.

The store also seemed deserted.

"Buenos dias!" Keys shouted. *"Hola!"*

A curtain that led to a back room was pulled aside slightly. A face peered through.

"Senor Jeff!!"

A man, short, stocky, mustachioed, stepped through the curtains, rushed toward Keys and threw both arms around him.

"Senor Jeff . . . my friend." He looked back toward the other room. "Benito! Benito, come out. Come here. Look! It's our friend, Senor Jefferson Keys come to see us!"

A boy, not more than fourteen, came into

the room smiling.

"Senor Jeff, do you remember my boy, Benito?"

"Of course I do, Andres, but now he's about a foot closer to the ceiling. Andres Martinez, Benito, this is my friend Billy Joe Bickford."

Andres Martinez extended his hand.

"Any friend of Senor Jeff, the liberator of Villa Nueva, is more than welcome."

"Cut out that 'liberator' stuff, Andres."

"It is true." Andres looked at Billy Joe. "Have you not heard what he did during the time we were occupied by the forces of Maximilian?"

"No." Billy Joe looked at Keys, then back to Martinez. "Tell me about it."

"Forget it, Andres," Keys said.

"Who can forget it?"

"Go ahead and tell me."

"Over a hundred of Maximilian's army had occupied our village and set up a barricade. They knew the Juaristas were coming, but only twenty or thirty of them, so they were ready with rifles behind the barricade.

"And then on the road out of the dawning sun, a wagon — pulled by four horses — a man cracking the reins — a lighted cheroot between his teeth — faster came the wagon

— the man, Senor Keys, swung down into the wagon bed, shielded by the driver's seat — bullets flying past him and into the wagon — taking the burning cheroot from his teeth — touching it to the end of a fuse attached to a stick of dynamite — the wagon is loaded with more dynamite — the horses gallop faster — Senor Jeff climbs below the driver's seat to where the tongue is attached to the wagon — more bullets fly by — he reaches down — pulls the cotter pin — now, rifle in hand, jumps from the wagon — horses swerve one way — the wagon straight ahead into the barricade — explosions — BOOM! BOOM! BOOM!

"Bodies here — there — everywhere — the occupiers scatter — Senor Jeff and the Juaristas charge through. Victory! Liberation!"

"You left out the most important thing, Andres."

"What was that?"

"You and all the other villagers with guns, machetes, pitchforks, rocks — everything they could get a hold of — swarmed into the fight and that's what won the day."

"We helped." Andres grinned. "But without you — helpless." He turned to Billy Joe. "Your friend did that, Senor Billy Joe."

"And that's what you called a 'set-to'?"

Billy Joe said, turning to Keys. "Not remembered in any history books?"

Keys just shrugged.

"But you haven't told me, my friend," Andres said, "what brings you to Villa Nueva, to Mexico? Are you here to help Juarez again?"

"No. Not this time. We had a job to do and we did it. There are seven of us, on our way back to Arizona and we got hit by a duster — tornado — hit bad. Not far from here. Our supplies got ruined." Keys took a piece of paper out of his pocket. "Here's a list of supplies we need. Thought maybe we could get them from you."

Andres took the paper and studied it, not for long.

"Yes. I can provide most of this, or something close to them. We heard about the tornado."

"Good. That will be of great help, my friend."

"Speaking of friends," Martinez said, "how is your friend — and mine — Doc Zeeger? Have you seen him since Mexico? Is he . . . in good health?"

"Saw him this morning. He's one of the seven on the job we came to do. His health? Better than before we started. He'll live to be a hundred."

"Good. Very good. He too fought valiantly that day. Give him my warm greetings."

"I will. But" — Keys looked at Billy Joe, then back to Martinez — "we were wondering about something here in Nueva . . ."

"Why there is no one outside in the streets?"

"That's it." Keys nodded.

"It is a bad time here. Very bad."

"Why?" Billy Joe asked.

"Six *pistoleros* rode in two days ago. They have taken over our village . . ."

"Six men," Billy Joe said, "take over a whole town?"

"Very bad *hombres.* Killed three people, including our sheriff. Every one is afraid. Stay inside. Maybe they go away, but not yet."

"Where are these bad men?" Keys asked.

"Where else? The cantina. They drink. Shoot off their guns. People are afraid. I am afraid."

"But you keep your store open," Keys said.

"They told me to. They come and take things. Don't pay. Very bad."

"You fought against greater odds — against Maximilian's army — now six *pistoleros* have cowed all of you. I don't believe . . ."

"We thought they might go away . . ."

319

"Or they might kill some more before they go away . . . if they go away."

Martinez closed his eyes for a moment, then shuddered. He turned to his son.

"Benito, go outside. Take our friends' animals to the stable. I'll get the supplies." He looked back at Keys. "Best you leave before they know you are here."

"They probably already know," Keys said.

"Benito, go."

Benito went.

"Billy Joe. I'd like a cold beer; how about you?"

"You picking the right side this time?" Billy Joe asked.

"I don't think we have much choice. You know damn well they saw us come in. They're not going to let us sneak out. You want that cold beer?"

"I believe I do." Billy Joe smiled.

"No! Please, my friend. Three of them are brothers. One is a giant, maybe seven feet tall. You can not reason with them . . ."

"Who's going to reason? Just going to have a beer and be on our way. Better than being ambushed with all our animals and supplies. Don't you think, Mister Bickford?"

"For once I agree, Mister Keys."

"We'll see you later, Andres."

"I hope so."

Keys and Billy Joe walked out the door and toward the cantina.

There was a man standing in front of the cantina. When he saw the two of them approaching, he turned and walked back inside.

Keys and Billy Joe entered side by side and looked around.

There were six men in the room. One was the biggest living creature Keys and Bickford had ever seen without hair all over its body. Three of them looked alike — all three like hogs. One of the hogs was obviously the leader. He rose and smiled.

"Hello, strangers. My name's Trace. Trace Watkins. You Americans?"

The strangers nodded.

"So are we." Trace smiled. "Sometimes. What're you doing here in this Mex town?"

"Thought we'd have a beer and be on our way," Keys said.

"Sure," Trace said, still smiling. "Joe, draw these fellow Americans a beer."

Joe, one of the nonbrothers behind the bar, pulled a lever and filled two glasses with beer and slid them down the bar.

As Keys and Bickford started to move, another nonbrother slugged Keys from behind with the barrel of a gun and the giant grabbed Billy Joe by both arms and pinned them behind his back. Another took both his guns and tossed them on a table.

Before Keys could stagger to his feet his gun was also in the palm of a *pistolero's* grip.

"Oh, I forgot to tell you," Trace said, "we don't welcome strangers, not here or any place. No strangers ever good news'd us, or bought us a beer."

"We can do without the beer," Keys managed to say.

"You're gonna do without a lot of things — like living — for starters."

"Gimme the word, Trace," the giant said, "and I'll snap this one's neck."

"That sounds like a good idea." Trace nodded. "Go ahead and snap."

In that instant there was the sound of a snap.

But not Billy Joe's neck.

A bullwhip.

It snapped off part of the giant's left ear — in the next instant, the giant's right ear was gone — blood spurting.

Both the giant's hands went to the sides of his head. He screamed in pain.

Billy Joe dove for his guns on the table.

Keys slugged the *pistolero* next to him and grabbed his gun.

Elijah's whip snaked again, this time

around Trace's neck with the sharp crack of bone.

Billy Joe fired twice. Two *pistoleros* dropped.

Keys fired. Another fell.

Through the doorway Andres and four other citizens stormed in with smoking guns.

Six men lay on the floor of the cantina dead as beaver pelts. Elijah walked over to Trace's body and unwound the whip from around the dead man's broken neck.

"Hello, Elijah," Keys said, "I'm glad you dropped by. So's Billy Joe. Arcn't you, Billy Joe?"

Billy Joe holstered both guns — then nodded.

"Thought you might need company," Elijah said. "Everything's quiet at the camp."

"Good." Keys turned to Andres Martinez and his *compañeros*. "Like old times, my friend."

"*Sí,* Senor Jeff. Like old times."

"Supplies about ready?"

"Just about." Martinez smiled.

"Fine. You'll see that these people get buried?"

"Good and proper, Senor Jeff."

"You'll excuse us," Keys said, "if we don't

stay for the funerals."

CHAPTER FIFTY-TWO

"Those mules don't want to move much," Billy Joe said, "or hardly at all . . . just poking along."

"They're overloaded," Elijah noted.

"And stubborn," Keys added, ". . . need encouraging."

"With Elijah's whip?" Billy Joe smiled.

"Not that much. Used to have the same trouble on cattle drives."

"Don't tell me you did that too." Billy Joe pushed the hat lower on his forehead.

"Did what?"

"Drove cattle."

"Across the Red River to Abilene. Three times. Last time as trail boss. Ol' Ned got sick — buried him along the way."

"And you took over . . . as usual."

"Somebody had to."

"Seems like that somebody's always you."

"Not always."

"What did you do?"

"About what?"

"About those slow-poke cattle."

"Sometimes we sang to 'em."

"Did it work?"

"Sometimes."

"Well then . . . why don't you try it on the mules?" Billy Joe suggested.

"You mean sing 'em the old drovers' song?"

"That's what I mean."

"What do you think, Elijah?"

"If the mules can take it . . . so can I."

Keys pushed his horse ahead, abreast of the lead mule, began to whistle, then sing.

There was an old cowboy called Ned,
With more miles behind than ahead,
Saddle-worn and trail-dusted,
On a horse that he trusted,
He pushed the young drovers ahead.
He whistled a tune as he led,
Then here's what the old trail boss said.

Put the sun in your pocket,
Put it there but don't lock it,
Save it for a rainy day.
See that lightning, hear that thunder,
Tearing blue skies asunder,
Warning herds that are under,
There's trouble along the way.

The trail will get dreary
And at night you'll be weary,
But take the sun from your pocket,
Let it lift like a rocket,

And the sun from your pocket
Will light a new day.

Keep them beeves tight and clustered,
Don't let 'em get flustered,
And the sun from your pocket
Will show them the way.

Put the sun in your pocket,
Put it there, but don't lock it,
Save it for a rainy day.

"I'll be damned," Billy Joe said. "They're moving right along."

"Said it works sometimes." Keys smiled.

"Maybe they just want to get away from your singing." Elijah grinned.

"You believe that?" Bickford asked.

"That they want to get away from my singing? Probably."

"No. About putting the sun in your pocket."

"In a way, I do."

"How?"

"Well, when things get rough and you think about something . . . I don't know . . . something good, sweet, strong, worthwhile . . . maybe something good will happen."

"Like what?"

"Like Elijah showing up with his bullwhip. That's what . . . and there's our camp just ahead."

Chapter Fifty-Three

"You think they're happier to see us — or the mules?" Elijah smiled.

"I think it's a toss-up," Keys replied.

It wasn't.

No contest.

At that moment there was more of a feeling of camaraderie in the camp than there had been since the caravan crossed the border.

Instinctively, Karla Olang ran to Billy Joe Bickford and stopped just short of throwing both her arms around him.

Elizabeth Shelby sauntered up to Keys with an unlit cigarette between her lips.

"Got a light?"

Keys took a match out of his pocket and struck it against the butt of his revolver.

"Can't shake the habit, huh?"

"Which habit you talking about?"

Keys let the flame touch the edge of her cigarette.

"Nicotine," Keys said.

"Oh, *that* habit."

Doc Zeeger made his way almost between them.

"Did you manage to get most of what was on the list?"

"Yep."

"Didn't happen to run into our friend Martinez, did you?"

"He's the one we got the supplies from. Sends you his warmest greetings. Son Benito's grown a foot and a half."

"Good. I s'pose," Doc said, "these days Villa Nueva's a sleepy little village."

"There's six" — Billy Joe took a step closer — "sleeping from here to eternity."

"How's that?" Doc frowned.

"We also had a little 'set-to' in Villa Nueva. Didn't we, Mister Keys?"

"Yes, we did, Mister Bickford."

"Six dead men ago," Billy Joe added.

"William!" This time Karla did put both her hands on Billy Joe's arms. "Are you alright?"

"Just fine." And after a slight pause, he pointed to Elijah. "Thanks to a timely entrance by this man and his companion."

"What companion?" Sandusky asked. "We saw you leave here alone."

"Not quite." Keys looked at Elijah. "Say, you got a name for that friend of yours?"

"Call her Cleo," Elijah said straight-faced, "short for Cleopatra."

"Yeah." Keys smiled. "She can wrap

herself around you. Is that it?"

It appeared as if Elijah was actually blushing, but then, it was hard to tell.

"Were there any senoritas?" Elizabeth inhaled the cigarette. "In that sleepy little village?"

"Come to think of it," Keys said, "I don't recall any. Do you, Mister Bickford?"

"No, I don't, Mister Keys. But something I *do* recall."

"What's that?"

"We never did have that beer."

"Alright," Doc said, "enough of this reminiscin'. Let's get them mules unloaded."

"Right." Keys nodded. "Doc, how are the rest of the animals and wagons?"

"They'll do," Doc answered.

"So'll the Gatling." Sandusky winked.

"Good. By morning we'll be heading north."

As he turned, Elizabeth Shelby was standing close to him with a fresh unlit cigarette between her lips.

"Got a light?"

A short time later Elijah, from a distance, had signaled to Keys. Keys nodded, moved away from the rest of the Trespassers, and stood next to the signaler.

"I've seen that look on your face before."

"Yeah, I guess you have."

"Usually means there's something on that wary mind of yours."

"Yeah, it does."

"What is it this time?"

"Couple of things. Tell you better when I get back."

"Back? Back from where?"

"There's plenty of daylight left. Be back by dark . . . or shortly after. Didn't want to leave without letting you know."

"Alright. Now I know."

Elijah nodded.

"See you later."

Keys nodded.

"Elijah."

"Yeah?"

"No need to say it, but I'm going to . . . thanks for getting us out of that tight spot."

"You're right. No need to say it. You'd've done the same for me . . . Matter of fact . . . you have."

Elijah mounted and headed north.

"Where's he going?" Elizabeth Shelby asked Keys.

"Fishing."

"Fishing?"

"Fishing."

"We're in the desert," she said. "There's no fish around here."

"I guess" — Keys shrugged — "he was misinformed."

The rest of the Trespassers had supper together . . . but as usual, not altogether together.

Doc next to Sandusky.

Karla Olang next to Billy Joe Bickford.

Elizabeth Shelby next to Keys.

"Still thinking about that poker game?" Sandusky slid a spoonful of hot beans into his mouth.

"And that warm woman." Doc gulped down a mouthful of hot coffee.

"And the . . . odds?"

"That too."

"What are they now, Doc?"

"What's the difference? We're playing with house money."

"That's one way to look at it."

"Only way. What're you thinking of . . . besides beans?"

"The good earth."

"Of Ohio?"

"Yep. I'd like to be buried there . . . but I'm in no hurry . . . say after ten, twelve crops."

"Would you settle for five?"

"I'd settle" — Sandusky slid another

spoonful of beans into his mouth — "for one."

"William . . ."

"Yes, ma'am."

"There you go again . . ."

"Sorry . . . Karla."

"Earlier you said something about what happened in that town . . ."

"Villa Nueva."

"Yes, Villa Nueva . . . you said 'six dead men ago,' didn't you?"

"I did."

"You killed them?"

"Not all six. All six are dead, mind you, but I didn't kill all six. There was Keys, Elijah, and then . . ."

"William."

"Yes."

"Why did you kill them?"

"Because they were trying to kill us."

"Why?"

"Why what?"

"Why were they trying to kill you?"

"I really don't know. They didn't much talk about it. They took over the town. They didn't like us being there — so they had it in mind to kill us. Damn near did — oh, excuse me — almost did — before we killed them."

"And how many did *you* kill?"

"Just my share. Why? You keeping track?"

"No, but are you?"

"Keeping track?"

"Yes."

"No, Karla, I'm not. But I'll tell you this, I've never killed anybody who wasn't trying to kill me first — not so far."

"What does that mean? 'So far?' "

"I don't know what it means. It just came out. Seems like no matter what I say, Karla, you take it wrong."

"I'm sorry, William, I don't mean to, it's just that . . ."

"That what?"

"It's just the way I was brought up. Until that day when those people broke into our house, killed my father and took my mother and me, I had never seen, or even thought about, any real violence. I'm beholden to all of you for saving my life, but ever since then, that's all I've ever seen or heard about — violence, killing."

"Karla, like I said, I just did my share. What about Keys and Elijah and . . ."

"William, I said I'm beholden to all of you, but . . ."

"But what?"

"Well, I don't feel about them the way I feel about . . . you."

"You don't?"

"Of course not. Don't you know that by now? Can't you tell . . ."

"Oh, God!"

"What is it?"

"I . . . I just wish we were someplace else."

"Where?"

"Anyplace where . . ."

"Where what?"

"Where there weren't any other people around and I could . . . Oh, God, what am I saying? Have I gone crazy? I don't even recognize myself."

"Sure you do, William. Maybe for the first time you realize who you really are."

"And who's that?"

"Someone with the same feelings as other people . . . people who don't rely just on those guns."

"Maybe so. But I'll tell you something else, Karla."

"Go ahead."

"Those guns . . . sure came in handy over at Villa Nueva."

"Young love." Elizabeth nodded toward Karla Olang and Billy Joe Bickford.

"You say 'love' like it was a dirty word."

"Oh, I forgot, you were in love once."

"Let's skip that."

"You're right. That was a dirty crack. I apologize. Got a light? And don't lecture me about that vice."

He lit her cigarette, then his cigar.

"What would life be," Keys said, "without a vice or two?"

"Or three or four?" She motioned over toward Karla and Billy Joe. "But for the two of them I don't think it's love . . . or ever could be."

"Why not?"

"Because he's already in love . . . or hadn't you noticed?"

"What do you mean?"

"Just what I said. He's already in love . . . with those two guns strapped around his waist. And a leopard doesn't change his stripes."

"Spots."

"What?"

"Spots. A tiger has stripes; a leopard has spots."

"Don't get technical. You know damn well what I mean."

"You don't think people can change?"

"Usually for the worse."

"You're just being cynical."

"It's a cynical world. I ought to know. Besides, you've got a reason for wanting him to change. You think if he does, maybe you two won't have to face each other."

"Oh, that."

"Yeah, that."

"Well, he could change . . . *after* we do face each other . . . if he's still alive."

"If he is — and to tell you the truth, I'm not sure either way — it'll be too late for him and her. Because she'll never look at him the way she does now. And that's not being cynical — just realistic — because every time she looks at him she'll be thinking about the man he killed — you."

"You think so?"

"I think so. She's young and impressionable — and that's the impression she'll have of him as long as she lives."

"Well then, I guess there's no easy answer."

"There never is."

"She's not that much younger than you."

"Oh, yes, she is. I'm as old as the oldest story ever told."

"Oh, that again."

"That again."

"Suppose you get all that money, won't you forget about San Francisco and . . ."

"How the hell could I ever forget about San Francisco?"

"I mean won't you go someplace else and . . ."

"Someplace else? Hell no. I'd go right back — only this time on my own terms.

336

I'd build a mansion on Nob Hill — the biggest and best — imported furniture, clothes made in Paris, a carriage trimmed with gold, a box at the opera. I'd buy my way into high society with donations to all the right charities and . . . and I know what you're thinking . . ."

"What am I thinking?"

"What if I run into some of my old . . . clients from Madam Pleasant's high-class whorehouse?"

"What if you did?"

"I probably will, and I hope I do, because then I'd probably smile — or spit in their face — because either way, the sons of bitches would be more reluctant to admit it than I would. And I'd lord it over them like the queen of England. How do you like them apples?"

"They're your apples, queenie. If that's what you'd like to do — do it."

"Well, I must say, your attitude surprises me."

"Yours doesn't, but in the meanwhile . . ."

"In the meanwhile, what?"

"A man called Elijah has returned."

Elizabeth Shelby had put together a tin plate of hot food and poured coffee into a tin cup. Elijah sat cross-legged near Keys, who smoked what was left of his cigar.

"Before I left, I said . . ."

"Elijah, go ahead and eat your supper, then we can talk."

"Why? I can chew and talk at the same time."

"Go ahead then."

"Well, first off, I was wondering about those two trackers . . ."

"Yeah, so was I."

"Last I saw them was before we hit the Yaquis."

"Right."

"So, I was wondering if they were still tracking us."

"And?"

"And the answer is no."

"You sure?"

"Sure as I can be under the circumstances, circumstances being that there was no sign of them, of a camp, or of any tracks, or any kind of signs that they or anybody else was dogging us."

"I'd take that as favorable, wouldn't you?"

"Partly yes."

"What's the other part?"

"Parts. One, why'd they quit? Two, who the hell are they, and three, where'd they go?"

"Any thoughts?"

Elijah chewed and nodded.

"I got to figure they're comancheros from Battu's bunch."

"Not bad figuring. What else?"

"No matter how we zigzag, in order to get back to Arizona, we got to go through Battu's terrain."

"So?"

"So I'm damn sorry we didn't kill 'em like we talked about, before they got away."

"So am I, but things happened too fast. First, Elizabeth being taken by those damn Yaquis, then Ruiz showing up, then hitting the stronghold, going after the gold, the duster. We had too many things on our minds."

"Yeah, but now we got to have *them* on our mind. If I spot 'em again I've got to kill 'em. You agree?"

"Be my guest. What else?"

"Won't be too long before we come across those three graves . . ."

"Don Carlos and company."

"Right."

"Well, he's dead at the present time."

"The lead wolf is dead alright, but what about the rest of the pack? They might be in the mood for a little revenge — and also to collect . . ."

"Karla?"

Elijah nodded and took a swallow of coffee.

"Well, Mister Elijah, we can zig and zag from here to doomsday — and if there were just the two of us maybe we could make ourselves invisible in this terrain — but not seven of us with slow-going wagons and pack mules, now, could we?"

"No, Mister Keys, we couldn't. So?"

"So, we do what my former commander, the boy general, George Armstrong Custer, would do . . ."

"What's that?"

"Go straight ahead. 'Ride to the sound of the guns.' But in this case hope we don't run into any."

"What if we do?" came a voice out of the darkness, then a body belonging to Elizabeth Shelby. "Then what?"

"You sure," Keys said to her, "you don't have some of that Yaqui blood in you? You certain as hell know how to sneak up like an Indian. Doesn't she, Elijah?"

"She sure does, and I ought to know, I'm part Indian myself."

"I'll ask it again," she said, "then what?"

"Then we fight," Keys said, " 'til we die — or they do."

Chapter Fifty-Four

"Senor Battu, permit me to introduce myself." He removed his sombrero, smiled sanctimoniously, and bowed from the waist as he stood next to Rinaldi and the two co-mancheros who brought him into the camp.

"I've permitted you to come this far. Go ahead and introduce."

"I am Miguel Smith."

"Smith? What the hell kind of a name is that? You a breed?"

"*Sí.* My father is unknown except for being a gringo who sailed away before I was born . . ."

"Alright, Miguel Smith, that's enough biography. Get to the point. You told my men you were sent here with a message."

"That is correct."

"Who's the message from and what is the message?"

"I am an emissary of . . ."

"Emissary?"

"Correct. That means . . ."

"I know what it means. You talk like a politician. Cut out the bullshit and talk straight."

"Yes, Senor Battu. I am an emissary of Don Ricardo Morales . . ."

"Who the hell is Don Ricardo Morales?"

Miguel Smith bowed again, then placed the sombrero back on his head.

"Don Ricardo Morales is the successor to Don Carlos Mondego."

"Successor?" Battu looked around at his men.

"*Sí,* Senor Battu, that means . . ."

"I know what that means, you son of a bitch. That means that Don Carlos Mondego is dead."

"Exactly. Dead."

"Continue."

"Don Ricardo — Don Carlos' successor — has sent me to tell you, pardon, to ask you to meet with him and come to an agreement."

"What kind of agreement?"

"I am only an emissary, Senor Battu, empowered only to deliver a message. The rest is up to you and Don Ricardo when you meet."

"*If* we meet."

"That too is up to you, but I believe Don Carlos' successor Don Ricardo wants to talk business."

"Business, huh?"

"*Sí,* business."

"Well, Don Carlos, dead or alive, owes me five hundred. Is that what Don Ricardo, his successor, wants to talk about?"

Miguel Smith shrugged.

"I am only an em . . ."

"Yes, yes, I know . . . emissary."

Miguel Smith nodded and smiled.

"Where does this Don Ricardo want to meet? Will he come here?"

"Oh, no, Senor Battu. The message he asked me to deliver includes the request that you meet him at the same place you used to meet Don Carlos."

"Chupadero Flats?"

"Exactly. Chupadero Flats."

"When?"

"Soon."

"How soon?"

"Soon as I deliver this message. He will be there with six of his men and he requests you come with six of your comancheros."

"Why the hell do we need so many with us, just to meet and talk business? Don Carlos and I used to meet with three men with each of us."

"I do not know the answer to that, Senor Battu. I am just an . . ."

"Yes, yes, I know. Go back and tell him we will meet tomorrow, noon."

"Very good, Senor Battu. With your kind permission I will leave now and see you tomorrow at noon."

"You?"

"Of course. I am privileged to be one of Don Ricardo's six. And now, having delivered the message, I . . ."

"Good-bye and get the hell out! You're giving me a headache with all your bullshit!"

"Thank you very much, Senor Battu." Miguel Smith bowed again. "And Godspeed."

"Get out!"

"No fire to night," Keys had said, "nor any other night 'til I say so. Cold camp. Don't want to draw any attention when we can't see what's out there. We'll eat something hot at noon when a fire won't make much difference."

"Good idea," Doc agreed. "I'll take the first watch after some cold beans and jerky."

"I'll relieve you in two hours if that's OK with you, Jeff," Sandusky said.

"Fine."

"I'll take the third watch," Elijah volunteered.

"No. I will," Keys said. "Give those eyes of yours some rest."

"Then I'll take the watch after yours," Billy Joe spoke to Keys, "if that's satisfactory?"

"It is. Let's have some of those cold beans and jerky."

"That's our department." Elizabeth

Shelby smiled. "Let's get to it, Karla."

The Trespassers ate.

"You're supposed to be giving those eyes a rest."

Elijah sat cross-legged, leaning against a rock, with his eyes wide open.

"They are resting."

"Don't you ever sleep?"

"I was sleeping." Elijah smiled.

"Well, you got a funny way of sleeping."

"Indian sleep."

"You're only part Indian."

"Yeah, but sometimes I can't tell which part."

"Neither can I. Well, Mister Part Indian, go back to sleep. It's my watch."

Keys moved out.

"I brought you some cold coffee."

"That's a good way to get shot, Miss Shelby, creeping up in the middle of the night like that."

"I wasn't creeping. You want that cold coffee?"

"Sure."

She handed him the tin cup and sat next to him.

"Mind if I sit down?"

"Looks to me like you're already sitting."

"So I am. Give me a sip of that coffee, will you?"

"Sure."

She drank and handed the cup back to him.

"Nothing worse," she said, "than a cup of cold coffee."

"Except a cold woman."

"I wouldn't know."

"No, you wouldn't."

"I keep thinking about what you said."

"What did I say? I forget."

"About riding to the sound of the guns . . . about fighting 'til we die . . . or they do . . . wasn't that it?"

"It was. But I don't even know who the hell *they* are. Might be comancheros. Might be Don Carlos' men. Might be anybody down here. But even if we gave up the gold, I don't think we'd get out alive . . . oh, hell . . . I guess I shouldn't have said that."

"And I guess you can't help it."

"Help what?"

"Telling the truth."

"Usually it's the best way." He drank the rest of the coffee and set the cup on the ground.

"Jeff, would you do something?"

"What?"

"Put your arm around me."

"Sure . . . Red."

CHAPTER FIFTY-FIVE

He dismounted from the coal-black, silver-saddled stallion that had formerly belonged to Don Carlos Mondego. Six soldados, Miguel Smith among them, also dismounted and stood by their horses.

He moved forward and extended his right hand.

Battu stood in the foreground beside his animal. Behind him, next to their horses, were six of his comancheros, including Rinaldi, Charly and Diaz.

A gentle breeze whispered across Chupadero Flats. The day was warm and clear. A mild sky — a milder wind.

"Senor Battu, I am Don Ricardo Morales, Don Carlos' cousin."

Battu and Morales smiled and shook hands.

"I did not know Don Carlos had a cousin."

"Neither did he until after he died."

Don Ricardo's face was that of a man without a soul. A face that, even with a smile, revealed nothing.

Miguel Smith started to move forward as if to join the twosome.

"Keep that one away." Battu pointed. "He gives me a headache."

Don Ricardo turned and looked at his emissary, who stopped frozen for an instant, then backed away.

"I see," Don Ricardo said, "that you have brought six of your men as we agreed."

"I always keep an agreement."

"So do I." Don Ricardo motioned toward his soldados.

"I can count. I also can see that you now have Don Carlos' horse."

"And everything else."

"Why have I not seen you before, Don Ricardo? I have done much business with Don Carlos."

"Because, Senor Battu, I have always made it my business to remain in the background until the appropriate time."

"And now you are no longer in the background."

"That is correct and that is why I wanted to meet with you."

"Now we have met. Now what?"

"In the past you have provided Don Carlos with much that was necessary for his business . . ."

"And pleasure."

"Correct again. And I wanted to assure you that as far as I am concerned we can still go on with that arrangement in the future. An arrangement that will continue to be profitable for both sides."

"An arrangement whereby I take many chances on both sides of the border."

"And reap many benefits. You understand that I have to be . . . discreet."

"And I don't. Is that it?"

"Precisely. You're in a position to provide . . ."

"Yes. Yes. I know what you need . . . and what I can provide."

"Good. Then we understand each other and can continue to do business along the same lines."

"You say that you have taken over all that belonged to Don Carlos."

"Obviously."

"Then there is a matter to be settled."

"What is that?"

"An obligation."

"Obligation?"

"A debt. To me."

"Senor Battu, I know of no such debt."

"Then I will inform you."

"Please do."

"Don Carlos owes me five hundred from our last transaction."

"What transaction is that?"

"I delivered to him one beautiful, untouched gringo girl for two thousand. He had only fifteen hundred with him and agreed to pay the remaining five hundred . . . which I never received. Since you have assumed everything, I expect to collect the five hundred from you. Is that not a fair expectation?"

"Oh, no, Senor Battu, I do not think so."

"Why not?"

"Where is this gringo girl now?"

"I do not know," Battu lied.

"Well, since I never received . . . the merchandise . . . have never even seen it, why should I be obliged to pay?"

"A matter of honor, Don Ricardo."

"On both sides, Senor Battu."

Battu looked back at Rinaldi, who responded with a slight shrug of both shoulders.

"Surely a man of your eminence, Senor Battu, does not look to a subordinate for counsel."

"I look to no one but myself . . . for anything."

A momentary pause.

"What about half?" Battu suggested. "Two hundred and fifty. As evidence of honor . . . and good faith."

"Miguel. Bring me my saddlebag."

Miguel Smith scurried to the black stallion, unfastened the saddlebag and scurried up next to Don Ricardo and delivered it to him.

"As you wish, Don Ricardo, it is my . . ."

"Get him away," Battu said. "He gives me a headache!"

Miguel Smith waited for no command before retreating to his former position.

"I never carry money on my person," Don Ricardo noted as he reached inside, "but in this saddlebag that formerly belonged to Don Carlos, there is a silver flask, which also formerly belonged to him, worth a great deal. It even has his initials engraved on it. Is it not beautiful?"

"It is beautiful."

The sun glinted on the flask and the initials.

"Then it is fitting that Don Carlos' debt be paid with Don Carlos' former property. Agreed?"

"Agreed." Battu smiled, took the flask, then shook it. "Ah-ha!" He smiled even wider, unscrewed the top, and lifted the flask to his mouth.

"To Don Carlos Mondego!" Battu emptied the fluid into his mouth. "May he rest in peace."

Don Ricardo nodded.

Both men had saved face and appeared

more than satisfied. So did their subordi-
nates.

"We will do much business," Battu said.

"I thought so," Don Ricardo agreed.

All concerned saddled up.

Battu and his men rode in one direction
where twenty of his comancheros waited
out of sight for his signal in case of trouble.

Don Ricardo and his men rode in another
direction where twenty-five of his soldados
waited out of sight for his signal in case of
trouble.

Chapter Fifty-Six

Elijah had circled back and made his report.

Keys nodded.

"Well, something like this had to come
sooner or later."

"Sooner," Elijah said. "I'd say in no more
than a half-hour."

"We'll be ready."

Keys summoned Doc, Billy Joe, Sandusky,
Elizabeth Shelby and Karla.

"This is the way we'll play it," he said and
proceeded with his instructions.

"Greetings." He removed his sombrero and
bowed from the waist even though he was
on horseback. "I am Miguel Smith, emis-

sary for Don Ricardo Morales, who you can see with five of his caballeros on the crest of that hill."

"Yes, we see him. Why is he up there and you down here?" Keys said.

"Oh, he will be down here soon. Don Ricardo wanted me to greet you first . . . in a friendly fashion."

"We consider ourselves greeted."

Miguel Smith waved his sombrero toward the crest of the hill, then placed it on his head at a rakish tilt.

The Trespassers waited as the riders from the hill approached.

Ironically, the convergence took place within sight of the three graves where Don Carlos and his two soldados rested — presumably in peace.

Don Ricardo Morales dismounted and so did one of the riders, then Miguel Smith followed suit.

"Don Ricardo Morales. These are my friends."

"Jefferson Keys. These are *my* friends."

"This is my land."

"Are you talking about the land that used to belong to Don Carlos?"

"That is correct. I am his cousin and his heir."

"But we're not on that land. We're on the

trail. We understood that his land began on the other side of the road. The side where he's buried."

"A detail." Don Ricardo smiled.

"An important detail." Keys did not smile.

"And what are you doing here . . . Senor Keys?"

"Passing through . . . Senor Morales."

"That's all?"

"That's all . . . unless we're forced to do something else."

"I see. And did you pass this way earlier?"

"We did. Going the other way."

"And you met my cousin, Don Carlos?"

"We killed him."

"You speak . . . forcefully."

"We act the same way . . . when we're forced to."

"I loved my cousin, Don Carlos."

"I see that you also love his horse."

"That too."

"Then maybe we did you a favor. We didn't want to kill him, or anybody — we still don't, but . . ."

"He forced you to?"

"Right."

"I must admit, he was sometimes . . . impetuous."

"Right again. What about you? Are you impetuous?"

"I would not say that. I use my brains, but still . . ."

"Still what?"

"We shall see. I also see that there are seven of you."

Keys nodded. "And seven of you," he said.

"Correct. But two of you are women."

"So?"

"So, the odds are in our favor."

"Don't depend on it."

"I also see that one of the women is fair-haired."

"What's that got to do with anything?"

"A woman traveling with Don Carlos was fair-haired, I am told. A woman who was his property."

"I don't know about that. But this woman is traveling with us. And she's not property. She's a free citizen of the United States and we're taking her back."

"Only if I say so, Senor Keys."

"You say you use your brains. Well, now's the time."

"How so?"

"We can go on our way and you can go on your way . . . or . . ."

"Or?"

Keys looked to his right.

"Or there can be more graves."

"Is that a threat, Senor?"

"A fact, Senor. Are you fast with a gun?"

"Fast. But not as fast as my man, Alvarez. He is the fastest."

Alvarez, who had been standing just behind and to the side of Don Ricardo, took a step forward and moved his hand slightly toward his low-slung gun and holster.

"This is my man, Billy Joe Bickford. Billy Joe, introduce yourself to Senor Alvarez."

Alvarez's hand moved fast; Billy Joe's hand moved faster. His gun exploded, shattering Alvarez's gun handle still in its holster. Alvarez stood trembling and a wet spot slowly took shape inside his pant leg.

"Billy Joe," Keys said, "is the slowest of my men. What about those odds now?"

"We will have to do something about that."

Don Ricardo Morales waved toward the top of the hill.

Twenty-five riders appeared on the ridge.

Don Ricardo waved again.

The twenty-five riders began their descent and made their way toward the group below.

Jefferson Keys nodded toward Sandusky, who stood atop his wagon. Sandusky pulled away the tarp that had been covering the Gatling. Doc jumped on the wagon next to Sandusky.

As the riders reached level ground, the

Gatling blasted a barrage of fire that riddled the area just in front of them.

Then another barrage even closer as Doc fed another cylinder into the Gatling.

Hundreds of missiles ripped an irregular trench in front of the horses. They reared and neighed and retreated as dirt splattered animals and horsemen.

The riders finally managed to rein their horses to an unsteady stop and looked toward Don Ricardo, who stood nonchalant.

"Now is the time," Keys said, "Senor Don Ricardo, to use your brains. Either that . . . or more graves. Your choice."

There was a pause, but not much of a pause.

"You and your friends," Don Ricardo said, "may continue your journey with my blessing."

"Blessed are the peacemakers," Keys said.

"We will pay our respects at my cousin's grave and light a candle for him on Sunday."

Don Ricardo Morales mounted the silver-saddled black stallion and rode across the trail. The rest of them followed their leader.

When Don Ricardo and his soldados were far enough away, Karla Olang rushed up to Keys and threw both arms around him.

"Thank you, Mister Keys, thank you. I hope you don't mind if I give you a hug."

"I don't mind a bit, but thank William here," Keys said. "He got us off to the right start. Give him the hug."

She did.

"Thank you, William."

Billy Joe Bickford blushed and it did show.

"Don't I get to hug anybody?" Elizabeth Shelby smiled.

"Let's all save the hugs and kisses," Keys said, " 'til this thing is over — one way or t'other."

Doc had descended from the wagon and stood next to Keys.

"Remind me of something, Jeff."

"What's that?"

"Never to play poker with you."

"The longer I am alive — the less I understand." Charly.

"Me too." Diaz.

"What do you mean, 'me too'?" Charly.

"What else can 'me too' mean — but 'me too'?" Diaz.

They had been observing the proceedings between the Trespassers and Don Ricardo and his soldados from above, behind a rugged rock on an outcrop formation of rugged rocks.

After the conference between Battu and Don Ricardo, Battu had instructed Charly and Diaz to follow Don Ricardo and make sure he didn't double back and double-cross the new owner of the late Don Carlos' initialed silver flask — and at the same time look for any sign of the gringos who had passed through Battu's territory without paying a passage fee.

Charly and Diaz had accomplished both phases of their mission without being detected.

Elijah had turned back toward the Trespassers' camp as soon as he had spotted Don Ricardo and his men and before he had a chance to spot Charly and Diaz. Charly and Diaz had observed Miguel Smith greeting the Trespassers, then Don Ricardo and five others coming down from the hill and parlaying with the Trespassers' leader. They were too far away to hear what had been said but close enough to see and hear the shooting confrontation between Billy Joe and Alvarez — then the charge of Don Ricardo's soldados from the hill — then the awesome display of firepower from the gun from hell — and finally, the discreet retreat of Don Ricardo toward the three graves and back toward his newly claimed domain.

Now the two of them had to decide what to do — and what not to do — next.

"I think we better get the hell out of here."
Charly.

"Me too." Diaz.

"We better make our report to Battu."
Charly.

"The sooner — the better." Diaz.

"Those gringos with the wagons are heading north." Charly.

"Back to where they came from." Diaz.

"Back across Battu's territory." Charly.

"Looks like." Diaz.

"That one wagon is loaded heavy." Charly.

"Very heavy." Diaz.

"I wonder what's in it?" Charly.

"Me too." Diaz.

"I think Battu will want to find out."
Charly.

"Me too." Diaz.

"Don't say 'me too' no more." Charly.

"OK. I'm done with 'me too.' " Diaz.

"Let's go." Charly.

"Let's go." Diaz.

"We're ready to roll," Doc said to Keys.

"No, we're not," Keys replied.

The rest of the Trespassers were standing nearby.

"Why not?" Billy Joe asked. "There's plenty of daylight."

"That's why," Keys said.

"I don't get it," Elizabeth Shelby said. "I want to get the hell out of this damn country, don't you?"

"I do."

"Are you out of your mind? Why don't we get a move on?"

"Because it'll be easier for them to see us during daylight."

"Who's *them?*"

"I don't know. Maybe Don Ricardo — maybe the comancheros. So we travel at night."

"For how long?" Doc asked.

"I don't know that either. 'Til I say so."

"Makes sense." Doc nodded.

"You know, Jefferson," Elijah said, "if we travel at night, I can't scout ahead and see much."

"I know, but it's still less of a risk that way."

"You think of everything." Elizabeth Shelby smiled.

"Not everything," Keys said. "Most things."

CHAPTER FIFTY-SEVEN

The sun came up smiling over Fort Canby.

But not everyone at Fort Canby was smiling.

Particularly not Colonel Crook.

The reason — the unexpected arrival of General Nelson Appleton Miles.

Miles carried with him a letter from the war department ordering him to inspect the forts within the Arizona Territory and make whatever recommendations he felt necessary to improve conditions in the area. Never mind that conditions had already been vastly improved under the command of Colonel George Crook.

There was no love lost between the two officers.

And there could be no more difference between the two officers.

Crook was a "wilderness soldier" who commanded according to conditions.

Miles was a "headquarters general" who went by the book and by whatever was politically expedient — and favorable to his career.

Years ago, during hostilities, Crook had been advanced over Miles by General Sherman. At the time Miles had been bitter with jealousy. And even though since then, while Crook had been in the field risking his life, and Nelson Appleton Miles had been in Washington currying favor and advancing his career with behind-the-desk promotions, Miles still bore a lingering grudge — mainly because those under his command never displayed the devotion and respect that Crook possessed from his officers and men. It was no secret, even to General Miles, that his officers and men often referred to him as "Ol' Fuss and Feathers."

And now Miles, who outranked Crook, was at Fort Canby after having visited Fort Whipple, Fort Apache, Fort Bowie, Fort Defiance, Fort Lowell and the other outposts in the territory and had called a meeting in Crook's office.

Captain Bourke and Lieutenant Crane were also in attendance and, of course, in spotless uniform. Crook hadn't bothered to dress any differently for the occasion.

General Nelson Appleton Miles was, as usual, dressed as if on his way to a gala ball. He was a big man with a trace of weakness in his girth. A pleasant enough face sat above a fat neck. His plump hands seemed effete. His skin was thin and resented the outdoor rigors. He wore an overdone uniform of his own design. He seemed bothered by the sight and smell of Crook's cigar but said nothing — about that.

"I'm happy to meet both of you gentlemen," Miles said to the two officers, "and would appreciate a résumé from each of you to include in my report."

"Yes, sir," Bourke and Crane said simultaneously.

"By the way, George" — Miles looked back at Crook — "how's Mary?"

"Fine." Crook let the smoke seep out of his mouth and nostrils. "How's Mary?"

"Fine." Miles smiled and glanced back at Bourke and Crane. "George and I do have something in common, gentlemen. Each of our wives is named Mary. Fortunately for me, I've been able to spend much more time with my Mary than George has with his." Then back at Crook. "Maybe I can do something about that, George."

"Like what?"

"Oh, recommend in my report that you be sent back to Washington for duty, where your Mary can join you."

"No, thanks, General. I'm hoping that . . . my Mary can join me out here soon, now that things seem to be settling down."

"Well, that's what I'm here to find out, George, just how settled down things are around here and make suggestions for further improvements. I'd like to start my inspection immediately, along with my staff."

"You and your staff are free to inspect away . . . anywhere, anytime you want, General."

"Very good."

"Let me know what my staff and I can do to help with your inspection."

"Of course. In the meantime, I'll just reconnoiter adroitly and let you know. Well" — General Nelson Appleton Miles lumbered toward the door — "I think that'll be all . . . for now."

Bourke and Crane saluted smartly. Miles returned the salute.

Colonel Crook didn't bother.

After the door closed, Captain Bourke gulped and addressed Crook.

"Permission to speak freely, Colonel?"

Crook nodded.

"How in the hell did someone like that come to outrank someone like you, sir?"

"I think you're speaking a mite too freely, Captain."

"Yes, sir."

"Colonel?"

"Yes, Lieutenant."

"Why didn't he include his staff in this meeting?"

"May I, Colonel," Bourke responded, "venture my opinion on that, sir?"

"Venture ahead."

"Maybe the general doesn't want witnesses around as to what happened when he makes out part of his report . . . sir."

"That'll do, Captain. You're speaking about my commanding officer . . . and yours."

"Yes, sir."

And that was part of the difference between a soldier's soldier and a politician's soldier.

"We have much to report, Jefe." Charly.

"Very much." Diaz.

"You better have, otherwise why the hell did you come back?"

Charly and Diaz stood in front of Battu and Rinaldi at the comanchero camp.

"Don Ricardo is sneaky." Charly.

"Very sneaky." Diaz.

"Explain." Battu took a swig from his silver flask.

"During the meeting at Chupadero Flats he had men hidden." Charly.

"We saw them later." Diaz.

"I had men hidden too. Twenty. How many with him?"

"We counted." Charly.

"Twenty-five." Diaz.

"The sneaky son of a bitch. You hear that, Rinaldi?"

"I heard, Jefe."

"You see that? You can't trust anybody. What else?"

"They came across the gringos." Charly.

"Near the three graves." Diaz.

"Good. Did they fight? Kill each other?"

"No, Jefe." Charly.

"No fight." Diaz.

"What the hell did they do?"

"They talked." Charly.

"At first." Diaz.

"Talked? Then what?"

"Then one of the gringos shot the pistol from one of Don Ricardo's soldados." Charly.

"Before the soldado could draw." Diaz.

"That's all?"

"No, Jefe." Charly.

"Don Ricardo's soldados, all twenty-five, charged from the hill." Diaz.

"Good. Then did they fight?"

"No, Jefe." Charly.

"The soldados quit charging." Diaz.

"Why?"

"The gun from hell." Charly.

"Many bullets. Thousands." Diaz.

"All bullets landed in front of the soldados." Charly.

"They quit charging." Diaz.

"Talked some more." Charly.

"Then Don Ricardo and his men rode away." Diaz.

"Dirty coward sons of bitches." Battu took

another swig from the silver flask. "What more?"

"One of the wagons is now heavy." Charly.

"Very heavy." Diaz.

"They're heading north." Charly.

"Coming this way, we think." Diaz.

"Good. With a heavy wagon they'll move slow. That's a pretty good report."

"Thank you, Jefe." Charly.

"We rest now, Jefe?" Diaz.

"No. Not here. Get your asses up to Lookout Point. One of you come back, let us know when you see them coming."

"But Jefe, we need food." Charly.

"And drink." Diaz.

"Take some with you. Let us know when you see them coming."

"It won't be for a long time." Charly.

"We rode like hell." Diaz.

"Can't we have our women first?" Charly.

"Then we go up? Please, Jefe?" Diaz.

"All right. All right. You gave a good report. Have your women first, then go up."

"Thank you, Jefe." Charly.

"Very much." Diaz.

"One more thing. Is that blond girl I sold to Don Carlos still with the gringos?"

"Yes, Jefe. We saw her." Charly.

"She's still with them." Diaz.

"Good. Go to your women."

Without further hesitation Charly and Diaz rushed off to their women.

"Rinaldi, tomorrow take some of your men and make a sweep. Make sure that son of a bitch, Don Ricardo, isn't sneaking up this way and everything is quiet before we welcome those damn gringos and that blond girl that's still with them. You understand?"

"I understand, Battu."

The Trespassers traveled that night and with first light found shelter and shade within a semicircle of boulders out of sight of the trail that led north.

They made cold camp, ate and tried to get some rest and sleep.

In spite of traveling all night, Elijah took it upon himself to make a wide early morning circle around the campsite for any sign of unwanted activity. He found none and returned to camp.

"Elijah, get some sleep," Keys said.

"I intend to."

"This time close your eyes. I'll keep mine open."

Elijah nodded and walked away.

Doc and Sandusky had no trouble sleeping under Sandusky's wagon.

After a couple of hours Elizabeth Shelby, who had been sleeping next to Karla, rose and walked toward where Keys was leaning against a rock.

Billy Joe moved to where Karla slept, leaned down and adjusted the blanket that had slipped off her body.

"Oh! William."

"Sorry," Billy Joe said. "Didn't mean to wake you."

"That's alright. For a second there, I thought I was back home."

"Go back to sleep." He started to move away.

"No. William, please sit here next to me."

He did.

"Home," she said. "It's hard to realize that I don't have a home."

"Sure you do. The ranch is still yours, isn't it?"

"Well, I own it, but . . ."

"But what?"

"I don't think I can live there without . . . the two of them. I've never lived alone. I don't think I could get used to it."

"You can get used to a lot of things if you have to. And you can do without things . . . if you have to."

"What about you?"

"What about me?"

"You're used to those guns . . . even sleep with them. Can you get used to being without them?"

"I never tried. Not in a long time. They're the only company I've had in a long time."

"Good company?"

"Good enough . . . so far."

"Then I guess that's all that matters."

"No, it isn't. Not anymore. You know that."

"William. Is it just because you feel sorry for me?"

"That isn't what I feel . . . sorry, I mean, and you know that too, but . . ."

"But what?"

"There's something I . . . I promised to do."

"With those guns?"

Silence.

"Then," she said, "I guess that answers that." And she turned away from him.

Billy Joe rose and walked back to his blanket.

"It's funny," Elizabeth Shelby said after she sat next to Keys by the rock.

"What's funny?"

"I could sleep during the day when I was at Madam Pleasant's, but not out here."

"Maybe you need a roof over your head."

"Maybe I need a cigarette." She pulled one already rolled out of the pocket of her blouse. "Got a light?"

"Sure, Red."

He struck a match and lit the cigarette between her lips.

"I like that," she said.

"Like what? The cigarette?"

"No. When you call me Red. That's the second time. You remember the first?"

"Sure I do."

"Keys . . ."

"What?"

"Don't make it the last."

"OK, Red."

"You know" — she smiled — "red stands for danger."

"I don't think you're as dangerous — or as bad — as you make out."

"Neither are you. Oh, as dangerous maybe, but not as bad."

"Right. We're just a couple of missionaries in search of a mission."

"I wouldn't go so far as to say that."

"Neither would I."

"Have you decided yet which way we get back to Arizona?"

"Decided a long time ago — Bottleneck Pass. Told your partners, Waxer and Kline, to stick as close as they could."

"You know something, Keys? I haven't had a bath in quite a while."

"Maybe you don't need as many baths

anymore." He smiled. "How about a drag from that cigarette?"

Elizabeth Shelby took the cigarette from her mouth and parted her lips.

"How about a drag from these?"

CHAPTER FIFTY-EIGHT

"Would you care for another cut of that beef before dessert, Nelson?" Kline asked General Nelson Appleton Miles.

"Don't mind," the general smiled and replied.

The general carried nowhere near the girth that one of his two hosts, Willard Oliver Waxer, toted, but the sash around his middle had been replaced twice in the last three years.

Waxer and Kline had met and hosted the general several times during their business trips to Washington, and when they heard of his arrival at Fort Canby did not hesitate to invite him for a gourmet supper in their private car.

Nor did the general hesitate to accept the invitation.

They had been of mutual assistance to each other in the past and would no doubt be of further assistance to each other in the future.

Waxer and Kline had contributed to the campaigns of senators and congressmen on both sides of the aisle, and had ready access to legislators who passed legislation favorable to entrepreneurs who made it their business to help in the winning of the West while helping themselves in the winning of business.

All parties concerned made sure that nothing illegal transpired in these transactions. It was a game of winks and nods in the right direction, or directions, piled high with profits from the flow of millions of dollars in expenditures involved in contracts.

President Grant believed that both North and South and the entire United States and Territories would benefit with the expansion and development of the West. He expressed that belief in words and deeds, favoring ". . . appropriations for river and harbor improvements and for fortifications and other advancements in whatever amounts Congress may deem proper."

The East and West were linked by rail two months after Grant's inauguration when the Union Pacific and Central Pacific railroads converged at Promontory Point, Utah. The Southwest was further flooded by federal disbursements throughout the region.

The War Department distributed over two

million dollars a year inside the Arizona border to entrepreneurs who supplied the Army with beef. Then there were beans and bacon at forty and fifty cents a pound, flour at twenty dollars a hundred weight.

Waxer and Kline were involved through their banks and other investments in all phases of supplying these and other necessities to the Army, to civilians and through the Army to the quiet, conquered Indians on their reservations.

But there were some men who didn't want the Indians to be too quiet or too conquered. So long as there was trouble in the Territory, there would be more government contracts. Colonel Crook was not too popular with those men. He had succeeded too well in quelling all sorts of trouble.

Waxer and Kline were among those men.

"Nelson," Waxer inquired, as he sipped from his tumbler of milk, "how long will you be in the Territory?"

"Just long enough to conclude my report."

"Yes." Kline nodded while already digging into his dessert. "We've heard about your assignment, and also about the rumor of you taking charge of the entire Territory."

"Oh, that's just a rumor, gentlemen. And I'm not sure I'd want to. I rather favor being in Washington."

"Well, sir," Waxer said, "it wouldn't be permanent and certainly would be an added feather in your cap to set things straight around here."

"So far in my report, I'd have to say that Crook is doing a pretty good job of it."

"Yes." Kline smiled. "But you'd do much better and we'd see to it that you'd have our fullest cooperation while you were here."

While at Fort Canby, General Miles had done his best to find fault with Crook's handling of his command, but there was little, or nothing, for him to contradict — so far.

"Well, I appreciate that, gentlemen, and if that situation does arise, I'll keep it in mind."

"Fine, sir." Waxer smiled.

"And how is Mrs. Miles, General?" Kline inquired between bites of dessert.

"Very well, thank you."

"Do give her our warmest regards," Kline added. "And we do look forward to seeing her again soon. Either in Washington — or out here."

They had waited in the tent that had been set up near the stationary engine and cars while their commanding officer dined in

Waxer and Kline's private car.

"They" were two members of General Nelson Appleton Miles' staff.

Major Andrew Bronson and Captain Homer Keeler. Bronson was tall, thin, dark of complexion and much darker of eyes — with pointed nose, pointed jaw and pointed hairline. Keeler was shorter, fairer and squarer. Both were capable, competent, and probably more loyal than their commander deserved.

Bronson had been Miles' aide-de-camp for over three years and eagerly looked forward to his retirement at the end of this year. Keeler was his likely replacement but looked forward to it none too eagerly.

"I make it about three hours, Andy," Captain Keeler said.

"Three and a half hours," Bronson replied without looking at his watch.

"You think they could be eating all this time?"

"That Waxer fellow looks like he's been eating morning, noon and night," Bronson noted.

"The general himself, he's got a pretty hearty appetite." Keeler grinned. "In more ways than one."

"Captain Keeler, I'm going to pretend that I didn't hear that remark — and you'd better be careful what you let slip. You never know who might be listening."

"Yes, sir. I'm sorry, Andy, uh, Major Bronson."

"But you're right, Homer. He has been putting on weight — what with food and medals and citations and such. You know I remember seeing Colonel Crook half a dozen years ago and he hasn't changed a whit, except for a few more gray hairs."

"Major, that's my idea of a soldier and officer. I sure would like to serve with him — uniform or no."

"Crook wears his uniform on the inside."

"Well, for some reason, our general's sure got it in for him. Been bustin' his butt trying to find something around here to criticize for that bloody report of his."

"He's found something everyplace else we've been," Bronson said.

"Yeah, some of it true and some of it . . . I better shut up, huh, Major?"

"You better, Homer. The feasting must be over because here comes our general now."

General Nelson Appleton Miles lay in his bed at Fort Canby digesting his sumptuous supper and thinking things over.

He wished that his wife, Mary, were in bed with him — for more than one reason

— not just physical. Through the years he had become used to talking things over with her. "Strategizing" about his career, as they put it.

Mary Miles was a handsome woman, large-boned but with patrician features and with more passion than Miles had expected before they married. And always, even after short separations, she reminded him what a hot-blooded woman he had married.

Miles looked forward to the physical facet of their relationship and just as eagerly to another aspect of their alliance. Mary was his best and certainly most appreciative audience and admirer. She believed what he believed — that Nelson Appleton Miles was the finest, brightest, most capable officer in uniform — and that someday, when he was out of uniform, he might very well rise to the highest political office, and thus become Commander-in-Chief of the United States Army. And they both knew that his rise to command would depend on politics as well as military campaigns.

But he would have to overcome one disadvantage as far as the vast majority of his military brethren were concerned. And that was that he was not really their "brother" — not a member of their fraternity.

Unlike Sherman, Sheridan, Grant, Mc-

Clellan, Crook, Custer — and even Robert E. Lee — he had not gone to West Point.

Miles always believed that the fraternity of West Pointers invariably stuck together and looked upon him as an alien. In his early twenties, Miles had been a dry-goods clerk when the Civil War broke out. He purchased a commission and discovered his life's profession. The Army suited him better than clerking and provided him with greater opportunities for advancement, especially when he made Mary his life's partner.

Through the years she gloried in watching and listening to him, and he reveled in posturing in front of her, while together they strategized about his future — and hers.

They had cultivated well-placed proponents and relatives, as well as highly successful entrepreneurs such as Waxer and Kline. And while not making any untoward promises, they had succeeded in coming to unspoken understandings of mutual expediencies.

In his report, which he had laboriously prepared, Miles had listed detailed suggestions for improvements at the other forts, but when it came to Fort Canby and Colonel Crook, he had been stymied. Crook's command had been exemplary.

Nelson Appleton Miles needed a dramatic

last act in his report.

A sudden Indian uprising in the Territory would provide a welcome denouement, but since that seemed unlikely under Crook's command, Miles would make it his business to stick around for a time and hope — if not for the worst — for something, anything, he could uncover and cash in on.

In the meantime, he missed Mary's physical presence and their discussions involving their mutual vaulting ambitions.

"Come," Colonel Crook responded to the knock on his office door.

Captain Bourke entered.

"I know it's late, sir, but I saw the light from your window . . ."

"Old Army habit, Captain. Stay up late and get up early."

"Yes, sir."

"Is there something wrong?"

"Well, no, sir. But I was just wondering . . ."

"About what?"

"If there's anything I can do to help as far as he's concerned."

"By 'he' I presume you refer to General Miles."

"Yes, sir. General Nelson Appleton Miles. He's bound and determined to . . ."

"Yes, I know, Captain. There's nothing you can do unless you can miraculously make a certain Gatling gun reappear before he finds out what happened. Or has he already found out?"

"No, sir. Not that I know. You know that none of the officers or men would say anything . . ."

"Yes, I know that too, Captain. Well, let's just hope that Keys and company don't show up with that damn gun before Ol' Fuss and Feathers decides to leave, otherwise we'll have some explaining to do and he'll have a field day writing that damn report of his for the boys back in Washington."

"You can always put it on Lieutenant Crane, he was . . ."

"I couldn't and I wouldn't."

"Yes, sir. I know."

"I'm in command of the post and whatever happens is my responsibility."

"Yes, sir. Have you thought about which way Keys would come back — if he does?"

"Oh, he'll be back, alright, if he lives. And I have thought about it . . . and the link."

"What link, sir?"

"That redheaded spitfire that kept company with Waxer and Kline before she went off with Keys."

"I don't understand, sir."

"What ever Keys is up to, I believe Waxer and Kline are in on it — and she's the link."

"Yes, sir. But that's not much to go on."

"No. But it's all we got. Now get some sleep, Captain, and hope that General Miles has a pleasant journey back to Washington before Keys shows up with that piece of Army property."

"Yes, sir. Good night, sir."

The midnight moon looked down in pale profile at the buttes and mystic monuments tearing themselves out of the barren, desolate terrain bisected by a narrow ribbon of road trailing north and south, to and from the United States and Mexico.

A lonesome coyote made known his craving and waited for a response in vain. The only other sound was a west wind weaving across rocks as old, or older, than the moon itself - - until, through the patient night, along that ribbon of road — came the creaking sounds of wagon wheels under a heavy strain. Plodding hoofbeats of ridden and riderless animals — horses and mules — and the Trespassers; Jefferson Keys, Elizabeth Shelby, Elijah, Doc Zeeger, Billy Joe Bickford, Sandusky, and Karla Olang, moving north, knowing they were drawing ever closer to their destination carrying five million dollars in gold but not knowing they were coming within sight of a place the comancheros called Lookout Point.

CHAPTER FIFTY-NINE

The toe of his boot struck the ribs of one of the sleeping men then swiftly slammed into the stomach of the other.

Both Charly and Diaz yelped with pain, braced themselves on their elbows and looked up at Battu, who glared at both of them. Rinaldi stood at his side beneath the sun that flared behind them.

"You sons of bitches! There's not a half a brain between the two of you!" Battu spat. "You hear me?"

"We hear you, Jefe!" Charly.

"We hear you!" Diaz.

"What is it, Jefe?" Charly.

"What's wrong?" Diaz.

"I'll tell you what's wrong." Battu picked up an empty whiskey bottle on the ground between the two of them, then hurled it against a rock, spraying it with shards of broken glass. "I'll tell you, you stupid bastards! Are you listening?"

"We're listening, Jefe." Charly.

"We're listening." Diaz.

"I send you up here to keep an eye on the trail down there, and you come up drunk, then drink some more — then pass out dead so you don't see what I sent you up here to see 'til Rinaldi finds out this morning. Tell them what you find out this morning, Rinaldi, tell them!"

"On the trail, tracks, wagon tracks and horses — they came through in the night going north. By now they . . ."

"Never mind! That's enough! Now you know what happened while you are dead drunk with too much food in your belly and too much women in your crotch. Now you know, huh?"

"We are sorry, Jefe." Charly.

"Very sorry." Diaz.

"It won't happen again, Jefe." Charly.

"Never." Diaz.

"No, it won't. Because you know what happens to sentries who fall asleep on duty?"

"No, Jefe." Charly.

"No." Diaz.

"I'll show you what happens."

Battu drew his gun and fired twice into the head of Charly, then twice into the heart of Diaz.

"That's what happens."

CHAPTER SIXTY

Battu was determined.

He would get the girls, the gun, the wagon, everything; the young girl with blond hair, the other girl with hair red as a fox, whatever made the heavy wagon so heavy, the horses, mules, everything — if he had to follow them across the border and kill every man in the caravan. It would be one of his best hauls.

But he remembered what Charly and Diaz said about the gun from hell shooting many bullets — many.

He would need every comanchero in the camp who could ride a horse and shoot a gun.

Rinaldi had only a half dozen men with him when he found the tracks on the trail and sent for Battu. Those men had stayed below while Battu and Rinaldi rode up to Lookout Point and dealt with Charly and Diaz.

Now Battu gave his instructions. Two of the comancheros would ride back to camp and bring back a full force while he and Rinaldi and the others followed the tracks until the full force caught up with them. They would attack, kill, collect the bounty, then head back across the border where the

U.S. Army could not follow.

The Trespassers had moved all through the night. By dawn they were tired and hungry. They made cold camp and listened to what Keys had to say.

"For the last few days we've been going at night and trying to hide out and sleep during the day. I know you're tired, so am I, and so are the animals. But we're getting close to the border, so this is the way it's got to be.

"We've been lucky so far, but we don't know what's behind us — or how close. So from now on we're going to move during the day. That way we can move faster and Elijah can let us know what's coming. I know it's tough, particularly on you women . . ."

"You hear that, Karla," Elizabeth Shelby said, "he's concerned about us, and here I thought that he was no more malleable than marble."

"What I was going to say is, while the animals are resting, you women can cook up a hot meal that'll keep us going for the rest of the day."

"Ah." Elizabeth Shelby smiled. "That's the Jefferson Keys we know and love."

"Elijah, after you eat . . ."

"I know, Jefferson, I'll be all eyes and ears."

Billy Joe moved closer to Karla.

"I'll gather up some mesquite so we can build a fire."

"Thank you, William."

"Jeff," Doc said, "I'll look over the animals, then Sandusky and me being the oldest, we'll just plop down for awhile if that be alright with you."

"That be," Keys said.

With a frying pan in hand and a rolled cigarette in her mouth, Elizabeth Shelby sidled up next to Keys.

"Tell me something . . . Jefferson."

"What?"

"When we get back . . ."

"Do you mean . . . if?"

"No. I mean when."

"OK."

"When we get back . . . are you going to miss all this?"

"That all depends."

"On what?"

"On whether you quit smoking."

Two hours later, the Trespassers were moving north again.

Still tired, but not hungry.

A quiet tension prevailed.

Keys thought of some lines from Samuel Taylor Coleridge's epic tome.

Like one that on a lonesome road
Doth walk in fear and dread,
And having once turned round, walks on,
And turns no more his head;
Because he knows a frightful fiend
Doth close behind him tread.

Keys was not sure about what kind of frightful fiend, or how close, but his every instinct told him to keep the Trespassers moving.

Elijah raced in from behind, rode past the wagons, pack mules and other riders, and reined his snorting horse up next to Keys.

"Bad news, brother!"

Billy Joe, Elizabeth Shelby and Karla moved their mounts up beside Keys and Elijah.

"How bad?" Keys said.

"A swarm of 'em, comancheros, I guess, just joined up with a dozen or so back there who'd been doggin' our trail. They'll be coming after us alright . . ."

"How far back?"

"Say half an hour unless we keep moving."

"That's just what we're going to do. As

fast we can."

It would be a race not just to the border, but beyond. Keys knew that as far as Battu was concerned there was no border for him — only for the U.S. Army. Keys also knew that if the Trespassers had to make a stand against the comancheros, the Trespassers would be better off doing it not in Mexico, but in Arizona.

And if they could get to Bottleneck Pass in time, he might prevent the comancheros from catching up to them — or at least make their passage a hell of a lot harder.

"Alright!" Keys hollered out. "We leave the pack mules behind. Everybody and everything else follow me and ride like hell!"

CHAPTER SIXTY-ONE

The Trespassers made it across the border and through Bottleneck Pass — animals and riders exhausted. They could go no farther, but Keys hoped they wouldn't have to, at least not for awhile — if his plan worked.

The Gatling gun was uncovered, loaded and ready with Sandusky and Billy Joe behind it. The others were all deployed and Keys was high up on a ledge of Bottleneck Pass placing enough dynamite on it to blow down the gates of hell, and with a wick long enough to get the hell out of there when the time was right before those gates came tumbling down.

Keys looked down and across to the south and saw that the time was right — now.

In the distance the dust swirled behind the riders pounding closer to the border and Bottleneck Pass.

If they continued at the same pace and he lit the wick at just the right time, the co-mancheros, or most of them, would be blasted away and buried under tons of granite boulders, jagged rocks and sling-stone rubble.

Jefferson Keys wiped the sweat off his mouth, took one last look toward the riders, struck a match, lit the wick, and scrambled down the slope of Bottleneck Pass as if his life depended on it.

It did.

CHAPTER SIXTY-TWO

Battu, Rinaldi and about a dozen other co-mancheros made it through the narrow pass when the mountain and all hell broke loose.

A thunderous blast pierced the air for miles around and echoed on both sides of the border, screams, yelps — human and animal, frenzied yells for help, the earth quaking, rumbling rocks cascading onto flesh and bone. A stone cemetery where the pass had been just minutes before.

From out of the tumult, chaos, turmoil and confusion, Battu, Rinaldi and the other survivors milled amid the dust and debris, but not for long.

Battu screamed an epithet and led the comancheros, with his gun firing, toward the Trespassers, as Keys made it behind one of the wheels of Doc's wagon.

But as Battu and his comancheros charged from one direction, another group of riders, about a dozen or more, led by Amory Valance, appeared from another direction with guns and rifles spouting lead.

Sandusky cut loose with the Gatling into the comancheros. Hundreds of rounds ripped into Battu, Rinaldi, and the rest, who tumbled off their horses, most of them dead before they hit the ground.

Elijah, Doc and Elizabeth Shelby fired away at Valance and his men.

Sandusky turned the Gatling toward Valance and squeezed, but after just a few rounds the Gatling jammed.

"Billy Joe!" Keys yelled. "Rifle!"

Billy Joe Bickford tossed him the Henry from the wagon and resumed firing with his handguns.

Keys took aim and fired the Henry twice. Both shots hit the target and Amory Valance fell from his horse. The rest of his men had had more than enough. With their leader on the ground and no more paydays, they spurred their mounts and scattered in all directions.

Keys looked around to make sure that all the Trespassers were alive and unwounded.

They were. Doc. Elijah. Billy Joe. Sandusky. And Elizabeth Shelby and Karla.

With the Henry still in hand, Keys walked, not fast, not slow, toward the direction he had previously aimed.

He stopped where Amory Valance had fallen and lay face up on the ground — unseeing eyes open.

"I don't know whether you can hear me, you son of a bitch," Keys said, "and I don't care. But thanks for giving me the chance to pay you back."

With his boot Keys rolled the body of Valance face down on the ground.

"And now you can see where you're going."

He turned and started to walk back toward the Trespassers. They all saw it at the same time.

A detachment of troopers on horseback led by Colonel George Crook.

Crook, Captain Bourke and Lieutenant Crane dismounted and approached Keys and the rest of the Trespassers.

"Well, Keys," Crook said, "I told you I'd be waiting." He pointed to what was the pass. "But you made it easy. We heard that blast from miles away."

"Figured you would, George. But had no choice."

"Uh-huh. What else did you figure?"

"Told you we'd get Battu for you. There he is." Keys pointed. "And on this side of the border, all legal. We brought back the Olang girl. Battu killed her mother and father. And then there's the matter of the reward. Five hundred, wasn't it?"

"Uh-huh. Anything else?"

Keys looked first at Elizabeth Shelby, then at the rest of the Trespassers. He knew that there was no longer any way of getting the gold to Waxer and Kline. He had no alternative.

"Oh, yeah, George — by the way . . ."

"I figured there'd be a 'by the way.' Go ahead."

"We brought back five million in Confederate gold that now legally belongs to the U.S. government. Happy to turn it over to you, George."

"I'll bet you are."

"It's right there in that wagon."

"Uh-huh. What about what's in the other wagon?" Crook motioned toward the Gatling gun.

That's when Keys, Crook, and the rest of them saw another group of riders in uniform approaching.

They were led by General Nelson Appleton Miles.

CHAPTER SIXTY-THREE

"What the hell is going on here?" General Nelson Appleton Miles barked as he looked around at the carnage.

He and two of his staff, Major Bronson and Captain Keeler, had dismounted and stood in front of the Trespassers and Colonel Crook.

"Looks like a damn abattoir," Miles said looking at Crook and the Trespassers. "What happened?"

"Well, first off" — General Crook cleared his throat — "you do know Jefferson Keys here . . ."

"Yes, I do know Keys, from the war, and from his reputation afterwards — which is none too good."

"To sum it up briefly, General, Keys led a small expedition into Mexico — where the

U.S. Army couldn't go — against a comanchero named Battu who had crossed the
U.S. border, killed a family and kidnapped
their daughter. He succeeded in rescuing
the young girl — that one over there — and
luring Battu back into the U.S. While he
was at it, Keys and his people uncovered
five million in Confederate bullion, which
belongs to the U.S., and just turned it over
to us as you rode up . . . General. Does that
about sum it up, Mister Keys?"

"I'd say so, Colonel." Keys smiled.

Nelson Appleton Miles did not smile.

"What about that bunch of dead people
over there?" He nodded toward Valance and
his erstwhile followers.

"Evidently" — Crook shrugged — "they
got wind of the gold and tried to take it
away for themselves — so Keys and his
group were protecting U.S. property."

General Miles seemed stymied for a moment, but only for a moment.

"Speaking of U.S. property, Army property." He pointed to Sandusky's wagon.
"How did they come to possess that Gatling
gun? That's U.S. property, isn't it?"

"We borrowed it, General," Keys said.

"You mean you stole it, don't you?"

General Nelson Appleton Miles in that
moment knew he had what he had been

looking for in his report and he intended to make the most of it.

"Borrowed, General," Keys said. "We did bring it back."

"That won't wash, Keys." Miles' tone was harsh. "Not for you and certainly not for Colonel Crook. This won't go easy on any of you. This should have been reported to the War Department and to me. Keys, you and the rest of your band are going to go to prison, and Colonel, you are going to be severely reprimanded and most likely demoted after I make my report. Do you understand, Colonel?"

"I understand, General."

"In the meanwhile, these people will be disarmed and escorted by my staff back to Fort Canby and detained there until I file my report, and I intend to remain here until justice is done."

"General Miles."

"What is it, Keys?"

"That young lady, Karla Olang, she had no part in any of this and she's gone through all four edges of hell. Is she also to be . . . detained?"

"Uh . . . well, no. She's free to . . . uh, go back home whenever she wants."

"Thank you, General," Keys said quietly.

"Major Bronson."

"Yes, sir."

"You will be in charge of disarming and escorting these people back to the fort. I'll see you there."

"Yes, sir."

They exchanged salutes. Nelson Appleton Miles mounted, restraining an unexpressed smile of accomplishment, and rode away in the direction of Fort Canby.

Jefferson Keys looked at Billy Joe Bickford, who stood next to him.

"Looks like our unfinished business is going to have to wait."

"I can wait," Billy Joe replied.

Keys took a step closer to Crook.

"I'm sorry, Colonel."

"So am I. Seems like the General has hung both of us out to dry and there's nothing I can do about it. He's my commanding officer."

"I know. But can you arrange for me to send a telegraph?"

"I think so. Sure I can. Who you going to send it to?"

"*His* commanding officer."

CHAPTER SIXTY-FOUR

Mister President,
A few friends of mine and I retrieved

from Mexico five million in Confederate gold bullion which we turned over to Colonel Crook for your government. Broke a few rules along the way. General Miles holding us for trial. Details upon request. Can you help, sir?

Jefferson Keys

"General Miles, thank you for coming."

Nelson Appleton Miles was in Crook's office along with Keys, Elijah, Doc, Billy Joe Bickford, Sandusky and Elizabeth Shelby.

"You said something about an important telegraph bearing on this case," Miles grumbled.

"That's correct, sir." Crook held up a piece of paper.

"I don't know what bearing it could have, but let's hear it. I've got work to do."

"Yes, sir."

Crook read.

Colonel Crook,

Regarding the matter of Keys and his friends concerning the five million in gold, which this government sorely needs. For whatever offense, or offenses, Keys and his friends may have committed in retrieving the gold, they are hereby pardoned by the President of the

United States and are to receive a 1 percent fee for their efforts. General Miles is to report back to Washington at once. The matter is closed except for my expressing my thanks once again to Jefferson Keys for saving my life from an assassin's bullet at Appomattox Courthouse.

Ulysses Simpson Grant
President, United States of America

A stunned silence reverberated through the room.

Without breaking the silence, General Nelson Appleton Miles walked to the door, opened it and walked out, not closing it behind him.

CHAPTER SIXTY-FIVE

The Trespassers unanimously decided on how to distribute the $50,000 fee.

Elizabeth Shelby:	$25,000
Jefferson Keys:	$10,000
Doc Zeeger:	$ 5,000
Elijah:	$ 5,000
Billy Joe Bickford:	$ 5,000

Sandusky refused to accept more than the

original deal but did collect the $500 reward for Battu.

"Not as much as it might have been," Doc said, "but not bad for a couple weeks' work, considering we got out with our skins whole and didn't have to go to Joliet."

"Thanks to Jefferson Keys," Elijah added, "and his friend, President Ulysses Simpson Grant."

"Well, Billy Joe," Keys said, "we still have that unfinished business . . . anytime you're of a mind to."

There was a pause.

"That assassin Grant referred to, the one you killed . . . my father?"

Keys nodded.

"Why didn't you tell me then?"

"He died for what he believed in. I thought that was enough to tell you."

"Even though I swore to kill you?"

"Just as sure as the setting of the sun," Keys added.

"Well, Mister Keys," Billy Joe said, "as far as I'm concerned, the sun has set."

Elizabeth Shelby put both arms around him and kissed Billy Joe Bickford lightly on the left side of his face.

"Now, if you'll excuse me." Bickford smiled. "I'm going to see a young lady about buying into a ranch . . . and about something else." He started to walk away, paused in front of Elijah. "I'd be pleased to have you come visit us."

Elijah smiled and nodded.

"Good luck . . ." Elizabeth Shelby waved, ". . . William."

William Joseph Bickford waved back.

"Well." Sandusky smiled. "We had a few laughs along the way."

"Yeah." Keys nodded. "A couple of times we almost died laughing."

"Me," Doc Zeeger said, "I'm going to see about a card game . . . and a warm woman."

"Hold on, Doc." Sandusky wiped at his whiskers. "I'll go along part way with you . . . then it's back to farmin' — in O-hi-o."

They left.

"How about you?" Keys asked Elijah.

"I might go back to the blanket," the big man said, "and then again I might not. I've got five thousand dollars to think it over. That's a hell of a lot more money than they paid for my father. So long, you two."

After Elijah moved off, Elizabeth Shelby took a step closer to Keys.

"What about us?" she said.

"What about us?" he stated.

"Don't we have some unfinished business? In bed?"

"We didn't get to keep the five million. Wasn't that part of the deal?"

"I don't remember."

"I don't think you're the same woman who made that deal. And I'm not the same man. With that twenty-five thousand, where do you go from here? San Francisco?"

"Nope. Change of mind. Change of venue."

"Where?"

"There's a little pueblo to the south of San Francisco. Been there once. It's going to grow and in a way I might grow with it. Place called Los Angeles . . . City of the Angels. And you?"

"Crook told me President Grant's ordered Custer back West . . . Dakota Territory. Might ride up there and pay Yellow Hair a visit."

"Well, in case you change your mind, I'll be in Los Angeles. I won't be hard to find."

"No, you won't . . . Red."

"Well, partner." Simon Ignatious Kline munched as they dined in their private car. "It was a game of chance and we lost."

"True," Willard Oliver Waxer said, sipping his milk, "but there are many, many more games for players like us."

"Yes, indeed," Kline said. "Willard, would

403

you pass me the butter?"

Jefferson Keys reined in his horse as he came to a fork in the trail.

He pulled a double eagle gold piece from his pocket.

Heads — north to the Dakotas and Yellow Hair.

Tails — west to Los Angeles and Red.

He flipped the coin and it spun in the air. But no matter which side came up, it didn't matter.

Jefferson Keys had already made up his mind.

ABOUT THE AUTHOR

Andrew J. Fenady has spent most of his adult life in the badlands of Hollywood creating, writing and producing motion pictures, television series, Movies of the Week, stage plays and songs, including the classic "Johnny Yuma Was A Rebel."

Fenady has received a passel of awards, among them The Golden Boot for Westerns, The Edgar Award for *The Man With Bogart's Face,* The Christopher Award for *The Green Journey* and three Emmys for *Confidential File.*

He's worked with the toughest top starts, such as John Wayne, Robert Mitchum, Charles Bronson and many, many more.

The employees of Thorndike Press hope you have enjoyed this Large Print book. All our Thorndike and Wheeler Large Print titles are designed for easy reading, and all our books are made to last. Other Thorndike Press Large Print books are available at your library, through selected bookstores, or directly from us.

For information about titles, please call:
(800) 223-1244

or visit our Web site at:
http://gale.cengage.com/thorndike

To share your comments, please write:
Publisher
Thorndike Press
295 Kennedy Memorial Drive
Waterville, ME 04901